THE HIVE

CAMILO JOSÉ CELA

THE HIVE

Translated by J. M. COHEN in
consultation with ARTURO BAREA

THE NOONDAY PRESS
FARRAR, STRAUS AND GIROUX • NEW YORK

For my brother Juan Carlos,
cadet in the Spanish Navy

This Noonday Press edition, 1990
Second printing, 1990
Published simultaneously in Canada by Harper & Collins,
Toronto
Printed in the United States of America

Library of Congress Cataloging-in-Publication Data
Cela, Camilo José.
[Colmena. English]
The hive / Camilo José Cela ; translated by J.M. Cohen in
consultation with Arturo Barea.
p.   cm.
Translation of: La colmena.
I. Title.
PQ6605.E44C613   1990   863'.64—dc20   89-25895   CIP

The original translation has been slightly revised for this edition.

THE HIVE

Chapter One

DON'T let's lose our sense of proportion, I'm sick and tired of telling you it's the only thing that counts."

Doña Rosa comes and goes between the café tables, bumping into the customers with her enormous backside. Doña Rosa often says "Damn it to hell" and "What a pain . . ." For Doña Rosa her café is the world, and everything else revolves around the café. Some people claim that Doña Rosa's little eyes begin to sparkle when spring comes and the girls go in short sleeves. I think this is sheer gossip; for nothing in the world would Doña Rosa ever sacrifice a solid five-peseta piece, spring or no spring. What Doña Rosa likes is simply to drag her great bulk about between the tables. When she is alone, she smokes cigarettes at ninety centimos the packet, and from the moment she gets up to the moment she goes to bed she drinks *ojén anís*, whole glasses full of the best. And then she coughs and smiles. When she is in a good mood, she sits on a stool in the kitchen and reads novels or serials, the bloodier the better: it's all grist for her mill. Afterwards she cracks jokes and tells people about the murder in the Calle de Bordadores or the murder on the Andalusia Express.

"Navarrete's father was friendly with General Miguel Primo de Rivera, so he went to him, fell on his knees, and said: 'General, sir, for God's sake reprieve my son!' and Don Miguel, though he had a heart of gold, told him: 'My dear Navarrete, I can't possibly do it, your son must pay for his crimes on the scaffold.' "

"They were men, those fellows," she thinks. "It takes guts."

Doña Rosa's face is covered with blotches; it always looks as if she were changing her skin like a lizard. When she is deep in thought, she forgets herself and picks strips off her face, sometimes as long as paper streamers. Then she snaps out of it, begins to walk up and down again, and smiles at the customers, whom at heart she loathes, showing her blackened little teeth encased in filth.

Don Leonardo Meléndez owes the shoeblack thirty thousand pesetas. The shoeblack, who is a heron—exactly like a bloated, rickety heron—had been saving money year after year only to lend it all to Don Leonardo in the end. It serves him right. Don Leonardo is a smart fellow who lives on credit and on business projects that never come off. Not that they turn out badly; they simply don't come off at all. Don Leonardo wears resplendent ties and puts brilliantine on his hair, so heavily scented that you smell it from afar. He has the airs and graces of a grandee and an immense poise, the poise of a widely experienced man. I don't believe he is so very experienced, but he certainly carries himself like one who has never gone short of a bank note in his wallet. He treats his creditors like dirt, and his creditors smile at him and pay their respects, at least outwardly. Someone or other actually thought of suing him and dragging him to court, but the fact remains that so far nobody has fired the first shot.

Don Leonardo has two favorite tricks of speech; he likes to use a little French word now and then, such as *Madame* and *rue* and *cravate*, and he likes to say: "We, the Meléndez . . ."

Don Leonardo is an educated man who makes it obvious that he knows a good many things. Every day he plays a few games of checkers; he never drinks anything but light coffee. If he sees someone at a near-by table smoking American cigarettes, he asks them courteously: "Could you help me out with a cigarette paper? I wanted to roll myself one, but now I find I've run out of paper."

Upon which the other confesses: "Sorry, but I don't use them myself. If you'd like one of these . . ."

Don Leonardo then looks doubtful and waits a couple of seconds before answering: "Oh, well, let's smoke light tobacco for a change. Not that I'm partial to the weed, you know."

Sometimes the guest at the other table only says: "I'm afraid I've no cigarette papers on me." And then Don Leonardo is left with nothing to smoke.

With their elbows on the encrusted marble of the round tables, the customers watch the proprietress go past almost without seeing her, while they ponder over this world which, alas, has not been all it might have been, this world in which everything has gone wrong bit by bit, though no one can ever quite understand why; perhaps because of some small thing without the least significance. Many of the marble tops were once tombstones in an old churchyard abandoned long ago; on some, a blind man passing his fingertips along the lower side of the table may still decipher the lettering: "Here lie the mortal remains of Señorita Esperanza Redondo, who died in the flower of her youth" or "R.I.P. His Excellency Señor Don Ramiro López Puente, Undersecretary in the Ministry of Public Works."

The customers of cafés are people who believe that things happen as they do because they happen and that it is never worth while to put anything right. At Doña Rosa's they all smoke and most of them meditate, each alone with himself, on those small, kindly, intimate things which make their lives full or empty. Some lend a vague air of dreamy recollection to their silence; and some review their memories with rapt faces wearing the look of a poor suffering beast, an affectionate, pleading, weary beast: their foreheads resting on their hands and their eyes full of bitterness, like a sea in dead calm.

There are certain evenings when the conversations between the tables die down, conversations about new kittens, or the food situation, or the little boy who died and there is someone who cannot remember him—"But *don't* you remember?"— the little boy with fair hair who was very sweet and rather thin, always wore a fawn hand-knitted sweater, and must have been five or so. On those evenings the heart of the café has an uneven beat, like a sick man's, and the air seems to get thicker and greyer, though now and then a cooler breath pierces it like a flash; no one knows where it comes from, but it is a breath of hope that opens, for a few seconds, a little window in each shuttered spirit.

Don Jaime Arce, with all his impressive manner, gets bills of exchange presented to him all the time. In the café everything is common knowledge, even though it may not seem so. Don Jaime applied at a bank for a credit, got it, and signed a few bills. Then what happened, happened. He made a business deal, was cheated and left without a penny, the bills were presented for payment, and he said he could not meet them. Don Jaime Arce is undoubtedly an honest man who has bad luck in money matters, simply bad luck. Admittedly he is not a hard worker, but then he has never had a chance. Others quite as lazy as he is, or even worse, have made thousands out of a few lucky coups, met their bills, and are now riding about in taxis the whole day long and smoking good tobacco. Things did not turn out that way for Don Jaime, on the contrary. He is looking round for a job and cannot find anything. He would have taken on any work, the first that came along, but nothing has cropped up that would seem worth while; and so he spends his whole day in the café, his head against the plush back of the seat and his eyes on the gilt scrolls of the ceiling. Sometimes he will hum snatches from a musical comedy, beating time with his foot. As a rule Don Jaime is not thinking of his misfortune; in fact, he usually thinks of nothing at all. He looks at the mirror and asks himself: "Now who invented the mirror?" Or he stares fixedly, almost insolently, at someone and wonders: "Has this woman any children? She may be a virtuous old spinster." Or: "How many consumptives are in this café just now?" Don Jaime will roll himself a very thin cigarette, no thicker than a straw, and light it. "Some people are artists at sharpening pencils to a point as sharp as a needle, and it never breaks off." Don Jaime changes his position; one of his legs has gone to sleep. "What a mystery this is: thump-thump, thump-thump, and so on all one's life, day and night, summer and winter—the human heart."

At the back of the café, by the stairs leading up to the billiard room, there usually sits a silent lady who lost her son a month ago. The boy's name was Paco. He was studying for the post-office exams. People at first said he'd had paralysis, but later it came out that he'd died from something different. He'd had meningitis. It was quickly over, and anyway he lost consciousness at the beginning. He already knew by heart all the place names of León, Old Castile, New Castile, and part of Valencia (the province of Castellón and about half the province of Alicante); it was a great pity he died. Now his mother is left alone, as her other son, the elder one, is knocking about in the world and nobody knows where he is. In the afternoons she comes to Doña Rosa's café, sits down by the foot of the little staircase, and stays there during the dead hours to warm herself. Since her son's death Doña Rosa has been very affectionate towards her. Some people get pleasure out of being kind to those in mourning. They seize the opportunity to give advice, or to recommend resignation and fortitude, and have a very good time. Doña Rosa likes to comfort Paco's mother by telling her that it is better that God took him than it would have been if he had lived on as a half-wit. The mother then looks at her with an acquiescent smile and agrees that, of course, if one comes to think of it, Doña Rosa is right.

Paco's mother is a widow by the name of Isabel, Doña Isabel Montes de Sanz. She is still rather good-looking; her short cape is somewhat threadbare. Apparently she comes of a good family. People in the café on the whole respect her silence, and it rarely happens that some acquaintance of hers—mostly one of the women coming back from the ladies' room—leans over her table and asks: "Well, how is it, are you beginning to buck up?"

Doña Isabel will smile but hardly ever answer; if she feels a little brighter than usual, she glances up at her friend and says: "You look very pretty today, dear." Much more frequently, however, she never says a word; a wave of her hand on leaving, and that is all. Doña Isabel knows that she belongs to another class or at least to another walk of life.

An unmarried woman who is getting a bit long in the tooth calls the cigarette boy: "Padilla!"

"Coming, Señorita Elvira."

"A Triton." She searches her bag stuffed with tender, indecent old letters, and puts thirty-five centimos on the table.

"Thank you."

"Thank you."

She lights the small cigar and, with a faraway look, puffs out a billow of smoke. Shortly afterwards she calls again: "Padilla!"

"Coming, Señorita Elvira."

"Did you give him my letter?"

"Yes, Señorita."

"What did he say?"

"Nothing, he wasn't at home. But the maid said I shouldn't worry, she'd give it to him at suppertime without fail."

Señorita Elvira says nothing more and goes on smoking. Today she feels a bit funny, she has the shivers and everything she sees seems to dance in front of her eyes. Señorita Elvira leads a dog's life, the sort of life that wouldn't be worth living if one looked closer at it. She is doing nothing, certainly; but because she does nothing, she has nothing to eat either. She reads novels, goes to the café, smokes from time to time a small cigar, and is ready for whatever may fall into her lap. The trouble is that windfalls are few and far between, and nearly always bruised and maggoty at that.

*   *   *   *

Don José Rodríguez de Madrid won one of the smallest prizes in the lottery at the last draw. His friends tell him: "You've had luck, haven't you?"

Don José has always the same answer, which he seems to have learned by heart: "Bah, a lousy forty pesetas."

"There, there, old boy, don't start explaining, we're not going to ask for a share in it."

Don José is a magistrate's clerk and seems to have some nice little savings. People say, too, that he married a rich wife, a girl from La Mancha who died soon afterwards, leaving all she had to Don José, and that he was in a great hurry to sell her four vineyards and two olive groves because he said the country air was bad for his respiratory tracts and the important thing was to look after one's health.

At Doña Rosa's café Don José always orders the common *ojén anís*; he is neither a snob nor one of those poor devils who go in for light coffee. The proprietress regards him with something like sympathy because they have this affection for the drink in common. "*Ojén* is the best there is in the world; it is tonic, diuretic, and an aid to digestion; it is blood-building and banishes the specter of impotence." Everything Don José says is apposite. Once, some years ago, shortly after the end of the Civil War, he had words with the violinist. Nearly everyone present maintained that the violinist was in the right, but Don José called the proprietress and said: "Either this impudent, rascally Red is kicked out at once, or I never set foot in this place again."

Upon this, Doña Rosa gave the violinist the sack, and that was the last anyone heard of him. The customers who had taken the violinist's side began to change their minds and ended by declaring that Doña Rosa had done quite right, that one had to be firm and set a warning example. "You never know where you might end up with this sort of effrontery." In saying this, the guests assumed a grave, judicious, somewhat apologetic air. "It's impossible to do anything right or worth while if there's no discipline," they were saying at the tables.

At the top of his voice a man already advanced in years tells a story about a joke he played on the notorious Madame Pimentón nearly half a century ago.

"That stupid fool thought she was playing me for a sucker. Some hope! I stood her a glass or two of white wine, and when she left, she bashed her face against the door. Haw, haw! She bled like a stuck pig. And all she said was 'Oh, la, la, oh, la, la,' and off she went spitting out her guts. Poor wretched soul, she was drunk all the time, you really couldn't help laughing."

From the neighboring tables, faces look at him in something like envy. They are the faces of people who smile, blissfully at peace, in those moments when they succeed in thinking nothing at all, without being quite aware of it. People are toadies out of stupidity, and at times they smile though they feel at the bottom of their hearts a boundless aversion, an aversion they have difficulty in restraining. It is possible to go to the length of murder out of flattery; surely more than one crime of violence has been committed to save face, to make up to somebody.

"That's the way to deal with spongers of her sort. We mustn't let them get the better of decent people like us. Just as my old father used to say: 'If you want grapes, come and get them— and you'll get it!' Haw, haw! The dirty old bitch didn't turn up there again, no fear."

A fat and glossy cat is running about between the tables. A cat full of health and good cheer, a pompous, self-important cat. It makes its way between a woman's legs, and the woman jumps.

"You blasted cat, get out of here!"

The teller of the story gives her a gentle smile: "But, madam, the poor cat—what harm has it done to you?"

A long-haired youth writes verse in all this hubbub. His mind is far away, he takes no notice of anything around him;

it is the only way to write fine verse. If he were to look right or left, his inspiration would elude him. This thing called inspiration must be rather like a little butterfly, deaf and blind, but luminous; otherwise many things would have no explanation.

The young poet is composing a long poem entitled "Fate." He had his doubts whether he should not call it "This Fate," but after consulting various better-established poets, he finally decided that it was best to call it "Fate," without any trimmings. It was simpler, more evocative, more mysterious. Also, calling it plain "Fate" would make it more suggestive, more —how to put it?—more indefinite and poetic. In this way it would not be clear whether fate as such was meant, or a particular fate, an undecided fate, a tragic fate, a blue fate, or a violaceous fate. "This Fate" would have tied it down too much and left less scope for imagination to take wing in free, untrammeled flight.

The young poet has been working for months on this poem. By now there exist some three hundred finished verses, a carefully laid out dummy of the future edition of the work, and a list of potential subscribers who will in due course be sent a leaflet with a subscription form, in the hope that they will sign it. He has also chosen the type for the printer (a simple, clear, classical type one can read with ease—in a word, Bodoni) and drafted the copyright and subscription notice. Two doubts, however, still harass the young poet: whether or not to put *Laus Deo* below the colophon and whether or not to take it upon himself to write the biographical note for the blurb on the dust jacket.

Doña Rosa is certainly not what one would call sensitive.

"And it's no news to you what I'm telling you. If I want scoundrels around I've got quite enough with that no-good, my brother-in-law! You're very green still, d'you hear me? Very green. A fine thing that would be! Whenever have you seen a fellow without education or morals coming to this place, puffing and blowing and stamping about as if he was a real gent? What's more, I'll take an oath that it won't happen while I've got eyes in my head."

Doña Rosa has drops of sweat on her brow and her hairy upper lip.

"And you there, you booby, slinking off to get the evening paper! There's no respect or decency in this place, that's all there is to it. One day I'm going to give you a proper thrashing if I'm really fed up. Has one ever seen such a thing?"

Doña Rosa pins her small rat's eyes on Pepe, the old waiter who came to town from the Galician village of Mondoñedo forty or forty-five years ago. Behind her thick lenses, Doña Rosa's eyes resemble the startled eyes of a stuffed bird.

"What are you looking at? What are you looking at like that, you fool? You're just the same as you were on the day you came here. Not even God Almighty Himself could make you people lose your farmyard smell. Come on, wake up, and let's have no more trouble. If you'd more guts, I'd have slung you out in the street long ago. D'you hear? What a pain . . . !"

Doña Rosa pats her belly and changes her mode of address.

"Now come, come, man . . . everybody to his job. You know, we mustn't lose our sense of proportion, damn it to hell, or the respect, d'you get me, or the respect!"

Doña Rosa lifts her chin and takes a deep breath. The little hairs of her mustache quiver as though in challenge, jauntily and yet ceremoniously, like the little black antennas of a courting cricket.

A kind of sorrow floats in the air and sinks into men's hearts. Hearts do not ache, and so they can suffer one hour after the other, for a whole lifetime, while we none of us ever understand with full clarity what it is that happens to us.

A gentleman with a white goatee feeds bits of bun soaked in light coffee to a swarthy little boy sitting on his knee. The gentleman's name is Don Trinidad García Sobrino, and he is a moneylender. Don Trinidad's youth had been turbulent, full of complications and distractions, but when his father died, he told himself: "From now on you'd better be careful, Trinidad my lad, or you'll land yourself in a mess." So he devoted himself to business and a well-ordered life and ended by being rich. It had been the dream of his life to become a deputy in the Cortes; he considered it no small distinction to be one of five hundred among a people of twenty-five million. For some years Don Trinidad cultivated a few third-rankers in Gil Robles's party, in the hope that they would make him a deputy; he did not mind for what constituency, having no predilection for any specific region. He spent money on entertaining them, contributed to the propaganda fund, was patted on the back, but in the end was neither nominated as a candidate nor even taken along to the informal circle of the Big Boss. Don Trinidad had some moments of bitterness and mental crisis, and finally turned himself into a follower of Lerroux. He seems to have done quite well in the Radical Party, but then came the Civil War and with it the end of his not very brilliant and rather brief political career. Nowadays Don Trinidad keeps aloof from the *res publica*, as Don Alejandro Lerroux put it on a memorable day, and is content to be left in peace and not reminded of the past while he continues to apply himself to the lucrative business of lending money at interest.

In the afternoons he takes his grandson to Doña Rosa's café, plies him with food, and stays quiet, listening to the music or reading his paper, interfering with no one.

Doña Rosa leans against a table and smiles. "Anything new, Elvira dear?"

Señorita Elvira sucks at her cigar and tilts her head just a little. Her cheeks are creased and her lids rimmed with red as if she had weak eyes.

"Did you settle that thing?"

"What thing?"

"The affair with . . ."

"No, it didn't work. He went round with me for three days, and after that he made me a present of a bottle of hair lotion."

"Some people have no conscience at all, my dear."

"Well—so what?"

Doña Rosa comes closer and speaks almost in her ear. "Why don't you make it up with Don Pablo?"

"Because I don't want to. After all, Doña Rosa, one has one's pride."

"What a pain . . . ! We've all got our weaknesses. But what I say to you, Elvira dear, is this—and you know I always want the best for you—what I say to you is that you were well off with Don Pablo."

"So-so. He asks a lot. And what's more, he slobbers. I loathed him in the end—but what can you do about it?—he made me feel quite sick."

Doña Rosa affects the sugary, persuasive voice of good advice: "You should have more patience, Elvira dear. You're still a little girl."

"You think so?"

Señorita Elvira spits under the table and wipes her mouth with the inside of a glove.

A printer by the name of Vega who has made money— Don Mario de la Vega is his name—is smoking a colossal cigar that looks as if it were part of an advertisement. The man at the next table tries to ingratiate himself.

"That's a fine cigar you're smoking there, my dear sir."

Vega answers gravely, but without looking at the man: "Yes, it's not too bad, it cost me a cool five pesetas."

The man at the next table, who is a smiling, undersized little man, would like to say something such as "I wish I were in your shoes," but he hasn't the courage; fortunately, shyness shuts him up at the last moment. He looks at the printer, smiles his meek smile, and says: "Only five? I'd have thought at least seven pesetas."

"No, five it was, plus thirty centimos for the tip. That's quite good enough for me."

"Yes, indeed."

"What d'you mean? I don't think one's got to be a millionaire like Romanones to smoke this sort of cigar."

"Not a millionaire, no, but . . . you see, I couldn't afford one, and most of the people in this place couldn't either."

"Would you like to smoke one?"

"Well . . ."

Vega smiles, almost as though he regrets in advance what he is going to say. "Then work as hard as I work."

And the printer gives a violent, a colossal guffaw. The smiling, undersized man at the next table stops smiling. He turns red and feels that his ears begin to burn, his eyes to smart. He looks down because he doesn't want to notice how the whole café stares at him; at least, he imagines that the whole café is staring at him.

While Don Pablo, a miserable fellow who sees everything upside down, is grinning over his tale about Madame Pimentón, Señorita Elvira drops the butt of her cigar and stamps on it. Now and then Señorita Elvira has the gestures of a real princess.

"What harm was that nice little cat doing you? Puss, puss, puss, come here!"

Don Pablo glances at the woman.

"And cats are such intelligent creatures! They're more reasonable than certain people. They're animals that understand everything. Puss, puss, puss, come here, come here. . . ."

The cat walks away without turning its head and disappears into the kitchen.

"I've a friend who's got money, he's a man with a lot of influence, don't you think he's one of those fellows without a penny to their name, and he has a cat called Sultan. That cat's a marvel."

"Is it really?"

"I'll say he is. 'Sultan,' my friend says, 'Sultan, come here.' And there he is, waving his beautiful tail that's just like a plume. 'Sultan, off with you,' he says, and off he goes like any great gentleman. I don't think there are many cats like him, he must be the Duke of Alba of the cat world. My friend loves him like his own child, but then he's a cat you can't help being fond of."

Don Pablo lets his eyes wander round the café. For an instant they meet Señorita Elvira's. Don Pablo blinks and turns his head.

"And then, cats are so affectionate. Have you noticed how affectionate they are? Once they get fond of a person, they go on being devoted to him all their lives."

Don Pablo clears his throat and makes his voice sound grave and important. "Their example might serve as a lesson to many human beings."

Don Pablo takes a deep breath. He is pleased with himself. The fact is that the bit about "their example might serve" and so on came out just right.

Pepe the waiter returns to his corner without saying a word. Once in his own domain, he puts one hand on the back of a chair and gazes at himself in the mirrors, as though at something very odd and strange. He sees himself fullface in the nearest mirror, he sees his back in the mirror on the rear wall, and his profile in those at the corners.

"What that damn old witch needs is somebody to slit her open one fine day. That old sow! That dirty old whore!"

Pepe is a man with whom things soon blow over. He is content to mumble a little phrase he would never have dared to say aloud.

"Bloodsucker! Old swine! Eating up the bread of the poor!"

Pepe is very fond of using sententious expressions in his moments of bad temper. Afterwards his mind begins to wander, and soon he has forgotten all about it.

Two little boys, five to six years old, are playing train between the tables, wearily and without any enthusiasm. When they are going towards the back of the café, one is the engine and the other the carriages. On the way back to the entrance they change places. Nobody takes any notice of them, but they go on stolidly, joylessly, running backwards and forwards with immense seriousness. They are a pair of thoroughly logical disciplinarians, two small boys who play train though it bores them stiff because they have decided to have fun, and, to have fun, they have decided that come what may they are going to play train the whole afternoon. If they don't get any fun out of it, it is not their fault. They are doing their best.

Pepe watches them and says: "It's going to fall, you are."

Pepe has lived in Castile for half a century and speaks Castilian, but he still translates every word directly from his native Galician. The children answer: "No, we won't," and go on playing train, without faith, without hope, and even without charity, as though carrying out a painful duty.

Doña Rosa enters the kitchen.

"How many ounces of chocolate have you put in, Gabriel?"

"Two, madam."

"There you are! There you are! Who could afford that? And on top of it, all those rules and regulations about wages, and overtime and whatnot. Didn't I tell you in so many words to put in an ounce and a half, and no more? But it's no good talking plain Spanish to you, you people don't want to understand and that's that."

Doña Rosa takes breath and resumes her attack. When she breathes, it is like a steam engine, panting and puffing rapidly, with her whole body shaking, and a hoarse whistle in her chest.

"And if Don Pablo thinks it isn't thick enough, he can take his wife and go where they'll give it to him stronger. A nice thing that would be! The cheek of him! That mean old beggar doesn't seem to know that if there's one thing we aren't short of here it's customers, thank the Lord. If he doesn't like it, he can lump it, it wouldn't be our loss. Who do they think they are—royalty? His wife's a poisonous snake and I'm fed up with her. Yes, I'm fed up to the teeth with Doña Pura, that's what!"

Gabriel warns her, as he does every day: "They may hear you, madam."

"Let them hear me if they like, that's why I'm saying it. My tongue isn't fur-lined, so what? The thing I can't understand is how that stupid old brute had the nerve to give Elvira the brush-off, and she an absolute angel, with no thought in her head except how to make him happy. And then he makes out like a lamb with Doña Pura, that old mischief-maker who's exactly like a fat snake and always laughing up her sleeve behind people's backs. Well, as my old mother used to say, God rest her soul: 'We live and learn.' "

Gabriel tries to straighten out the mess. "Would you like me to take out some of the chocolate I put in?"

"You know for yourself what you ought to do as an honest man, as a man who's got his wits about and isn't a thief. When you feel like it, you know perfectly well what's good for you."

Padilla, the cigarette boy, is talking with a new customer who has just bought a whole packet of tobacco.

"Is she always like that?"

"Yes, but she isn't so bad. She's got a strong temper all right, but she isn't really bad."

"But she called the waiter over there a fool."

"Goodness, that's nothing. Sometimes she calls us perverts and Reds."

The customer cannot believe his eyes and ears. "And you don't mind, then?"

"No, sir, we don't mind."

The new customer shrugs his shoulders.

"Well, well. . . ."

The cigarette boy walks off to make another round of the place. The customer is left to his thoughts.

"I don't know who is worse, that dirty old walrus in her black dress or this bunch of clowns. If they only got together one day and took hold of her and gave her a good walloping, she might see reason. But not they, they wouldn't dare. In their heads they're sure to call her names all day long, but outwardly—what we've seen just now. 'Out with you, you fool, you wretch, you thief.' And they're delighted. 'No, sir, we don't mind.' I can see it all. My word, what people! That's the way it goes."

The customer goes on smoking. His name is Mauricio Segovia and he works at the Central Telephone Exchange. I mention all this because he may turn up again. He is a man of thirty-eight to forty, with red hair and freckles. He lives a long way off, in Atocha, and it was by pure chance he came to this part of the city. He was following a young girl who suddenly turned a corner and disappeared through the first doorway before Maurico had made up his mind to speak to her.

The shoeblack is calling out: "Señor Suárez! Señor Suárez!"

Señor Suárez, who isn't a regular customer either, gets up from his seat and goes to the telephone. He walks with a limp, not of the foot but from higher up. He wears a fashionable suit of a light color and a pince-nez. He looks about fifty and might be a dentist or a hairdresser. If one looks closer, one might well take him for a pharmaceuticals salesman. Señor Suárez has all the signs of an extremely busy man, one of those who say in a single breath: "A *café exprès*, nothing with it; send me the shoeblack; and, boy, get a taxi for me."

When these very busy men go to the barber's they have a shave, a haircut, a manicure and a shoeshine, and a look at the paper. Sometimes, in saying good-by to a friend, they announce: "From such-and-such an hour to such-and-such an hour, I'll be at the café, then I'll have a look in at the office, and in the evening I'll drop in at my brother-in-law's. You'll find the numbers in the telephone book. Now I must go, I've still a lot of small things to see to." With such men you can tell at once that they are the conquerors, the outstanding figures, the men used to giving orders.

Señor Suárez talks quietly into the telephone, in the high-pitched, rather affected voice of a pansy. His jacket is a little too short and his trousers are tight-fitting like a bullfighter's.

"Is that you? . . . Naughty, very naughty! You are a

tease. . . . Yes . . . yes. . . . All right, just as you like. . . .
Good-by, precious. . . . He, he, you're always the same. Bye-
bye, ducky, I'll pick you up in no time."

Señor Suárez walks back to his table, smiling. Now his limp
has something tremulous about it, something shivery: it is an
almost lustful limp, coquettish and provocative. He pays for
his coffee, asks for a taxi, gets up as soon as it arrives, and
leaves, holding his head high like a Roman gladiator, oozing
satisfaction, radiating bliss.

Some people follow him with their eyes until the revolving
door swallows him up. No doubt there are persons who attract
attention more than others. You recognize them by the sort
of little star that marks their foreheads.

The proprietress makes a half-turn and goes to the counter.
The nickel-plated coffee machine bubbles away, producing
cups of *café exprès* ceaselessly, while the cash register, coppery
with age, never stops tinkling.

Several waiters with flabby, sorrowful, sallow faces, envel-
oped in worn-out dinner jackets, are standing there, the edges
of their trays resting on the marble, and waiting for the manager
to hand them the orders and the small gilt or silverplate saucers
with the change.

The manager puts the telephone back and hands out what
the waiters ask for.

"So you've been gossiping again, as if there wasn't any work
to do."

"I was only ordering more milk, madam."

"What, more milk? How much did they bring us this morning?"

"The usual, madam, sixty litres."

"And isn't that enough?"

"No, I don't think that will see us through."

"This place is worse than a Maternity Hospital. How much
more did you order?"

"Twenty litres, madam."

"Won't there be some left over?"

· 18 ·

"I don't think so."

"What d'you mean, 'you don't think'? What a pain! And if there is some left, eh?"

"There won't be—at least, I believe so."

"Yes, 'I believe,' it's always 'I believe.' It's easy enough to say that, but what if there is?"

"You'll see, madam, there won't be any left. Look how full the place is."

"Yes of course, 'Look how full the place is, look how full the place is.' That's quickly said. But why? Because I'm fair and give good value; if not, you'd see where they'd all go to. They're a lousy lot."

The waiters look at the floor and try to escape notice.

"And you there, put a bit more pep into it. There are too many straight coffees on those trays. Don't people know we have buns and sponge cake and tarts? No, they don't, and I know why. You're quite capable of not telling them on purpose. What you'd like is to see me ruined and selling lottery tickets in the street. But you'll be damned first. I know who I'm dealing with. A nice lot! Now come on, get along. And pray to any saint you like that I don't lose my head."

The waiters march away from the counter with their trays. With them, it's like water off a duck's back. No one gives Doña Rosa a glance. Not one of them gives Doña Rosa a thought either.

A man of the sort who put their elbows on the table—you remember?—and rest their pale foreheads in their hands, their eyes sad and bitter, their expression almost timorous, such a man is speaking to the waiter. He attempts a meek smile, looking like a lost child that begs water at a house on the roadside.

The waiter wags his head and calls the server. The server goes up to the proprietress.

"Madam, Pepe says the gentleman there won't pay."

"Well, it's up to him to get the cash any way he can. If he doesn't get it, tell him it'll come out of his pay packet and that's all there is to it. It really is the limit!"

The proprietress adjusts her lenses and looks around.

· 19 ·

"Which one is it?"

"The one over there, with the steel-rimmed spectacles."

"What a type! That's a good joke, that is. And such a face, too. Tell me, what's his reason for not wanting to pay?"

"Well, you see . . . he says he's come out without money."

"Now that's the last straw! In this country we've got more rascals than we need."

The server speaks in a thin voice without looking Doña Rosa in the eyes: "He says he'll come and pay as soon as he's got it."

The words that come from Doña Rosa's throat sound like brass.

"They all say that, and then what happens is that for one who comes back a hundred clear out, and out of sight, out of mind. Don't talk to me. If you breed ravens they'll peck out your eyes. Tell Pepe, he knows what to do: Into the street with the fellow, but gently, and when he's got him out there on the pavement, two good kicks where it hurts most."

The server ambles off, then Doña Rosa calls out to him: "Listen, tell Pepe to remember the face."

"Yes, madam."

Doña Rosa stays to watch the spectacle. Luis, still carrying his milk jugs, goes up to Pepe and whispers in his ear.

"That's all she says. For my part, God knows. . . ."

Pepe goes back to the customer, who rises slowly. He is a small man, stunted, pallid, and feeble, who wears spectacles framed in thin wire. His jacket is threadbare and his trousers frayed. He covers his head with a dark-gray felt hat, its ribbon grease-stained, and clutches a book in a newspaper cover under his arm.

"If you wish I'll leave you this book."

"No, no. Look here, get out into the street and don't make more trouble and upset for me."

The man walks to the door, followed by Pepe. They both go out. It is cold, and people are hurrying past. Newsboys are crying out the evening papers. A tram comes down the Calle de Fuencarral, clattering sadly, tragically, almost lugubriously.

The man is not a nobody, not one of the *hoi polloi*, not a vulgar man, one of the herd, an ordinary, standardized human being: he has a tattoo mark on his left arm and a scar in the groin. He is well read and translates a little from the French. He has assiduously followed the trends of intellectual and literary life, and would be able to quote by heart, even now, some of the essays published in *El Sol*. As a young man he had a fiancée who was Swiss, and he used to write futurist poetry.

The shoeblack is talking to Don Leonardo Meléndez. Don Leonardo says: "We, the Meléndez, an age-old line connected with the most ancient families of Castile, were once upon a time the masters of lands and lives. Today, as you see, we're practically in the middle of *la rue*."

The shoeblack feels admiration for Don Leonardo. The fact that Don Leonardo has robbed him of his savings seems to be something that fills him with awe and loyalty. Today Don Leonardo is affable with him, and the shoeblack takes advantage of this to frisk around him like a little lap dog. There are days, however, when he is less lucky and Don Leonardo treats him like dirt. On those days of misfortune, the shoeblack approaches him submissively and addresses him quietly, humbly.

"Anything new, sir?"

Don Leonardo does not trouble to answer. The shoeblack is not discouraged and persists.

"Terribly cold today, sir."

"Yes."

The shoeblack smiles. He is happy and would gladly give another thirty thousand pesetas for the response he elicited.

"A little more polish, sir?"

The shoeblack kneels down, and Don Leonardo, who hardly ever gives him a glance, peevishly puts his foot on the iron footrest of the box.

Not today. Today Don Leonardo is in a good mood. No doubt the draft project for the floating of an important limited company is taking shape in his mind.

"There was a time, *mon dieu*, when it was sufficient for one of us to look in at the Exchange to make everybody stop buying or selling until they saw what we were doing."

"That was something, wasn't it, sir?"

Don Leonardo purses his lips in an ambiguous grimace while his hand draws hieroglyphs in the air.

"Have you got a cigarette paper?" he says to the man at the nearest table. "I'd like to roll myself one with cut tobacco, but I find I've run out of papers."

The shoeblack keeps quiet and pretends not to have heard: he knows his place.

Doña Rosa comes up to Elvira, who has been watching the scene between the waiter and the man who did not pay for his coffee.

"Have you seen, dear?"

Señorita Elvira tarries a little with her answer.

"Poor boy . . . perhaps he's had nothing to eat all day, Doña Rosa."

"What, are you going all romantic on me, too? Then we've had it. Nobody could have a softer heart than I have, I assure you, but that's too much."

Elvira does not know how to reply. The poor girl is a sentimentalist who took to a loose life so as not to starve to death, or at least not quite so soon. She has never learned to do any work and, what is more, she is neither pretty nor accomplished. At home, as a small girl, she knew nothing but abuse and disaster. Elvira came from Burgos and is the daughter of a dangerous fellow called, in his lifetime, Fidel Hernández. Fidel Hernández killed his wife Eudosia with a cobbler's awl, was sentenced to death, and garroted by Gregorio Mayoral, the public hangman, in 1909. All he said was: "If I'd done her in with Bordeaux mixture, God himself wouldn't have known."

Elvira was eleven or twelve when she was left an orphan; she went to Villalón to live with her grandmother, who went round the parish with the collection box for St. Anthony's

Loaf. The poor old woman had a hard life, and when they had garroted her son, she began to waste away and died soon after. The other village girls had their fun with Elvira, pointing at the gibbet and telling her: "On one just like this they strung up your father, you nasty thing." One day, when Elvira could stand it no longer, she ran off with an Asturian who had come to sell sugar almonds at the village fair. She stuck to him for two long years, but as he nearly broke her back with the drubbings he gave her, she sent him to hell one day, in Orense, and set up as a whore in the bawdy house kept by La Pelona in the Calle del Villar; there she had a friend, the daughter of La Marraca, who used to gather faggots in the field of Francelos, by Rivadavia, and had twelve daughters, every single one a whore. From then on, it was all plain sailing for Elvira, let's put it like that.

The poor girl is somewhat embittered, but not overmuch. She has good instincts and, timid though she is, a remnant of pride.

Don Jaime Arce, bored with doing nothing but gaze at the ceiling and think sheer drivel, lifts his head from the back of the seat, and explains to the silent lady who watches life pass by from the foot of the spiral staircase that leads up to the billiard room: "All humbug . . . bad organization . . . mistakes as well, I don't deny it. But that is all, believe me. The banks do not function properly and the notaries, with their fussiness and haste, barge in ahead of time and create an entanglement that nobody could make head or tail of."

Don Jaime's face expresses a worldly-wise resignation.

"And so things take their course: writs—complications—the whole mess."

Don Jaime speaks slowly, with a great economy of words and a certain solemnity. He is deliberate in his gestures and takes care to let his words fall one by one, as though wanting to watch, measure, and weigh their impact. At bottom he is not insincere. The woman whose son died, on the other hand, seems like a nitwit with nothing to say; she only listens, opening her eyes wide in an odd fashion, as if she were trying to keep awake rather than to pay attention.

"That's all, madam. Anything else, let me tell you, is just bilge."

Don Jaime Arce is a well-spoken man, even though in the middle of a polished phrase he is apt to use unrefined words such as "mess" or "hodgepodge" or others of the same style.

The woman looks at him and says nothing. She simply moves her head back and forth, with a gesture that doesn't mean anything either.

"And now, if you see—everybody's talking. If my poor old mother were to return to this life now!"

When Don Jaime had reached his "let me tell you," the woman, Doña Isabel Montes, widow of Sanz, began to think of her dead husband as he was when she first knew him, handsome, elegant, very straight in the back, with a waxed mustache, and twenty-three years old. A misty wave of happiness drifted vaguely through her head, and Doña Isabel smiled, most discreetly, for half a second. Then she remembered her poor little Paco and the foolish look on his face when he had meningitis, and turned sad again, abruptly, almost violently.

When Don Jaime Arce opens his eyes properly, after having turned them heavenwards to reinforce his "if my poor mother were to return to this life now," he becomes aware of Doña Isabel and asks her gallantly: "Are you not feeling well, madam? You look a little pale."

"Oh, no, it's nothing, thank you very much. Just one of those ideas one gets."

Almost against his will, Don Pablo is always looking at Señorita Elvira out of the corner of his eye. Though it is all over and done with, he cannot forget their time together. All things considered, she was good, docile, and compliant. Outwardly Don Pablo pretends to despise her; he calls her a dirty prostitute; but inwardly it is different. In his moments of soft whispers and tenderness, Don Pablo used to think: "This isn't a matter of sex, no, it's a matter of the heart." Afterwards he forgot this and would have let her die of hunger or of leprosy without a pang. Don Pablo is like that.

"Luis, come here. What's wrong with that young man?"

"Nothing, Don Pablo, only that he didn't feel like paying for the coffee he had."

"You ought to have told me, man. He looked a decent sort."

"Don't you believe it. There are a lot of spongers and rascals about."

Doña Pura, Don Pablo's wife, says: "Of course there are a lot of spongers and rascals about, that's quite true. If one only knew them! What everybody should do is to work as God ordains, isn't it so, Luis?"

"Yes, maybe, madam."

"There you are. Then there wouldn't be any problem. The man who works can have his coffee, and a bun as well if he feels like it, but the man who doesn't work . . . Now look here: the man who doesn't work deserves no pity. The rest of us don't live on air."

Doña Pura is very pleased with her speech; it came off very well indeed.

Don Pablo turns again to the woman who had been frightened by the cat: "With those types who don't pay for their coffee one has to take care, great care. You never know what sort of man you come across. The chap they've just put out in the street may be one of two things—a gifted creature, what you might call a true genius, like Cervantes or like Isaac Peral, or an impudent rogue. I, for one, I'd have paid for his coffee. What does a coffee more or less matter to me?"

"Of course."

Don Pablo smiles like someone suddenly discovering that he has been absolutely right.

"That's the sort of thing you would never find among the dumb animals. Dumb animals are nobler, they never cheat. A dear thoroughbred cat like the one that gave you such a fright just now—he, he!—is God's own creature and all it wants to do is to play, only to play."

A beatific smile lights up Don Pablo's face. If his breast

could be opened, his heart would be found to be black and sticky like pitch.

After a short while Pepe comes in again. The proprietress, her hands in the pockets of her apron, her shoulders thrown back, legs apart, calls for him in a dry, cracked voice sounding like the clatter of a bell with a broken clapper.

"Come here!"

Pepe scarcely dares look at her. "What is it, madam?"

"Did you kick him?"

"Yes, madam."

"How often?"

"Twice."

The proprietress rolls her eyes behind her glasses, takes her hands from the pockets, and passes them slowly over her face where the coarse stubble begins to show, not quite hidden by her rice powder.

"Where did you kick him?"

"Where I could. On the legs."

"Well done. That'll teach him. Another time he won't try to steal decent people's good money."

Doña Rosa, her fat little hands on her belly, which is swollen like a goatskin filled with oil, is the very image of the revenge of the well-fed upon the hungry. Rascals! Dogs! Her fingers, like sausages bursting out of their skin, reflect the electric light in beautiful, almost voluptuous glints.

Pepe moves away from his mistress with a humble look. At bottom, though he is not fully aware of it, his conscience is clear.

Don José Rodríguez de Madrid talks with two friends who are playing checkers.

"There you see, forty pesetas, forty lousy pesetas. And then people go round talking their silly heads off."

One of the players grins at him. "It's more than you'd get out of a stone, Don José."

"Oh, well, just a little more. What can you do with forty pesetas?"

"Admittedly, old man, you can't do much with forty pesetas, and that's the truth. But after all, what I say is, everything's welcome but a kick in the pants."

"That's true, too. When all's said and done it didn't give me much trouble to earn them."

The violinist who was fired because he had answered back to Don José would have made forty pesetas last a week. He ate little and badly, he only smoked what he was given, but he managed to eke out forty pesetas over a whole week; no doubt there were others who kept alive on still less.

Señorita Elvira calls the cigarette boy. "Padilla!"

"Coming, Señorita Elvira."

"Give me two Tritons. I'll pay tomorrow."

"All right."

Padilla takes the two cigars from the packet and puts them in front of Señorita Elvira.

"One's for later, you know, for after supper."

"That's right. We trust you here, you know."

The cigarette boy's smile has a touch of gallantry. Señorita Elvira smiles back.

"Listen, would you give Macario a message for me?"

"Yes."

"Ask him to be so kind as to play *Luisa Fernanda.*"

The cigarette boy drags his feet towards the musicians' dais. A gentleman who has been exchanging glances with Señorita Elvira for some time now decides to break the ice.

"These *zarzuelas* have some pretty tunes, haven't they, Señorita?"

Señorita Elvira agrees with a pout. The gentleman is not discouraged; he interprets her grimace as a sign of sympathy.

"And they are very sentimental, too, don't you think?"

Señorita Elvira rolls her eyes. The gentleman gathers new strength.

"Do you like the theater?"

· 27 ·

"If it's good . . ."

The gentleman laughs as if to applaud a wisecrack. He clears his throat, offers Señorita Elvira a light, and resumes: "Of course, of course. And the pictures? Do you like the pictures, too?"

"Sometimes . . ."

The gentleman makes a gigantic effort, an effort that makes him blush to the roots of his hair: "Those dark little cinemas, eh, what about them?"

Señorita Elvira answers in a tone of dignity and mistrust. "I only go to the cinema to see the film."

The gentleman beats a retreat.

"Of course, naturally, so do I. . . . What I said was meant for the young people, of course, for those nice young couples—we've all been young once. . . . But say, Señorita, I've noticed you're a smoker; I think it's a very good thing if women smoke, a very good thing, naturally. After all, what's wrong with it? The best thing for everyone is to live one's own life, don't you think? I mention this because, if you'll allow me—I've got to go now, I'm in a great hurry, but we'll meet another time to continue our chat! If you'll allow me. I'd be delighted . . . well, I mean . . . to offer you a packet of Tritons."

The gentleman speaks hastily and in trepidation. Señorita Elvira answers with a certain distaste, as one who has the upper hand: "All right, why not? If you're set on it. . . ."

The gentleman calls the cigarette boy, buys the packet, and hands it to Señorita Elvira with his best smile. Then he gets into his overcoat, takes his hat, and leaves. But first he says to Señorita Elvira: "Well, Señorita, it has been a pleasure. Leoncio Maestre, at your service. As I've said, we must meet another time. We may well become very close friends."

The proprietress calls the manager. The manager's name is López, Consorcio López; he comes from Tomelloso in the province of Ciudad Real, a big, beautiful, and very prosperous market town. López is a young man, handsome and rather natty, with large hands and a narrow forehead. He is a little indolent and doesn't give a hoot for Doña Rosa's tempers. "The best thing with that woman," he always says, "is to let her talk, then she stops by herself."

Consorcio López is a practical philosopher and, really, his philosophy is serving him well. Once in Tomelloso, ten or twelve years ago and shortly before his coming to Madrid, Consorcio had refused to marry a girl friend whom he had saddled with twins. Her brother had said to him: "Either you marry Encarna, or I'll geld you next time I get you in a corner." As Consorcio wished neither to marry nor to be made a eunuch, he took the next train and departed for Madrid; and the affair must have been forgotten as time went by, for the fact was that they never bothered him again. Consorcio always carried two photos of his twins in his wallet. One was taken when they were a few months old and lying stark naked on a cushion, and the other on the day of their first Communion; the second photo was sent to him by his former girl friend, Marujita Ranero, who by then had become Señora de Gutiérrez.

Doña Rosa, as we have said, calls the manager: "López!"

"Coming, madam."

"How are we off for vermouth?"

"All right for the moment."

"And for *anís?*"

"Not too bad. We're getting short of one or two brands."

"Then let them drink others. I won't go in for extra expense now, I just don't feel like it. The things people expect to get! Now listen, did you buy that stuff?"

"The sugar? Yes, they'll bring it tomorrow."

"At fourteen-fifty, after all?"

"Yes, madam. They wanted fifteen, but we agreed that they'd come down by fifty centimos the kilo because it's a bulk order."

"Good. And now you know, a little sugar in a paper bag

with every order, and no second helping for anyone. Is that clear?"

"Yes, madam."

The young man who is writing verse licks his pencil and stares at the ceiling. He is one of those poets who write poems with "ideas." This afternoon he has his idea but not yet his rhymes. He has got a few down on paper. What he is looking for is something to rhyme with *stream*, which must be neither *seem* nor *team*. He is turning *redeem* and *gleam* round in his mind.

"I'm shut up in a stupid armor, in the shell of a common clod. *The girl with the deep blue eyes.* . . . But I want to be strong, more than strong. . . . *The girl, blue-eyed and fair.* . . . Either the work kills the man or the man kills the work. *She of the wheat-gold hair.* . . . To die! To die, just that, and leave a slender book of poetry behind. How fair, how fair she is!"

The young poet is pale, he is very white and has two pink spots on his cheekbones.

"*The girl of the deep blue eyes* . . . stream, stream, stream. . . . *The girl, blue-eyed and fair* . . . seem, team, seem, team. *She of the wheat-gold hair* . . . redeem. *And suddenly his free will to redeem.* The girl of the deep blue eyes. . . . *In rapture his free will so to redeem.* The girl of the deep blue eyes. . . . *And free again my will I shall redeem.* The girl of the deep blue eyes. . . . *Or turn your face towards the gentle gleam.* The girl of the deep blue eyes . . . the girl with. . . . What sort of eyes has the girl? . . . *And reap the corn in golden summer gleam* . . ."

Suddenly the young man sees the café all blurred.

"*Kissing the universe, a golden gleam.* That's funny."

He sways a little like a child that gets dizzy, and feels a wave of intense heat mount to his temples.

"I feel rather . . . perhaps my mother. . . . Yes, gleam, that's it, gleam. . . . *Over a naked woman flies a man.* . . . *What a team.* . . . No, not team. . . . And then I shall say to her: 'Never!' . . . That's funny. Very funny . . ."

At a table in the background, two women, both living on pensions and both smothered in paint up to their eyebrows, are discussing the musicians.

"He's a real artist; I love to listen to him. As my poor dear Ramón used to say, God rest his soul: 'Matilde, just watch the way he brings the violin up to his chin.' There you see how things are in this life; if that young man had somebody to pull strings for him, he'd go far."

Doña Matilde shows the whites of her eyes. She is fat, grubby, and pretentious. She smells and she has a huge dropsical belly.

"He's a real artist, a first-class artist."

"It's quite true. I look forward to this hour the whole day. He's a real artist, I absolutely agree. Whenever he plays the waltz from *The Merry Widow* as only he can, I feel a different woman."

Doña Asunción has the condescending mien of a sheep.

"Don't you think it was a different kind of music in those days? More refinement, I mean, and more feeling."

Doña Matilde has a son who is an impersonator and lives in Valencia.

Doña Asunción has two daughters: one is married to a clerk at the Ministry of Public Works called Miguel Contreras, and the other is unmarried, a reckless creature who lives with a university professor in Bilbao.

The moneylender wipes the little boy's mouth with a handkerchief. He has shining, kindly eyes and shows a certain distinction, although he is not really well groomed. The boy has had a mugful of light coffee and two buns and is ready for more. Don Trinidad García Sobrino neither thinks nor moves. He is a mild man, an orderly man, a man who wants to live in peace. His grandson looks like a little gypsy, thin yet potbellied. He wears a knitted cap and knitted leggings; he is a child who wears a good many warm clothes.

"Is there anything wrong, young man? Are you not feeling well?"

The young poet does not answer. His eyes are wide open and bewildered, and he seems to be struck dumb. A tuft of hair has fallen onto his forehead.

Don Trinidad puts his grandson down on the seat, gets up, and takes the poet by his shoulders.

"Are you ill?"

A few heads turn. The poet smiles a foolish, listless smile.

"Would somebody help me to hold him up? It looks as if he'd been taken ill."

The poet's feet slide, and his body falls under the table.

"Lend me a hand, somebody. I can't manage alone."

People get up. From the counter, Doña Rosa is watching: "Some people like to make trouble. . . ."

The boy knocked his forehead against the table when he collapsed.

"Let's take him to the lavatory. It must be a dizzy spell."

While Don Trinidad and three or four other guests take the poet to the W.C. so that he should recover a little, Don Trinidad's grandson amuses himself with eating the crumbs of the buns off the table.

"The smell of the disinfectant will bring him round. It must be a dizzy spell."

Seated on the lavatory, his head resting against the wall, the poet smiles as if in bliss. Even though he does not know it, he is happy at heart.

Don Trinidad returns to his table.

"Is he better now?"

"Yes, it wasn't much, just a dizzy spell."

Señorita Elvira gives the two Tritons back to the cigarette boy.

"And here's one for yourself."

"Thanks. That was lucky, wasn't it?"

"Well—better than nothing."

Once Padilla called an admirer of Señorita Elvira's a mug,

and she was offended. Since then the cigarette boy has been more respectful.

A tram nearly knocks down Don Leoncio Maestre.

"Idiot!"

"Idiot yourself, you poor fool. What are you dreaming about?"

Don Leoncio Maestre is dreaming about Elvirita.

"She's pretty, yes, very pretty. I should say so! And she seems a well-bred girl. . . . Surely she isn't a tart. How can one know? Everybody's life is a novel by itself. To look at, she's a girl of good family who has quarreled with her people. Now she will be working in an office, most probably in one of the syndicates. She's got sad, deliberate features. What she needs is, I think, affection and a lot of petting and somebody to show her his admiration the whole day long."

Don Leoncio Maestre's heart leaps beneath his shirt.

"I'll go back there tomorrow. I certainly shall. If she's there it's a good sign, and if not . . . is she isn't . . . I must find her."

Don Leoncio Maestre turns up the collar of his overcoat and makes two little hops.

"Elvira, Señorita Elvira. It's a nice name. I imagine that packet of Tritons must have pleased her. Every time she smokes one she'll remember me. . . . Tomorrow I'll tell her my name again. Leoncio, Leoncio. Leoncio. Perhaps she'll one day call me by a more affectionate name, something based on Leoncio. Leo. Oncio. Oncete . . . I'll have a glass of beer now, I feel like it."

Don Leoncio Maestre enters a bar and has a glass of beer at the counter. A girl sitting on a stool next to him gives him a smile. Don Leoncio turns his back to her. To tolerate that smile would be like a betrayal, his first betrayal of Elvirita.

"No, not Elvirita. Elvira. It's a simple name and a very pretty name."

The girl sitting on the stool addresses him from the rear.

"Would you give me a light, misery?"

Don Leoncio almost trembles as he lights her cigarette. He pays for his beer and hurries out into the street.

"Elvira . . . Elvira . . ."

Before Doña Rosa leaves the manager, she asks: "Have you given the musicians their coffee?"

"Not yet."

"Then give it to them now. They look exhausted."

The musicians on their dais drag out the final notes of a piece from *Luisa Fernanda*, the lovely bit that begins:

> "Among the oak woods
> Of my Extremadura
> Lies my little house
> Quiet and secure."

Before it they had played the *Moment Musical*, and before that something from *The Girl with the Bunch of Roses*, the number about the "pretty girl from Madrid, flower of the fair."

Doña Rosa walks over to them.

"I've told them to bring you your coffee, Macario."

"Thank you, Doña Rosa."

"Not at all. You know I never go back on my word. A promise is a promise with me."

"Oh, I know, Doña Rosa."

"So there."

The violinist, who has the large, bulging eyes of a weary ox, is looking at her while he rolls himself a cigarette. He purses his lips as though in scorn, and his hands are unsteady.

"And you'll get yours too, Seoane."

"Good."

"Well, well. You don't exactly waste words, I notice."

Macario intervenes to pour oil on troubled waters.

"The fact is, he's got stomach trouble, Doña Rosa."

"That's no reason for being so dull, I should say. The manners of some people . . . When one's got to tell them something, they kick, and when one's doing them a favor they ought to be pleased with, all they say is 'Good,' just as if they were noble lords. My foot!"

Seoane keeps quiet while his colleague appeases Doña Rosa. Then he asks the nearest guest: "What about that young boy?"

"Recuperating in the Gentlemen's. It was nothing."

Vega, the printer, offers his tobacco pouch to the flatterer at the next table.

"Go on, roll yourself a fag and don't snivel. I was once worse off than you are. And d'you know what I did? I got down to work."

"That's a great thing."

"Of course, man, of course, work—and no thought for anything else. And now, as you see, I can afford my cigar and my drink every afternoon."

The other makes a movement with his head which means exactly nothing.

"And if I told you that I want to work and can't find anything to work at?"

"Nonsense. There's only one thing needed for working, and that's to want to. Are you quite sure you want to work?"

"Goodness, yes."

"Then why don't you carry luggage to the station?"

"I couldn't. I'd crack up in three days. I'm a graduate . . ."

"And what good has it done you?"

"Not much, I admit."

"What's wrong with you, friend, is just what's wrong with a lot more people. They sit about in a café in comfort, twiddle their thumbs, and never do an honest stroke of work. Then one day they fall down in a faint like the sissy they've just carried indoors, and that's that."

The graduate gives back the printer's tobacco pouch and does not contradict him. "Many thanks."

"Don't mention it. Are you really a graduate?"

"Yes, sir. Of the curriculum of 1903."

"Good, then I'll give you a chance so you don't have to end

up in a poorhouse or on line for leftovers at a barracks. Do you want to work?"

"Yes, sir. I told you so already."

"Come and see me tomorrow. Here's my card. Come in the morning before twelve, say at half past eleven. If you want to, and can do it, you may work for me as a proofreader. The one I had was a good-for-nothing, and I had to chuck him out just this morning. He was not exact."

Señorita Elvira takes a sidelong glance at Don Pablo. Don Pablo is lecturing a youngster at the adjoining table: "Bicarbonate is good stuff, and perfectly harmless. The only thing is that the doctors won't prescribe it because nobody goes to a doctor just to be given a prescription of bicarbonate."

The youth nods without paying much attention and looks at Señorita Elvira's knees, which show a little beneath the table.

"Don't look over there and don't play the fool. I'll explain to you later, but don't you meddle with her."

Don Pablo's wife, Doña Pura, is deep in conversation with a friend, a stout woman bedecked with jewelry who scratches at her gold teeth with a toothpick.

"I'm absolutely tired of repeating the same thing. So long as there are men and women in the world, there will always be affairs. Man's the fire and woman's the yarn, and so things happen. What I told you about the platform of the forty-nine tram is the sober truth. I don't know what the world is coming to."

The stout lady absent-mindedly breaks the toothpick between her teeth.

"Yes, I agree with you, there isn't much modesty to be found these days. It all started with mixed bathing, you may be sure. We weren't like that before. . . . Now they present a young thing to you, you shake hands with her, and you're left all atremble the whole blessed day. After all, you may catch something you haven't got."

"True enough."

"And I think the cinemas are much to blame, too. People sitting there higgledy-piggledy and in the pitch dark, that can't come to any good."

"I quite agree with you, Doña María. What's needed is better morals, otherwise we poor decent women will pay for it."

Doña Rosa picks up the thread where she dropped it.

"And what's more, if you've got a stomach-ache, why don't you ask me for a pinch of bicarbonate? Have I ever refused you a pinch of bicarbonate? Anyone would think you haven't got a tongue in your head."

Doña Rosa turns round and raises her shrill, unpleasant voice above all the conversations going on in the café: "López! López! Send some bicarbonate for the violinist!"

The server leaves his jugs on a table and brings on a plate half a glass of water, a coffee spoon, and the sugar bowl of nickel-silver in which the bicarbonate is kept.

"What, have you stopped using trays?"

"That's how Señor López gave it to me, madam."

"All right, all right. Put it down here and clear off."

The server ranges everything on the piano and goes away.

Seoane fills the little spoon with the powder, throws back his head, opens his mouth, and in it goes. He chews it as if he were munching nuts, and washes it down with a sip of water.

"Thank you, Doña Rosa."

"Now do you see, do you see how little it costs to have manners? You've a stomach-ache, I send for bicarbonate, and everything's all right. We're here to help one another, but the fact is we can't because we don't want to. That's life."

The children who were playing train have suddenly stopped. A gentleman is explaining to them that they ought to behave more politely and quietly, and they watch him with curiosity, not knowing what to do with their hands. The older one,

Bernabé, is thinking of a boy next door, more or less his own age, who is called Chús. The younger one, Paquité, is thinking that the gentleman smells from his mouth. "It stinks like rotten rubber."

Bernabé is tickled as he remembers a funny thing that happened to Chús with his aunt. "Chús, you're a pig not to change your pants till you've got them all mucky. Aren't you ashamed of yourself?"

Bernabé holds back his laugh on remembering this; the gentleman would be furious. "Oh, no, auntie, I'm not. Dad makes his pants mucky too." It was enough to laugh oneself to death.

Paquité spends a little while in deep thought.

"No, it isn't of rotten rubber his mouth smells. It smells of red cabbage and of feet. If I was that gentleman, I'd stuff a melted candle in my nose. Then I'd talk like cousin Emilita, through the *dose*; they'll have to operate on her throat. Mamma says when she's had her operation she won't have her idiot face any longer and she won't sleep with her mouth open. But perhaps she'll die when they operate on her. Then they'll put her in a white coffin because she hasn't got tits yet and doesn't wear high heels."

The two ladies who live on pensions lean back on the seat and have a good look at Doña Pura.

The two old parrots' ideas about the violinist still float in the air like roving bubbles.

"I can't understand how it is that such women exist—she's just like a toad. She spends her whole time tearing people's reputations to pieces, and then she doesn't even see that the only reason her husband stands her is that she's got some money left. That Don Pablo there is a crook, a nasty bit of work. If he looks at a woman it's just as if he was stripping her with his eyes."

"Yes, indeed."

"And the other one, that Elvira, she's got her faults, too. What I mean to say, it isn't the same as with your girl, Paquita, who leads a respectable life when all's said and done, even if her papers aren't in order; that creature over there's something else, she flits around from one man to the next, squeezing a little money out of every one to fill her stomach."

"And another thing, Doña Matilde, you can't compare that nobody, that Don Pablo, with my daughter's friend who's a real professor of psychology, logic, and ethics and a perfect gentleman."

"Of course I don't. Paquita's friend has got respect for her and keeps her happy; and as far as she's concerned, he's handsome and agreeable and so she lets him love her, that's what she's made for, after all. But these hussies have no conscience and all they know is how to open their mouths to ask for something. They ought to be ashamed of themselves."

Doña Rosa carries on her conversation with the musicians. Her whole fat, bulging little body inflated, she shivers with joy as she makes her speech: she is like a civil governor.

"So you've your troubles? Tell me, and if I can, I'll fix them for you. So you think you're doing a good job, standing up here and scratching the fiddle as God meant you to? All right, here I am at closing time to pay you your five pesetas, and we're quits. Everything's all right if we're all friends together. Why d'you think I'm at swords' points with my brother-in-law? Because he's a tramp who goes whoring round, twenty-four hours a day, and then comes home to get his free supper. My sister's a damn fool to stand for it, but she's always been like that. Now if it were me . . . For all his beautiful eyes, I wouldn't let him trail round the whole day lifting skirts and pinching bottoms. Not me! Now if my brother-in-law were to work like I do, and if he were to put his back into it and bring home something at least, it would be another story. But it suits him better to soft-soap Visi, simple fool that she is, and to have a good time without doing a stroke."

"Yes, I see."

"So that's it. That guy's a miserable drone, he was born to be a pimp. And don't you imagine I say this only behind his back, the other day I told him the same thing right to his face."

· 39 ·

"Well done."

"Well done indeed. What's that beggar take us for?"

"Is that clock right, Padilla?"

"Yes, Señorita Elvira."

"Will you give me a light? It's still early."

The cigarette boy gives Señorita Elvira a light.

"You look happy, miss."

"Do you think so?"

"Well, it looks like it to me. I'd have said you're cheerier tonight than other evenings."

"Sometimes one has to put up a good front."

Señorita Elvira has a weak, sickly, and almost depraved air. The poor girl does not eat enough to be either depraved or virtuous.

The mother of the dead boy who was studying for the post office says: "Well, I must go now."

Don Jaime Arce rises with great courtesy and says, smiling: "Your devoted servant, Señora. Till tomorrow, by God's grace."

The lady moves a chair out of the way. "Good night and keep well."

"And the same to you, Señora. At your service."

The widowed Isabel Montes de Sanz walks like a queen. In her threadbare little cape, more for show than for use, Doña Isabel looks like an elegant courtesan past her prime who has lived like the proverbial grasshopper and has saved nothing towards old age. She crosses the room in silence and glides through the door. In the glances that follow her there is everything but indifference; there may be admiration, envy, sympathy, mistrust, or tenderness—who knows?

Don Jaime Arce no longer thinks of mirrors, or of virtuous old spinsters, or of the number of people with T.B. within the café (approximately 10 per cent), or of artists at pencil-sharpening, or of blood circulation. In the last hour of the evening Don Jaime Arce falls prey to a sleepiness that stupefies him.

"What are seven times four? Twenty-eight. And six times nine? Fifty-four. And nine times nine? Eighty-one. Where is the source of the Ebro? At Reinosa in the province of Santander."

Don Jaime Arce smiles, satisfied with his self-examination; while his fingers pull cigarette stubs to shreds, he repeats under his breath: "Ataulph, Sigerich, Walia, Theodored, Turismond . . . I bet that imbecile there doesn't know the list of the Visigoth Kings!"

That imbecile is the young poet, who emerges, white as chalk, from his rest cure in the W.C.

"As running water blurs the gentle gleam . . ."

Doña Rosa has gone in mourning, no one knows for whom, ever since she was a very young girl, which was many years ago; she is dirty and is hung with diamonds worth a fortune. Every year she grows a little fatter, nearly at the same rate at which she accumulates money.

She is a very rich woman. She owns the house with the café, and in the Calle de Apodaca, the Calle de Churruca, the Calle de Campoamor, and the Calle de Fuencarral dozens of tenants tremble like schoolboys on every first of the month.

"The more you trust them," she likes to say, "the more they take advantage of you. They're wasters, regular wasters. If there weren't honest judges in the world, I don't know what we'd come to."

Doña Rosa has her own ideas about honesty.

"Straight accounts, my dear, straight accounts, and no tampering."

She has never let anyone off by a penny and never permitted payment in installments.

"Why is there such a thing as a law of eviction," she would say, "unless it is applied? The way I see it, the law exists so that it is respected by everybody, first of all by myself. Anything else would be the Revolution."

Doña Rosa is a shareholder in a bank, where she drives the whole board mad, and according to the gossip in the district, she has trunks full of gold hidden away so carefully that they weren't found even during the Civil War.

The shoeblack has finished cleaning Don Leonardo's shoes.

"Here you are, sir."

Don Leonardo looks down at his shoes and gives him a cigarette from a ninety-centimos packet.

"Thank you very much, sir."

Don Leonardo pays no fee for the service, he never does. He permits his shoes to be cleaned in exchange for a small gesture. Don Leonardo is so mean that he rouses abject admiration in imbeciles.

Each time the shoeblack wipes Don Leonardo's shoes he remembers his thirty thousand pesetas. At bottom he is delighted to have been able to help Don Leonardo out of a fix. On the surface it irks him a little, next to nothing.

"The gentry are the gentry, that's as clear as day. Nowadays things are a bit upside down, but you can still tell a born gentleman at a glance."

If the shoeblack were an educated man, he would no doubt be a reader of Vásquez Mella's traditionalist writings.

Alfonsito, the messenger boy, is back from the street with the newspapers.

"Now look here, kid, wherever have you been to for the paper?"

Alfonsito is a sickly child of twelve or thirteen with fair hair and a constant cough. His father, who was a journalist, died two years ago in King's Hospital. His mother, who used to be a finicky young lady before her marriage, took to cleaning offices in the Gran Vía and having her meals in the soup kitchen of Auxilio Social.

"There was a line for it, madam."

"Of course, a line! It's simply that people now line up for the news, as if they hadn't anything more important to do. Come on, give me the paper."

"They were out of *Informaciones*, madam. I've brought you *Madrid*."

"Never mind. What d'you get out of them anyway? Tell me, Seoane, do you understand why there's so much government fuss and bother all over the world?"

"Well . . ."

"Now listen, there's no need for you to pretend. If you don't want to say anything, you don't. Goodness me, all that secrecy!"

Seoane smiles, with the bitter face of a dyspeptic, and says nothing. Why speak?

"As if I didn't know what's behind all this silence and smiling—as if I didn't know very well what's going on here! You don't want to know? All right, it's your business. I tell you one thing: it's the facts that speak. And how!"

Alfonsito leaves copies of *Madrid* at various tables.

Don Pablo produces his coppers.

"Any news in it?"

"I don't know, sir. You'll see for yourself."

Don Pablo spreads the paper on the table and reads the headlines. Over his shoulder Pepe tries to pick out the news.

Señorita Elvira beckons to the boy.

"Let me have the house copy when Doña Rosa's finished with it."

Doña Matilde, who has a chat with the cigarette boy while her friend Doña Asunción has gone to the toilet, comments scornfully: "I can't see why they want to find out about everything that's going on. As long as we're left in peace . . . don't you agree?"

"That's just what I always say, madam."

Doña Rosa reads the war news.

"They're going back a long way, it seems to me. . . . Well, if they come out on top in the end, it's all right. D'you think they'll come out on top in the end, Macario?"

The pianist looks doubtful.

"I don't know, it's possible. If they invent something that works."

Doña Rosa stares at the piano keys. Her face is sad and has

a faraway look, she seems to be talking to herself, thinking aloud.

"The trouble is, the Germans—who are gentlemen as true as God made them!—the Germans relied too much on the Italians, who are more afraid than a herd of sheep. That's the long and the short of it."

Her voice sounds thick and her eyes, behind her glasses, appear veiled and almost dreamy.

"If I'd met Hitler, I'd have told him: 'Don't you trust them, don't be foolish, those Italians are frightened of their own shadow.' "

Doña Rosa heaves a gentle sigh.

"What a fool I am! If I'd been face to face with Hitler I wouldn't have dared to raise my voice, not even that. . . ."

Doña Rosa is worried about the fate of the German armies. Every day she studies the communiqué from Hitler's headquarters and associates, through a series of vague forebodings she dare not try to see clearly, the fate of the Wehrmacht with the fate of her café.

Vega buys himself a paper. His neighbor asks: "Any good news?"

Vega is an eclectic. "It all depends for whom."

The server continues to say "coming" and to drag his feet along the floor of the café.

"If I were face to face with Hitler, I'd be frightened out of my wits, he must be a most frightening man. He's got a look in his eyes like a tiger."

Doña Rosa heaves another sigh. For a moment her enormous bosom makes her throat disappear from sight. "He and the Pope must be the two most frightening men there are." Doña Rosa taps on the piano lid with her fingertips.

"But after all, he must know what he's doing, that's what he's got his generals for."

For an instant Doña Rosa keeps quiet, then her voice changes: "Right."

She lifts her head and looks at Seoane: "How's your wife getting on with her trouble?"

"She's pulling through. Today she seems a bit better."

"Poor Amparo, and she's such a good soul!"

"Yes, it's true, she's having a bad time."

"Did you give her those drops Don Francisco told you about?"

"Yes, she's taken them. The worst of it is that she can't keep down anything, she throws it all up."

"Good Lord!"

Macario softly touches the keys and Seoane picks up his violin.

"What next?"

" 'La verbena,' don't you think?"

"Come on."

Doña Rosa steps from the platform as the violinist and the pianist, with the expression of resigned schoolboys, break into the din of the café with the familiar old bars, so often—oh, God, how often—repeated and repeated:

> "Where to in your Manila shawl, my pretty?
> Where to in your printed cotton dress?"

They play without their music. They don't need it.

Like an automaton Macario thinks: "And then I'll tell her: 'Look here, my girl, there's nothing to be done. With a miserable five pesetas for the afternoon and another five for the night, and two coffees—well, I ask you!' Then she'll answer, sure enough: 'Don't be silly. You'll see: with your ten pesetas and with a few lessons I can get . . .' Really, Matilde is an angel, nothing short of an angel."

Macario smiles inwardly and very nearly smiles outwardly as well. Macario is an undernourished sentimentalist who celebrated his forty-third birthday a few days ago.

Seoane stares vaguely at the customers of the café and thinks nothing. Seoane is a man who prefers not to think. All he asks for is that the day may pass rapidly, as quickly as possible, to be over and done with.

Half past nine strikes on the old clock with its tiny figures that shine like gold. The clock is an almost sumptuous piece. It was brought here from the Paris Exhibition by a hare-brained, penniless young marquis, who courted Doña Rosa 'way back in 1905. The little marquis, whose Christian name was Santiago and who was a grandee of Spain, died in his early youth of consumption, in El Escorial; and the clock stayed on the wall above the café counter, as if in remembrance of the hours that passed without bringing a man for Doña Rosa or a daily hot meal for the man who died. Such is life.

At the other end of the café Doña Rosa has words with a waiter, waving her arms about. Somewhat treacherously, the other waiters watch the scene in the mirrors, with hardly any interest.

Within half an hour the café will be empty. It will be like a man who has suddenly lost his memory.

Chapter Two

NOW scram."

"Good-by and thank you. You're very kind."

"You're welcome. Now off with you. And we don't want to see you here again."

The waiter tries to make his voice sound stern and awe-inspiring. He has a strong Galician accent that robs his words of any sting of authority or violence and sweetens even his sternness. When external pressure drives a meek man to asperity, his upper lip begins to tremble as though brushed by an invisible fly.

"I'll leave you the book if you wish."

"No. Keep it."

Martin Marco, pale and skinny in his threadbare jacket and frayed trousers, takes leave of the waiter by touching the brim of his greasy, dismal gray hat.

"Good-by and thank you. You're very kind."

"Forget it. Get out of here. And don't come near us again."

Martin Marco peers at the waiter and would like to say something memorable.

"Count on me as a friend."

"All right."

"I shall know how to repay."

Martin Marco straightens his wire-rimmed glasses and starts walking. A girl passes him whose face seems familiar to him.

"Good night!"

The girl looks at him for a second and continues on her way. She is very young and very pretty. She is not well dressed. Probably she is a milliner. All milliners have an air that borders on distinction. Just as all good wet nurses come from Asturias and all good cooks from the Basque provinces, the girls who make pleasant mistresses, manage to dress well and hold their own wherever you may take them, are usually milliners.

Martin Marco drags himself slowly down the boulevard in the direction of Santa Bárbara.

The waiter hovers for an instant on the pavement before pushing open the swinging door.

"There he goes, without a penny in his pocket!"

The people hurry past, muffled in their greatcoats, fleeing from the cold.

Martin Marco, the man who has not paid for his coffee and who looks at the city with the eyes of a sick and harassed child, pushes his hands into his trouser pockets.

The lights in the square glitter with a baleful, almost offensive brilliance.

Don Roberto González raises his head from the fat ledger and speaks to the boss.

"Would you mind letting me have fifteen pesetas in advance? Tomorrow is my wife's birthday."

The boss is a kind-hearted and decent man. He deals on the black market like every mother's son, but there isn't a mean bone in his body.

"That's quite all right, it makes no difference to me."

The baker takes a fat calfskin wallet from his pocket and hands Don Roberto twenty-five pesetas.

"I'm very pleased with you, González, the bakery accounts are in good shape. Here you've ten pesetas extra so you can buy a little something for the kids too."

Señor Ramón pauses briefly, then scratches his head, and mumbles:

"Don't say anything to Paulina."

"Don't worry."

Señor Ramón stares at the tips of his shoes.

"I've my reasons, you see. I know you're a reliable man and won't let your tongue run away with you. But it might happen, after all, that you somehow let the cat out of the bag, and then we wouldn't hear the end of it from her for the next fortnight. You know I'm the boss here, but you also know what women are like . . ."

"Don't worry and many thanks. I shan't talk, in my own interest."

Don Roberto lowers his voice. "Many thanks again."

"No reason to thank me. All I want is that you go on being happy in your work."

The baker's words touch Don Roberto to the quick. If the baker were to be lavish with his kind phrases, Don Roberto would do his bookkeeping for nothing.

Señor Ramón is between fifty and fifty-two. He is sturdy, with a ruddy complexion and a mustache—a man healthy in mind and body, who leads the decent life of an old-fashioned craftsman, rising at dawn, drinking red wine, and pinching the servant girls' bottoms. When he first came to Madrid at the beginning of this century, he carried his boots slung over his shoulder so as not to wear them out.

His biography can be told in a few lines.

When he came to the capital, he was not yet ten years old. He took a job in a bakery and saved his earnings till his twenty-first year, when he had to do his military service. From the moment he came to the city to the moment he was called up he spent not as much as a centimo; he saved all his money. He ate bread, drank water, slept behind the counter, and never had a woman. When he went off to serve the King, he left his money at the Post Office Savings Bank; when he was released from the army he drew it out and bought a bakery; in twelve years he had saved twenty-four thousand reales, six thousand pesetas, all that he had ever earned, which was at an average of little over a peseta a day. In the army he had learned to read, write, and do sums, and he had lost his innocence. He opened his bakery, married, had twelve children, bought himself an almanac, and sat down to watch the days go by. The ancient patriarchs must have been very much like Señor Ramón.

The waiter enters the café. Suddenly he feels his face go hot; he would like to cough, but rather softly, as though to get rid of the phlegm which the cold of the street has brought into his throat. Afterwards it might be easier to talk. On coming through the door he has noticed a slight pain in his temples; he has also noticed, or thought he did, that Doña Rosa's hairy upper lip is aquiver with lascivious joy.

"Come here!"

The waiter goes up to her. "What is it, madam?"

"Did you kick him?"

"Yes, madam."

"How often?"

"Twice."

"Where did you kick him?"

"Where I could. On the legs."

"Well done. That'll teach him. Another time he won't try to steal decent people's good money."

A shiver runs down the waiter's spine. If he were a determined man, he would throttle the proprietress; fortunately he is not. The proprietress is laughing on the sly, a cruel little laugh. There are people whom it amuses to see others having a bad time; to get a close view of it they haunt the slums, they take battered old things as gifts to dying people, to consumptives huddling under a vile blanket, to anemic little children with swollen bellies and soft bones, to girls who have become mothers at the age of eleven, to whores in their forties, eaten up by pustules and looking like Red Indian chiefs with the scab. Doña Rosa doesn't even come up to this category. She prefers her emotion at home, she prefers that quiver.

*   *   *   *

Don Roberto smiles contentedly. The poor man has been worrying because his wife's birthday might have caught him with nothing in his pocket. It would have been rotten luck.

"Tomorrow I'll get Filo some chocolates," he thinks. "Filo's like a kid, exactly like a little child, like a child of six. . . . With the ten pesetas I'll buy some little thing for the children and stand myself a vermouth. . . . A ball is what they would like best. . . . You can get quite a decent ball for six pesetas. . . ."

Don Roberto is thinking slowly, with a certain enjoyment. His wooly head is full of good intentions.

Harsh, shrill, jarring notes from a cheap, vulgar flamenco song drift through the panes and wooden slats of the skylight. At first, nobody can tell whether the singer is a woman or a young boy. Don Roberto is scratching his lips with the penholder when the concert catches his ear by surprise.

On the opposite pavement, at a tavern door, a little boy is howling fit to burst his throat:

> "Unhappy he who takes
> From a stranger's hand his bread,
> Ever watching the face
> If it bodes good or bad."

People in the tavern throw the boy a couple of coins and three or four olives, which he picks up from the ground in great haste. The boy is small, dark, and puny, as lively as a cricket. He goes bare-footed, his chest is naked, and he looks about six. He sings all by himself, clapping his hands to encourage himself and waggling his little bottom rhythmically.

Don Roberto shuts the skylight and remains standing there in the middle of the room. It has occurred to him to call the boy and give him a copper. One real—twenty-five centimos.

"No . . ."

Common sense triumphant, Don Roberto recovers his optimism.

"Yes, a few sweets . . . Filo's like a kid, she's just like

a . . ." In spite of the twenty-five pesetas in his pocket, Don Roberto's conscience isn't quite easy.

"But that's simply wanting to see everything black on black, isn't it, Roberto?" a timid, leaping little voice asks in his breast.

"Just so."

Martin Marco stops at the show windows of a sanitary fittings shop in the Calle de Sagasta. The shop glows like a jeweler's or a hairdresser's at a big hotel, and the washbasins look as if they belonged to another world, basins in paradise, with shining taps, smooth porcelain, and bright, clear, immaculate mirrors. There are white basins, green, pink, yellow, mauve, black basins, basins of every possible color. The things people think of! There are bathtubs beautifully gleaming like diamond bracelets, bidets with dashboards like a motor car's, luxurious lavatory bowls with two lids and bellied curves, elegant low cisterns where one surely might rest one's elbow and even keep a few select, finely bound volumes: Hölderlin, Keats, Valéry, for occasions when constipation asks for company; Rubén Darío, Mallarmé—but especially Mallarmé—for diarrheas. . . . What filthy nonsense!

Martin Marco smiles, as if in self-forgiveness, and turns from the shop window.

"Life," he thinks, "life is like this. With the money some people spend to do their necessary jobs in comfort, the rest of us might keep fed for a whole year. A nice state of things. It ought to be the aim of wars to reduce the number of people who can do their necessary jobs in comfort, and to let the rest eat a little better. The worst of it is, goodness knows why, that we intellectuals go on eating too little and doing our little duties in cafés. What can one do about it?"

Martin Marco worries about the social problem. He has no very clear ideas about anything, but he worries about the social problem.

"It's a bad thing," he sometimes says, "that there are rich and poor. It would be better if we were all equal, not too poor and not too rich, but somewhere in between. Humanity needs reforming. A scientific commission should be appointed and given the task to change mankind. At the beginning they would deal with small things such as teaching people the metric system, but later, when they get into their stride, they would tackle the most important matters. They might even decide to pull down the big cities and build them up again, all alike, with perfectly straight streets and central heating in every building. It would cost rather a lot, but there must be money to spare in the banks."

A cold gust blows down the Calle de Manuel Silvela, and Martin is assailed by a suspicion that what he thinks is nonsense.

"To hell with those nice washbasins!"

As he crosses the street, a cyclist has to give him a push to prevent a collision.

"Clumsy ass—I bet they let you out on a 'conditional' release!"

The blood rushes to Martin's head.

"Stop—listen—stop!"

The cyclist merely turns his head and waves him good-by.

A man walks down the Calle de Goya, reading a newspaper. We catch up with him as he passes a small secondhand bookshop that boasts the name "Give Food to Your Mind." A young servant girl crosses his path.

"Good night, Señorito Paco."

The man turns round.

"Oh, is it you? Where are you going?"

"Home, Señorito. I've been to see my sister, the married one."

"Nice for you."

The man looks into her eyes.

"What about it, have you got a boy friend? A girl like you can't possibly be without a young man. . . ."

The girl bursts into laughter.

"Well, I'm off, I'm in an awful hurry."

"Good night, then, and don't you get lost, my girl. Listen,

if you see Señorito Martin, tell him I shall drop in at the bar in the Calle de Narváez at about eleven."

The girl walks on, and Paco follows her with his eyes until she disappears amid the crowd.

"She moves like a fawn."

Paco, Señorito Paco, finds all women pretty, either because he is so amorous or because he is a sentimentalist. The young girl who just spoke to him was indeed pretty, but if she hadn't been, it would have made no difference: for Paco, they all are beauty queens.

"Just like a fawn!"

The man turns round again and thinks vaguely of his mother, who died years ago. His mother used to wear a black silk ribbon round her neck to restrain her double chin and held herself very well. One could see at the first glance that she came of a great family. Paco's grandfather was a general and a marquis and died in a duel at Burgos. He was killed with a pistol shot by a deputy named Don Edmundo Páez Pacheco, who belonged to the Progressist Party, was a Freemason, and held disruptive ideas.

The girl's curves had shown under her thin cotton overcoat. Her shoes had begun to lose their shape. She had nice clear hazel eyes, slightly slanting. "I come from my married sister's." Tut, tut . . . do you remember that married sister of hers, Paco?

Don Edmundo Páez Pacheco died of smallpox at Almería in the year of the great disaster.

The girl had been looking into Paco's eyes while she talked with him.

A woman, a child wrapped in rags on her arm, begs alms, and a fat gypsy woman sells lottery tickets. A few couples love each other there in the cold 'gainst wind and tide, close to each other, arm in arm, and warming themselves by holding hands.

Celestino is talking to himself in the back room behind the bar, surrounded by empty casks. Celestino does talk to himself occasionally. When he was a young lad, his mother used to exclaim: "What was that?"

"Nothing, I was talking to myself."

"For God's sake, boy, you'll go out of your head!"

Celestino's mother was not so much of a lady as Paco's.

"No, I won't give them away, I may smash them up, but I won't give them away. Either they pay me what they're worth or they don't take them away from here. I won't let anyone pull my leg, I just won't, and nobody's going to rob me either. It's sheer exploitation of the businessman, that's what it is. Either one has got will power, or one hasn't. That's clear. Either one is a man or one isn't. Robbers belong in the Sierra Morena!"

Celestino pushes his denture back into place and spits furiously on the floor.

"Whatever next?"

Martin Marco pursues his way, promptly forgetting the affair with the cyclist.

"If this thing about the miserable situation of intellectuals had occurred to Paco, what a to-do! But no, Paco's a bore, he doesn't get ideas any more. Ever since they let him out he runs round like a nitwit without doing anything worth while. Before, he at least wrote verse now and then. But look at him now. I'm sick and tired of telling him, I shan't do it again. It's up to him. If he thinks he'll be left in peace just because he's doing nothing, he can think again."

Martin is shivering with cold and buys himself twenty centimos worth of roast chestnuts—four chestnuts—at the mouth of the underground station on the corner of the Calle Hermanos Alvarez Quintero, that mouth which gapes like the mouth of a man in the dentist's chair and seems made to gobble up cars and lorries.

While he eats his chestnuts, he leans against the railing and absent-mindedly spells out the name on the street sign.

"The brothers Quintero—they were in luck, those two! Here they are: a street in the center of the town and a statue in the Retiro Park. Nothing to sneeze at!"

Martin has occasional vague fits of respectfulness and conservatism.

"Damn it all, they must have done something to be so famous. Only—oh, well—who's the bright lad who dares say it?"

Like fluttering clothes moths, unruly chips of conscious thought drift through his mind.

"Yes: an era of the Spanish stage . . . a cycle which they undertook to complete and succeeded in completing . . . theater faithfully mirroring the healthy customs of Andalusia . . . It all smacks somehow of charity to me, it belongs with suburban life and flag days and all that. What can one do about it? Anyway, nobody will budge them now. Here they are, and not God Almighty Himself can budge them."

It perturbs Martin that there exists no strict classification of intellectual values, no tidy list of brains.

"Everything is the same, everything topsy-turvy."

Two of his chestnuts are cold and two burning hot.

Pablo Alonso is a young man who affects the sporting manner of the modern businessman and has had a mistress called Laurita for the last fortnight.

Laurita is pretty. She is the daughter of a portress in the Calle de Lagasca and is nineteen years old. Before, she never had so much as five pesetas to spend on fun, let alone fifty pesetas to buy a handbag. With her young man, who was a postman, she never went out anywhere. Laurita was sick of getting frozen on walks in the Paseo de Rosales; her fingers and ears began to be covered with chilblains. Her friend Estrella had been set up in a flat of her own, in the Calle de Menéndez Pelayo, by a gentleman who supplied olive oil on the black market.

Pablo Alonso looks up.

"A Manhattan."

"We've no Scotch, sir."

"Tell them at the bar that it's for me."

"Very well, sir."

Pablo takes the girl's hand once more.

"As I was telling you, Laurita, he's a great chap, he couldn't be a better sort. Only nowadays you see him when he's poor and shabby, perhaps with a dirty shirt he's worn for a whole month, and with his toes sticking through his uppers."

"Poor boy! Doesn't he do any work?"

"No, nothing. He goes round with all sorts of ideas revolving in his head, but when it comes to it he never does anything. It's a pity, because he's nobody's fool."

"And has he got anywhere to sleep?"

"Yes, at my place."

"At your place?"

"Yes, I had a bed put up for him in a box room, and that's where he sleeps. At least he's out of the rain and can keep warm."

The girl, who is familiar with poverty, looks into Pablo's eyes. She is a little moved at heart. "How kind you are, Pablo!"

"No, silly. He's an old friend of mine, a friend since before the war. It's just that he now has struck a bad patch. Really, he's never had a good time."

"And he is a graduate, is he?"

Pablo laughs. "Yes, darling, he is. Come, let's talk of something else."

Laurita, for a change, falls back on the litany on which she started a fortnight back.

"Do you love me a lot?"

"A lot."

"More than anyone else?"

"More than anyone else."

"Will you always love me?"

"Always."

"Will you never leave me?"

"Never."

"Even if I were going about as dirty as your friend?"

"Don't talk drivel."

Bending down to set the drink on the table, the waiter smiles. "There was a drop of White Label left, sir."

"You see?"

*　　*　　*　　*

The little flamenco singer has been kicked by a drunken whore. His only comment is prim: "Lord, what a time of day to be drunk! Doesn't she leave anything for later?"

The boy does not fall, he only hits his nose against the wall. From a safe distance he shouts a couple of home truths after the woman, gently pats his face, and resumes his singing:

> "A master tailor was
> Cutting a pair of trousers,
> When a gypsy lad came past,
> Who was a young shrimp seller.
>
> " 'Now listen, master tailor,
> Make them nice and tight for me,
> So, when I go to Mass,
> The gentry will look and see.' "

The boy has the face, not of a person, but of a domestic animal, of a poor dirty beast, a perverted farmyard beast. He is too young in years for cynicism—or resignation—to have slashed its mark across his face, and therefore it has a beautiful, candid stupidity, the expression of one who understands nothing of anything that happens. For the little gypsy, every thing that happens is a miracle: he was born by a miracle, he eats by a miracle, has lived by a miracle, and has the strength to sing by sheer miracle.

Days are followed by nights and nights by days. The year has four seasons: spring, summer, autumn, and winter. There are truths one feels in one's body, such as hunger or the need to make water.

The four chestnuts are soon finished, and with his one remaining twenty-five-centimo piece Martin buys a ticket on the underground to the Calle de Goya.

"Here we go rushing on, underneath all the people sitting in their lavatories. Colón Station: top class, dukes, notaries, and a few guards from the mint. How aloof they are, reading their newspapers or staring down at the folds across their bellies. Serrano: gentlemen and ladies. Ladies don't go out by night; this is a district where life only goes on till ten o'clock. Now they'll be having their suppers. Velázquez: more ladies. Most agreeable. This is a very smart underground line. 'Shall we go to the opera?' 'All right.' 'Did you go to the races last Sunday?' 'No.' *Goya*: end of the show."

On the platform Martin pretends to limp, as he sometimes does.

"Perhaps I'll get supper at Filo's—don't push, Señora, there's no hurry!—if not, well, it won't be the last time."

Filo is his sister, the wife of Don Roberto González—that beast González, his brother-in-law calls him—who is a clerk at the City Council and a Republican of Alcalá Zamorra's crowd.

The González family lives at the end of the Calle de Ibiza in one of the small flats created after the Salmón Act. They manage to make ends meet, though it costs them much toil and trouble. She works till she drops, what with five small children and a little maid of eighteen to look after them, and he takes on whatever work he can get outside office hours, and wherever he can get it. At present he is in luck; he goes twice a month to a perfumery to do its bookkeeping and get twenty-five pesetas for that, and he also keeps the books of a rather flashy bakery where he is paid thirty pesetas a month. At other times, when Fortune turns her back on him and he cannot find an odd job for his spare hours, Don Roberto grows melancholy and broody. Then he is bad-tempered.

For some odd reason, one of those things that happen in life, the two brothers-in-law cannot stand each other. Martin says that Don Roberto is a greedy swine, and Don Roberto says that Martin is a savage, ill-bred sort of a swine. Goodness knows which of them is right. Only one thing is certain: poor Filo, caught between the devil and the deep blue sea, spends her time inventing ingenious devices to weather the storm as best she can.

If her husband is not at home, she fries her brother an egg

or warms a drop of light coffee for him. And if this is out of the question because Don Roberto, in his old coat and slippers, would make a terrible row, calling Martin a loafer and a parasite, Filo saves the leftovers of their meals for him in an old biscuit tin which she sends downstairs with the maid.

"Is this right, Petrita?"

"No, sir, it isn't."

"Oh, my dear, if it weren't that you make this nasty mess taste a little sweeter to me . . ."

Petrita blushes.

"Come on, sir, let me have the tin, it's cold here."

"No colder for you than for the rest of us, you wretched girl."

"Oh, I'm sorry."

Martin responds at once: "Don't take any notice of me. Do you know that you've become a real woman by now?"

"Get along, stop it."

"All right, I'll stop it, if you say so. Do you know what I'd give you if I hadn't too much of a conscience?"

"Stop it."

"A good fright!"

"Stop it . . ."

Tonight Filo's husband happens not to be at home, and Martin can have his egg and drink his cup of coffee.

"There isn't any bread. We've even got to buy some on the black market for the children."

"It's all right like this, thank you. You're very good, Filo, you're a real saint."

"Don't be silly."

Martin's eyes mist over.

"A saint, yes, but a saint married to a skinflint. Your husband's a skinflint, Filo."

"That's enough. He's very decent."

"Have it your own way. After all, you've given him no less than five pups."

For a few moments there is silence. From the other side of the flat sounds the reedy voice of a child saying his prayers.

Filo smiles. "That's little Javier. Tell me, have you got any money?"

"No."

"Here, take these two pesetas."

"No. What for? What can I do with two pesetas?"

"That's true enough. But you know, he who gives what he has . . ."

"Yes, I know."

"Have you ordered your clothes as I told you, Laurita?"

"Yes, Pablo. The coat fits very well, you'll see, you'll like me in it."

Pablo Alonso dons the benevolent, bovine smile of a man who gets his women, not through his looks, but through his pocketbook.

"I'm sure I shall. . . . At this time of the year you've got to wrap up, Laurita. You girls can well look smart and keep warm at the same time."

"Of course."

"It's perfectly possible to do both. It seems to me you women go out with not enough clothes on. Just think if you were to fall ill now!"

"Not now, Pablo. Now I'm taking great care of myself so that we can be very happy together. . . ."

Pablo accepts her love.

"I should like to be the prettiest girl in Madrid, then I'd please you for ever and ever. . . . You can't imagine how jealous I am."

The chestnut vendor is talking with a lonely unmarried woman who has creased cheeks and reddened eyelids, as if she had weak eyes.

"Lord, it's cold!"

"Yes, it's a filthy night. One day I'm going to pass out just like a sparrow."

The lonely woman puts a peseta's worth of roast chestnuts into her bag: her evening meal.

"See you tomorrow, Señora Leocadia."

"Good night, Señorita Elvira, and sleep well."

The lonely woman walks on in the direction of the Plaza de Alonso Martínez. Two men have a conversation behind one of the windows of the café on the corner of the boulevard. Both are young, one twenty-odd, the other thirty-odd. The older one looks like a member of the jury for a literary award, the younger one looks like a novelist. It is evident that their conversation runs more or less on the following lines: "I've submitted the manuscript of my novel under the title 'Teresa de Cepeda,' and in it I've treated a few neglected aspects of that eternal problem which . . ."

"Oh, yes. Will you pour me a drop of water, if you don't mind?"

"With pleasure. I've revised it several times and I think I may say with pride that there is not a single discordant word in the whole text."

"How interesting."

"I think so. I don't know the quality of the works my colleagues have sent in, but in any case I feel confident that good sense and honest judgment . . ."

"Rest assured, we proceed with exemplary fairness."

"I don't doubt it for a moment. It does not matter if one is defeated, provided the work that gets the award has unmistakable qualities. What's so discouraging is . . ."

In passing the window, Señorita Elvira gives them a smile —simply out of habit.

Another silence falls between brother and sister.

"Are you wearing an undershirt?"

"Of course I'm wearing an undershirt. Who'd go out on the street with no undershirt!"

"An undershirt marked P.A.?"

"An undershirt marked as I please."

"Forgive me."

Martin has rolled himself a cigarette with Don Roberto's tobacco.

"You're forgiven, Filo. But don't talk so tenderly. It makes me sick to be pitied."

Filo suddenly bridles.

"Here you go again!"

"No. Tell me, hasn't Paco been round? He should have brought a parcel for me."

"He hasn't been, but Petrita met him in the Calle de Goya and he told her he would be waiting for you at eleven at the bar in the Calle de Narváez."

"What's the time?"

"I don't know. It must be past ten."

"And Roberto?"

"He'll be some time yet. Today was his day to go to the bakery, and he won't be back till after half past ten."

A short silence, unexpectedly rich in gentle sweetness, envelops brother and sister. Then Filo speaks, infusing her voice with tenderness and looking into Martin's eyes: "Have you remembered that I'll be thirty-four tomorrow?"

"That's true!"

"Didn't you remember?"

"No—why should I tell you a lie? But I'm glad you told me now. I want to give you a present."

"Don't be foolish. As if you could go in for presents!"

"Just a little something to remember me by."

The woman puts her hands on the knees of the man.

"What I would like is that you write me a poem, as you used to years ago. Remember?"

"Yes. . . ."

Filo stares sadly down at the table. "Last year neither you nor Roberto wished me many happy returns. You both forgot."

She gives her voice a plaintive inflection; a good actress would have made it sound dark and heavy.

"I cried that whole night. . . ."

Martin gives her a kiss. "Don't be a silly. Anyone would think you were going to be fourteen tomorrow."

"I have gotten old, haven't I? Look at the wrinkles in my

· 63 ·

face. Now all that's left is to wait till the children grow up, get older and older, and then die. Like Mamma, poor dear."

At the bakery Don Roberto carefully blots his entry of the last transaction in the ledger. Then he shuts it and tears up several sheets with the drafts of the accounts.

The song about the tight trousers and the gentry at Mass sounds through the street.

"Good-by, Señor Ramón. Till next time."

"Good luck to you, González, till next time. Many happy returns to your good lady, and may you all keep well."

"Thank you, Señor Ramón. The same to you."

On the way home, two men cross the building sites by the bullring.

"I'm frozen stiff. It's cold enough to wean a vulture."

"Hear, hear!"

Brother and sister carry on their talk in the small kitchen. On the cold iron plaque of the coal range stands a little gas burner, which is lit.

"We've got no pressure up here at this time of the night. Downstairs they have a gas stove that eats up the lot."

A stewpot, not very large, is simmering on the gas. Half a dozen pilchards are laid out on the table, ready for the frying pan.

"Roberto's very fond of fried pilchards."

"What a queer taste. . . ."

"Leave him alone. What harm has he done to you? Martin dear, why do you hate him so much?"

"As far as I'm concerned . . . I don't hate him, it's he who hates me. And I notice it and defend myself. I know our ways are different."

Martin assumes a somewhat declamatory manner and sounds like a schoolmaster.

"To him, all things are the same, he believes the best he can do is to muddle along. I disagree. To me, all things are not the same, on the contrary. I know that there are good things and bad things, things one is bound to do and things one has to avoid."

"Now, stop it and don't make speeches."

"Indeed! That's what I get for it."

The light flickers for an instant in the lamp bulb, flares up, and is gone. The timid bluish gas flame is slowly licking the sides of the stewpot.

"Now, there!"

"It sometimes happens at night. The light has been very bad lately."

"There's no reason why the light shouldn't be as good as ever it was, it's simply that the company wants to force the price up. Until they get their increase, they won't let you have good light, mark my words. How much do you pay now?"

"Fourteen to sixteen pesetas, it varies."

"Soon you're going to pay twenty to twenty-five."

"Well, it can't be helped."

"If that's how you want things to improve, you're on the right way!"

Filo says nothing, and Martin gets a glimpse of one of those solutions that never work out. In the uncertain little glow from the gas flame, he has the vague, incorporeal air of a magician.

The blackout surprises Celestino in the back room.

"Now we're in for it. Those black-souled rascals are capable of looting my whole place."

The black-souled rascals are his customers.

Celestino tries to grope his way out when he overturns a crate full of fizzy lemonade. Clattering on the tiled floor, the bottles make an infernal noise.

"Blast and damn the electric light!"

From the door a voice asks: "What's up?"

"Nothing. Just smashing what's mine."

Doña Visitación holds the opinion that it would be one of the most effective means towards a betterment of the working classes if the ladies of the Women's Association were to organize pinochle competitions.

"The workers," she thinks, "have got to eat, too, even if many of them are so Red that they don't deserve so much consideration."

Doña Visitación is a kindly woman; she does not believe that one should kill the workers by slow starvation.

After a short while the light comes back, first reddening the filament so that it looks for seconds as if made of blood-filled little veins, and then suddenly filling the kitchen with radiance. The light is whiter and stronger than before, and the small packets, cups, and plates on the dresser stand out more clearly, as though they had filled out, as though they were newly made.

"It's all very pretty, Filo."

"It's clean . . ."

"I should say so!"

With curiosity, as if he had not seen it before, Martin glances round the kitchen. Then he gets up and takes his hat. He squeezes his butt out in the sink and throws it, most considerately, into the garbage can.

"Well, Filo, thanks a lot, I'm off."

"Good night, dear, and don't say thanks. I'd love to give you more. . . . That egg was meant for me, the doctor told me I ought to have two eggs a day."

"Oh, dear!"

"Never mind, don't worry. Your need is quite as great as mine."

"True enough."

"Oh, Martin, what times we live in!"

"Yes, what times, Filo! But things will straighten out, sooner or later."

"D'you think so?"

"You may be sure of it. It's a matter of destiny, it's something that can't be stopped, something that has the force of the tides."

Martin goes to the door and says in a changed tone: "Anyway . . . where's Petrita?"

"At it again?"

"No, no, I only wanted to say good night to her."

"Don't worry her. She's with the two babies. They're frightened at night and so she stays with them till they go to sleep."

Filo smiles as she adds: "I'm frightened too. Sometimes I imagine I'm going to drop dead out of the blue. . . ."

Going down the stairs, Martin crosses with his brother-in-law, who is coming up in the lift. Don Roberto is immersed in his newspaper. Martin feels like opening a door to the lift and leaving Don Roberto stuck in the cage between two floors.

Laurita and Pablo are seated face to face, a slender vase with three small roses between them.

"Do you like this place?"

"Very much."

The waiter comes to the table. He is a young waiter, well dressed, with curly black hair and a genteel manner. Laurita contrives not to look at him. Laurita has a simple, straightforward view of love and faithfulness.

"For the young lady, consommé, a grilled sole, and chicken Villeroy. For me, consommé and stewed bass with oil and vinegar."

"Won't you have more?"

"No, honey, I don't feel like it."

Pablo turns to the waiter. "A half-bottle of sauterne and a half-bottle of Burgundy. That will do."

Beneath the table, Laurita strokes one of Pablo's knees. "Aren't you well?"

"No, not exactly that. My food has been disagreeing with me the whole evening, but that's gone now. Only I don't want it to start all over again."

The pair look into one another's eyes and hold hands, elbows propped on the table, and the flower vase pushed to one side.

A couple in a corner, no longer at the stage of holding hands, stare at them without much discretion.

"Who's this conquest of Pablo's?"

"I don't know. Looks like a housemaid. D'you like her?"

"H'm, not so bad."

"Then go off with her, if she appeals to you. I don't think you'd find her too difficult."

"There you go again!"

"The one who's at it again is you. Listen, sweet, leave me alone, I don't feel like a row. Nowadays I'm not in the mood to give popular concerts."

The man lights a cigarette.

"Now listen, Mari Tere, this won't get us anywhere, you know."

"What a nerve! Leave me, if you want. Isn't that what you're after? I've still got people left who like to look at my face."

"Don't shout, we don't have to tell our affairs to the town-crier."

Señorita Elvira puts her novel on the night table and turns off the light. *The Mysteries of Paris* is left in the dark, next to a tumbler half filled with water, a pair of used stockings, and a lipstick worn down to its last stump.

Before falling asleep, Señorita Elvira always does a little thinking.

"Doña Rosa may be right. Perhaps it is better if I make it up with the old man. I can't go on like this. He is a slobberer, but after all I haven't so much to choose from any more."

Señorita Elvira asks very little from life, but she hardly ever gets even that much. It took her a long time to get wise to things, and when she did, her eyes were already ringed with crow's feet, her teeth decaying and blackish. Now she only asks not to have to go to the hospital, to be allowed to stay on in her miserable lodgings; within a few years, her golden dream may well be a bed in the hospital, close to the pipes of the central heating.

The little gypsy boy is counting a pile of coppers by the light of a street lamp. It hasn't been a bad day for him. By singing from one o'clock till eleven at night he has collected five pesetas sixty centimos. In any bar they will give him five-fifty for the five pesetas worth of copper coins; bars are always badly off for small change.

When he can afford it, the gypsy boy has an evening meal at an inn behind the Calle de Preciados, as you go down the little slope of the Calle de los Angeles. There he gets a plateful of beans, bread, and a banana for three-twenty.

The little gypsy sits down, calls the waiter, gives him the three-twenty, and waits to be served.

After his supper, he goes on singing till two o'clock in the Calle de Echegaray, after which he tries to get on the bumper of the last tram. The little gypsy—I believe I said so before—must be about six.

At the bottom of the Calle de Narváez is the bar where Paco is going to meet Martin, as he does nearly every night. It is a small bar on the right-hand side coming up, near the garage of the Armed Police. The owner, Celestino Ortiz by name, rose to the rank of major under Cipriano Mera* during the war. He is on the tall side, thin, his eyebrows meet, and his face is slightly pock-marked. On his right hand he wears a heavy iron ring with a miniature portrait of Leo Tolstoy in

* Cipriano Mera was the commander of an anarchist unit in the Republican Army during the Spanish Civil War. (*Translator's note.*)

colored enamel, which he had specially made in the Calle de la Colegiata; and he wears a denture which he leaves on the counter when it bothers him too much. For many years Celestino has cherished a dirty, tattered copy of Nietzsche's *Aurora*, his bedside book and catechism. He reads in it on every occasion and never fails to find a solution for his spiritual problems there.

"*Aurora*," he says, "*Meditation on Moral Prejudices*—what a beautiful title!"

The front cover shows an oval with the author's photograph, his name, the title, the retail price—one peseta—and the publisher's imprint at the bottom: "F. Sempere & Co., Publishers, Calle del Palomar 10, Valencia; Olmo 4, Madrid (Branch Office)." The translation is by Pedro González Blanco. The title page carries the publisher's emblem: the bust of a young woman in a Phrygian cap, with a laurel wreath below and, above, a motto that reads: "Art and Liberty."

There are entire passages which Celestino knows by heart. When the police guard from the garage come into the bar, Celestino Ortiz hides the book under the counter on top of the crate with the little vermouth bottles.

"They're sons of the people like me," he reflects, "but—just in case."

With the village priests, Celestino believes that Nietzsche is something very dangerous indeed.

What he usually does when he talks to the policemen is to quote bits and pieces, as a kind of joke, without ever telling them where he has got them from.

" 'Compassion comes to be the antidote to suicide, since it is an emotion that affords pleasure and provides us, in small doses, with the delight of feeling superior.' "

The policemen begin to laugh.

"Tell us, Celestino, haven't you been a priest once?"

"Never. 'Happiness,' " he continues, " 'of whatever kind gives us air, light, and freedom of movement.' "

The policemen roar with laughter.

"And running water."

"And central heating."

Celestino grows angry and scornfully spits at them: "You're a lot of poor ignoramuses."

Among the Regulars there is one, a reticent policeman from Galicia, with whom Celestino gets on well. The two always address each other with a certain formality.

"Tell me something, landlord, do you say this always with the same words?"

"Always, García, and I don't make a single mistake ever."

"Well, that's something, now."

Señora Leocadia, huddled up in her woolen shawl, extracts one hand from its folds.

"Here you are, eight nice fat ones."

"Thank you."

"Could you tell me the time, Señorito?"

The Señorito unbuttons his coat and looks at his thick silver watch.

"Yes, it's just on eleven."

At eleven her son comes to fetch her. The war left him with a limp; now he has a job as store clerk at the construction works for the new ministry buildings. The son, who is very good-hearted, helps his mother to collect her gear and then the two go off, she hanging on his arm, home and to bed. They walk up the Calle de Covarrubias and turn into the Calle de Nicasio Gallego. If there are any chestnuts left, they eat them; if not, they drop into some cheap little place and have a cup of light coffee, steaming hot. The old woman puts the tin with the charcoal next to her bed; there are always some embers left that go on smouldering till the morning.

Martin Marco enters the bar just as the policemen leave. Celestino goes to him and says: "Paco hasn't come yet, but he was here this afternoon and said you should wait for him."

Martin Marco adopts the peevish mien of a great lord. "Oh, well."

"What will it be?"

"Just black coffee."

Ortiz fiddles with the coffee machine, sets out saccharine, cup, saucer, and a spoon, and sallies forth from behind the counter. He puts the coffee on the table and begins to speak. A faint flicker in his eyes indicates that it costs him a great effort to bring the words out.

"Have you got paid?"

Martin gazes at him as if at a very strange being.

"No, I haven't. I told you I get my money every fifth and twentieth of the month."

Celestino scratches his neck.

"It's just that . . ."

"What?"

"Well, with this coffee it comes to twenty-two pesetas."

"Twenty-two pesetas? You'll get them from me, don't worry. I believe I've always paid you as soon as I got the money."

"I know."

"So what about it?"

Martin frowns and deepens his voice.

"It's incredible that you and I should always have trouble about the same thing when we have so much in common."

"That's a fact. I'm sorry, I didn't mean to bother you. It's just—you know—it's just that they came to collect the income tax today."

Martin raises his head, as a gesture of profound pride and scorn, and fixes his eyes on a pimple on Celestino's chin. For a fleeting moment he makes his voice sound soft. "What have you got there?"

Celestino is flustered. "Nothing, just a pimple."

Once more, Martin furrows his brow and speaks with a hard, impersonal inflection. "Do you wish to blame me for the fact that there is such a thing as income tax?"

"But, man, I never said anything like that."

"You said something very like it, my dear friend. Haven't we talked often enough about the problems of the distribution of income and the fiscal system?"

Celestino feels reminded of his schoolteacher and resents it. "Fine speeches won't pay my taxes for me."

"And that worries you, you unspeakable pharisee?" Martin stares at him, with a smile half of scorn, half of pity. "And you read Nietzsche? He can't have made much of an impression on you. You're a mean petty bourgeois."

"Marco!" Celestino lets out a lion's roar.

"Just so, shout away, call your friends the police."

"The police aren't my friends."

"Beat me up, if you like, I don't mind. I've no money, get that into your head. I have no money! And that's nothing to be ashamed of."

Martin gets up and leaves the bar with the gait of a triumphant hero. In the door he turns round: "And don't you weep, my honest tradesman. As soon as I have those twenty-odd pesetas in my possession, I shall bring them to you so that you can pay your income tax and rest in peace. Square it then with your conscience. This coffee goes on my account, and you put it where you've room for it, I don't want it."

Celestino is left in confusion, not knowing what to do. He thinks of hitting Martin over the head with a siphon for his cheek, but then he remembers: "To surrender to blind anger is a sign that one is close to the animal stage." He takes his book from the top of the bottles and shoves it into the drawer. There are days when the patron saint himself turns his back on you, when even Nietzsche seems almost to cross over to the other camp.

Pablo has sent the bellboy for a taxi.

"It's too early to go anywhere. If you like we'll go to the pictures first, to kill time."

"Just as you wish, Pablo. The main thing is that we can be very close together."

The bellboy is back; since the war hardly any wear caps.

"Your taxi, sir."

"Thanks. Shall we go, baby?"

Pablo helps Laurita into her coat. Once in the car, she calls his attention to the meter:

"It's sheer robbery! Look at it when we pass the next street lamp—he's got six pesetas up already."

On the corner of the Calle de O'Donnell Martin stumbles against Paco.

At the very moment when he hears a "Hello!" he is thinking: "Byron was right: if I ever have a son, I'll make him something prosaic, a lawyer or a pirate."

Paco slaps him on the shoulder. "You're quite out of breath. Why didn't you wait for me?"

Martin is like a sleepwalker, a man in delirium.

"I could have killed him! He's a swine!"

"Who is?"

"The barkeeper."

"The barkeeper? What has the poor wretch done to you?"

"He reminded me of what I owe him. He knows well enough that I pay as soon as I've got it."

"But, my dear friend, he probably needs it."

"Yes, to pay income tax. They're all alike." Martin looks at the ground and lowers his voice. "I've already been kicked out of one café today."

"Did they beat you up?"

"No, they didn't beat me up, but it was only too clear what they meant. I've had more than enough of it, Paco!"

"Now, don't get so excited, it isn't worth it. Where are you going?"

"To bed."

"That's the best thing. Shall we meet tomorrow?"

"As you like. Leave me a message at Filo's, I'll be dropping in there."

"All right."

"Take this, it's the book you wanted. Have you brought me the quarto sheets?"

"No, I couldn't get them. I'll see if I can tomorrow."

*   *   *   *

Señorita Elvira is tossing and turning in her bed, just as if she had bolted down an enormous supper. She thinks of her childhood and of the gibbet at Villalón; it is a memory that overcomes her at times. To throw it off, Señorita Elvira begins to recite the Credo until she falls asleep. There are nights—during which the memory is more obstinately persistent—when she reels off as many as one hundred and fifty or two hundred Credos.

Martin spends his nights at his friend Pablo Alonso's place, on a couch in the box room. He has a key to the apartment, and in return for this hospitality he has to observe only three rules: never to ask for money, be it a peseta; never to bring anyone else into the room; and to be out of the way from half past nine in the morning till past eleven at night. There is no provision for illness.

When he leaves Alonso's house in the morning, Martin goes to the Central Post Office or the Bank of Spain, where it is warm and one can write verse on the backs of telegraph forms or deposit sheets.

If and when Alonso lets him have one of his odd jackets, discarded while they are still almost as good as new, Martin dares to stroll into the lobby of the Palace Hotel after dinner. He is by no means greatly attracted by luxury, but he tries to make himself familiar with every kind of milieu.

"Everything is an experience," he thinks.

Don Leoncio Maestre sits down on his trunk and lights a cigarette. He has never been happier. In his mind he sings "*La Donna è mobile*" in a special version. When he was young, Don Leoncio Maestre won the rose at the "floral games" of literary and musical competition, which were celebrated in Minorca, his native island.

The text of the song Don Leoncio is soundlessly singing is, of course, in praise and homage of Señorita Elvira. What bothers him is that the stresses in the first line are inevitably misplaced. There are three possible solutions:

1. Oh, faír Elvírita!
2. Oh, fair Élvirí-ita!
3. Oh, faír Élvirita!

None of the three is much good, but the first one clearly is the best, if only because it has the stresses in the same place as *"La Donna è mobile."*

His eyes turned skywards, Don Leoncio thinks ceaselessly of Señorita Elvira.

"Poor little darling! She so wanted a smoke. Leoncio, I believe you hit the bull's eye when you gave her that packet of cigarettes. . . ."

Don Leoncio is so deeply immersed in his tender recollections that he never feels the chill of the metal sheeting of the trunk under his behind.

Señor Suárez lets the taxi wait at the front door. By now his limp has become positively alluring. He adjusts his pince-nez and gets into the lift. Señor Suárez lives with his mother, an old lady. They are so fond of each other that she has the habit of tucking him up in bed and giving him her blessing before she goes to bed herself at night.

"Are you comfy, pet?"

"Yes, quite comfy, Mummy dear."

"Then, till tomorrow, please God. Wrap yourself up well and don't catch cold. Sleep well."

"Thank you, darling Mummy. You, too. Give me a kiss."

"There, my pet. Don't forget your prayers."

Señor Suárez is fifty-odd, his mother twenty to twenty-two years older.

Señor Suárez arrives at the fourth floor, apartment C, produces his latchkey, and opens the door. He intends to change his tie, give his hair a good brush, put on a drop of eau de cologne, invent a charitable excuse, and depart in haste, again by taxi.

"Mummy!"

Every time Señor Suárez enters the apartment, he calls to his mother from the door, and then his voice is a feeble imitation of the Tyrolese mountaineers one hears yodeling in films.

"Mummy!"

The light in the front room is burning, but nobody answers.

"Mummy, Mummy!"

Señor Suárez begins to feel apprehensive.

"Mummy! Mummy! Oh, God! Oh, I can't go in there. Mummy!"

Urged by some strange force, Señor Suárez hurries down the passage. This strange force is probably curiosity.

"Mummy!"

With his hand almost on the door handle, Señor Suárez turns back and flees. From the entrance to the flat he calls once more: "Mummy! Mummy!"

After this he notes that his heart is beating very fast. He runs down the stairs taking two steps at a time.

"Take me to the Carrera de San Jerónimo, opposite Congress."

The taxi takes him to the Carrera de San Jerónimo, opposite the Congress Building.

Mauricio Segovia is sick of seeing and hearing how Doña Rosa insults her waiters; he gets up and leaves the café.

"I don't know who's more wretched, that dirty old walrus in black or her bunch of clowns. I hope they gang up one day and give her a sound thrashing."

Mauricio Segovia is kind-hearted, like all redheads, and cannot bear an injustice. If he favors the idea that the waiters would do best to give Doña Rosa a good hiding, it is because he has seen her treat them badly; at least they would be even, then, one and all, and could start a fresh score.

"It's simply a question of guts. Some people's guts must be large and soft, like slugs, and others' small and hard, like the flint of a lighter."

Don Ibrahim de Ostolaza y Bofarull faces the looking glass, lifts his head, strokes his beard, and proclaims: "Gentlemen of the Academy, I do not wish to hold your attention much longer—and so on, and so forth." (Yes, this works out beautifully. . . . The head in an arrogant pose. . . . Must be careful with the cuffs; sometimes they stick out too much and look as if they were about to fly off.)

Don Ibrahim lights his pipe and paces up and down the room. Then, with one hand on the back of a chair and the other holding his pipe aloft, as though it were the scroll habitually brandished by the statues of important gentlemen, he continues: "How could we admit, as Señor Clemente de Diego would have us do, that usucaption is the method of acquiring rights by exercising them? The inconsistency of this argument, Gentlemen of the Academy, leaps to the eye. Pardon my insistence and allow me to stress once more my old appeal to logic; without logic, nothing is possible in the world of ideas. (Here, no doubt, there will be murmurs of approval.) Is it not evident, Gentlemen, that in order to use anything, one must first possess it? I can read it in your glances that you agree. (Possibly a member of the audience says at this moment, in a low voice: 'Of course, of course!') Now, since in order to use a thing one must possess it, we may transfer this statement into the passive mode and assert that nothing can be used without previous possession!"

Don Ibrahim makes a step towards the footlights and strokes, with an elegant gesture, the lapels of his dressing gown; that is to say, of his tail coat. Then he smiles.

"Very well, Gentlemen of the Academy: As, in order to use a thing, one must first possess it, one also must first acquire it in order to possess it. Under what title does not matter; as I have stated, the only precondition is to acquire it, since nothing, absolutely nothing, can be possessed without having previously been acquired." (Here I may well be interrupted by applause. I shall have to be ready for it.)

Don Ibrahim's voice sounds as solemn as a bassoon. On the other side of the flimsy partition wall, a husband just back from his day's work asks his wife: "Has our girlie done her big business?"

Don Ibrahim feels chilly and tightens his muffler. In the looking glass he sees himself wearing the black bow tie that goes with a dress coat in the evening.

Don Mario de la Vega, the printer with the cigar, has taken the graduate—curriculum of 1903—to supper.

"Now listen, d'you know what I say? Don't come to see me tomorrow, come to start work. That's how I like doing things, on the hop."

First the graduate feels somewhat put out. He would like to say that for him it would be better to start in a couple of days because it would give him time to settle one or two small matters; but he tells himself that he would only risk a "No" for an answer.

"As you wish, and thank you very much. I shall try to do my best."

"That will be to your own advantage."

Don Mario de la Vega grins.

"So that's agreed. And for a good start, I invite you to supper with me."

Things grow misty before the graduate's eyes.

"But—well. . . ."

The printer cuts him short.

"Come on, then. That's to say, if you haven't got another engagement, of course. I don't want to intrude."

"Oh no, no, I assure you, you wouldn't intrude, quite the opposite. I have no engagement."

The graduate summons his courage and adds: "I've no other engagement tonight. I'm at your disposal."

In the restaurant, Don Mario makes quite a bore of himself, explaining that he likes to treat his subordinates well, that his subordinates are a happy crowd, that his subordinates are well off, that his subordinates look on him as on a father, and that his subordinates come to feel an affection for the printing works.

"No business will ever prosper without co-operation between the chief and his subordinates. And if a business prospers, everybody profits, the boss and his subordinates. Just a moment, I'll make a telephone call, I've got to leave a message."

After the peroration of his new boss, the graduate is amply aware that his role is that of a subordinate. Just in case he had not grasped it completely, Don Mario suddenly throws at him, halfway through the meal: "You start at sixteen pesetas a day, but I won't hear of a labor contract, is that understood?"

"I understand, sir."

Señor Suárez gets out of his taxi in front of Congress and turns into the Calle del Prado; he has to find the café where he is expected. To make his eagerness less obvious, Señor Suárez has decided not to drive up to the café door in his taxi.

"Oh, my dear boy, I'm most upset. Something dreadful must have happened at home—Mummy didn't answer when I called her."

On entering the café, Señor Suárez's voice becomes more affected than ever; it sounds nearly like the voice of a tramp in a bar with waitresses.

"Leave her alone and don't worry. She'll be asleep."

"Oh, do you think so, really?"

"Quite sure. Old women drop off to sleep just like that."

His friend is a smart fellow with the air of a rogue, a green tie, oxblood shoes, and striped socks. His name is José Giménez Figueras; although he looks fearsome with his hard stubble and Moorish stare, his incongruous nickname is Pepe the Chip.

Señor Suárez smiles and almost blushes. "How handsome you look, Pepe!"

"Shut up, you beast, or people'll hear you."

"Oh, you beast, you're always so affectionate!"
Señor Suárez makes a face. Then he falls into a brown study. "What can have happened to Mummy?"
"Can't you shut up?"
Señor Giménez Figueras, alias the Chip, twists the wrist of Señor Suárez, alias Lady Photographer.
"Listen, ducky, are we here to have fun, or do you want to play me the record about your darling mamma?"
"Oh, Pepe, how right you are! But please, don't be angry with me, it's only that I'm shaking all over with fright."

Don Leoncio Maestre has reached two fundamental conclusions. One: It is evident that Señorita Elvira is not just anybody. It shows in her face. Señorita Elvira is a refined young woman of good family, who had some sort of row with her parents and ran away from them. And a good thing too, damn it all. Or is it right and proper for parents to keep their children in bondage all their lives, as many of them believe? No doubt Señorita Elvira left home because her family had made life impossible for her for years. The poor girl! Well, every human existence is a mystery, but the fact remains that every face is the mirror of the soul.
"However could it occur to anyone that Elvira might be a common slut? For God's sake, man!"
Don Leoncio Maestre is a little vexed with himself.
Don Leoncio's second conclusion is that he has to go back to Doña Rosa's café after supper, to see if Señorita Elvira is about again.
"Who knows? Girls like her, who are sad and depressed because they've had a little trouble at home, are very partial to cafés where they can hear music."
Don Leoncio eats his supper in haste, gives himself a good brush-up, once again puts on his overcoat and hat, and departs for Doña Rosa's café.

*   *   *   *

Mauricio Segovia has supper with his brother Hermenegildo, who has come to Madrid to try to get the job of secretary
to the National-Syndicalist Center in his home town.

"How are you getting on with your things?"

"Well, I'm getting on . . . Quite well, really, I think."

"Have you had any fresh news?"

"Yes, this afternoon I was with Don José María, you know,
the man who's private secretary to Don Rosendo, and he told
me he'll push the proposal as much as possible. Now we shall
see what they'll do among the lot of them. Do you think they're
going to appoint me?"

"I should think so. Why shouldn't they?"

"I don't know. Sometimes I feel I've got it in the bag and
other times I feel that all I'll get from them in the end is a
kick in the pants. The worst of it is this hanging about, not
knowing which card to play."

"Don't get discouraged. God made us all of the same clay.
And then you know, nothing ventured, nothing gained."

"That's what I think."

Over the rest of their meal the brothers sit almost in silence.

"Say, the Germans have run into trouble head on."

"Yes, it smells to me as if they'd burned their fingers."

Don Ibrahim de Ostolaza y Bofarull pretends not to hear
the discussion on the little girl's big business in his neighbor's
apartment. He fiddles again with his muffler, again places his
hand on the back of the chair, and goes on.

"Yes, Gentlemen of the Academy, I, who have the honor
to express my opinions before you, believe that my arguments
are watertight. (This 'watertight'—wouldn't it sound too popular, and rather uncouth?) Applying the conclusions from the
syllogism previously used to the jurisprudential concept that
concerns us (applying the conclusions from the syllogism previously used to the jurisprudential concept that concerns us
—this might be a bit long-winded . . .), we may assert that,
just as we must first possess a thing in order to use it, we must

equally, in order to exercise a right of whatever nature, possess this right first." (Pause.)

The tenant next door asks about the color of the little girl's big business. His wife tells him it was the normal color.

"And now, may I remind this distinguished gathering that a right cannot be possessed unless it has been previously acquired. I believe my words to be as clear as the flowing waters of a crystal brook. (Voices: 'Hear, hear!') Then if a right must first be acquired in order to be exercised, since one cannot exercise what one does not possess ('Quite right!'), how is it thinkable, by the rules of strict logic, that there should exist a mode of acquisition by use, as Professor Diego, a man famed for much original thought, would have it, when this would be tantamount to the proposition that a right can be exercised before having been acquired, hence before being possessed?" (Insistent murmurs of approval.)

Behind the partition, the neighbor asks: "Did you have to give her a dose?"*

"No, I had it all ready, but then she did it nicely on her own. Look, I had to buy a tin of sardines because your mother told me the oil from the tin is better for that sort of thing."

"Never mind, we'll have them for supper and that's that. The story about the sardine oil is just one of those things of Mother's."

Husband and wife smile affectionately at each other, they hug and they kiss. There are days when everything goes well. The little girl's constipation had threatened to become a permanent worry.

Don Ibrahim considers that in the face of the insistent murmurs of approval, he ought to make a short pause, inclining his forehead and gazing, as though far away in his thoughts, at the portfolio and the glass of water.

"It seems redundant, Gentlemen of the Academy, to explain how necessary it is to remember that the use of an object—

---

* Literally "the parsley stalk," an old-fashioned Spanish household remedy for small children's constipation. (*Translator's note.*)

not the use or exercise of the right to use it, since this right does not yet exist!—which leads, by prescription, to its possession by the occupier in his capacity of owner, is a situation *de facto,* but never *de jure.*" (Very good!)

Don Ibrahim smiles triumphantly and stays so for a few moments, without a thought in his head. At bottom—and on the surface as well—Don Ibrahim is a very fortunate man. What if nobody pays any attention to him? It does not matter. That's what history is for.

"Finally and in the long run, history metes out justice. And if in this base world genius is neglected, why should we worry, when within a hundred years we shall none of us have a hair left on our heads?"

Don Ibrahim is roused from his gentle stupor by a violent, thundery, frantic ringing of his doorbell.

"Disgraceful—what a riot! Some people are quite uncivilized. It would be the last straw if they're at the wrong door."

Don Ibrahim's wife, who had been knitting next to the brazier, while her husband held forth, gets up to open the door.

Don Ibrahim lends an attentive ear. It is the man from the fifth floor who has been ringing.

"Is your husband in, Señora?"

"Yes, he is, he's rehearsing his lecture."

"May I see him?"

"Yes, of course."

The lady raises her voice: "Ibrahim, it's our neighbor from upstairs."

Don Ibrahim replies: "Show him in, dear, show him in, don't keep him out there."

Don Leoncio Maestre is pale.

"Let's see, my dear neighbor, what has brought you to my modest hearth?"

Don Leoncio Maestre's voice trembles: "She's dead!"

"Eh?"

"I say she's dead."

"What?"

"She is, sir, she's dead. I touched her forehead and it was ice-cold."

Don Ibrahim's wife opens her eyes wide.

"But who?"

"The old lady next door."

"Next door?"

"Yes."

"Doña Margot?"

"Yes."

Don Ibrahim cuts in.

"The mother of the 'queer'?"

Just as Don Leoncio answers "Yes," Don Ibrahim's wife reprimands her husband: "For goodness sake, Ibrahim, don't talk like that!"

"And she's dead, definitely?"

"Yes, Don Ibrahim, stone dead. She's been strangled with a towel."

"With a towel?"

"How frightful!"

Don Ibrahim begins to issue orders, rush to and fro, and beg everyone to keep calm.

"Genoveva, get on the telephone and call the police."

"What's their number?"

"How should I know! Look it up in the book, dear. And you, friend Maestre, keep watch on the stairs and don't let anyone up or down. You'll find a stick on the hatrack there. I'm going to notify the doctor."

When the door of the doctor's flat opens to him, Don Ibrahim asks with unruffled calm: "Is the doctor at home?"

"Yes, sir, please wait a moment."

Don Ibrahim is well aware that the doctor is at home. When he comes out to see why he is wanted, Don Ibrahim, apparently not quite sure where to begin, gives him a smile and asks: "How's your little girl? Her tummy all right by now?"

After supper, Don Mario de la Vega stands a coffee to Eloy Rubio Antofagasta—the graduate, curriculum of 1903. It is clear that he means to exploit his position.

"Would you care for a good cigar?"

"Yes, sir, thank you very much."

"My word, you don't pass by much, do you?"

Eloy Rubio Antofagasta smiles humbly. "No, sir." After which he adds: "It's because I'm so glad to have found a job, you see."

"And to have had supper?"

"Yes, sir, and to have had supper, too."

Señor Suárez is smoking a cigar, to which he has been treated by Pepe the Chip.

"Oh, how nice it tastes! It has your own aroma, dear."

Señor Suárez looks deeply into his friend's eyes.

"Let's go and have some sherry, shall we? I don't feel like having supper. When I'm with you, I lose my appetite."

"Right, let's go."

"Will you let me stand treat?"

Arms entwined, the Lady Photographer and the Chip walk up the Calle del Prado, on the left-hand side where there are a few billiard saloons. Several people turn their heads on seeing them.

"Shall we drop in here for a bit, to watch postures?"

"No, leave it alone. The other day they almost bashed my teeth in with a cue."

"What foul beasts! Some people have no culture at all, I'm sure. What savages! It would have given you an awful shock, wouldn't it, Chiplet?"

Pepe the Chip gets angry. "Now listen, you can call your mother 'chiplet,' not me."

This gives Señor Suárez an attack of hysteria. "Oh, oh, my poor mummy! Oh, what can have happened to her! Oh, God!"

"Will you be quiet?"

"Forgive me, Pepe, I won't mention my mamma to you again. Oh, the poor dear! Listen, Pepe, will you buy me a flower? I'd like you to buy me a red camellia. Going with you, it's best to wear a keep-off sign. . . ."

Pepe the Chip smiles with great pride and buys a red camellia for Señor Suárez.

"Put it in your buttonhole."

"Wherever you like."

After establishing that the lady is dead, quite dead, the doctor looks after Don Leoncio Maestre, for the poor man is suffering from a nervous attack, is almost senseless, and kicks about in all directions.

"Oh, doctor, what if this one dies on us now?"

Doña Genoveva Cuadrado de Ostolaza is profoundly alarmed.

"Don't worry, madam, there's nothing much the matter with him—a severe shock and that's all."

Lying back in an easy chair, Don Leoncio shows the whites of his eyes and foams at the mouth. Meanwhile, Don Ibrahim has organized the residents of the house.

"Keep calm, above all keep perfectly calm. Let every head of household make a conscientious search of his apartment. Let us all serve the cause of justice by lending it all the support and co-operation within our power."

"Yes, sir, very well put. At moments like these it's best if one man commands and the rest of us obey."

The tenants of the house of the murder, being Spaniards to a man, contribute, each in his fashion, a lapidary phrase.

"Would you make a cup of lime-blossom tea for him?"

"Yes, doctor."

Don Mario and Eloy, the graduate, both agree to go to bed early.

"Okay, fellow. And tomorrow we'll get going, huh?"

"Yes, indeed, sir, you'll see how satisfied you're going to be with my work."

"I hope so. Tomorrow at nine you can start showing me. Where are you going to?"

"Home. Where else should I go? Home to bed. Will you go to bed early, too?"

"Have done so all my life. I'm a man of regular habits."

Eloy Rubio Antofagasta feels like toadying. Being a toady is, in all probability, his natural condition.

"Well, if you've nothing against it, Señor Vega, I'll see you home first."

"Just as you like, friend Eloy, and much obliged to you. One can see you know well enough that a few more cigarettes will come your way."

"That's not the reason, Señor Vega, believe me."

"Come on and don't be a fool, man. As the bishop said to the monk, we've all been cooks before being friars."

Although it is a rather cold night, Don Mario and his new proofreader take a stroll, with the collars of their coats turned up. If Don Mario is allowed to speak of his favorite subjects, he heeds neither cold nor heat nor hunger.

After quite a long walk, Don Mario and Eloy Rubio Antofagasta run into a huddle of people standing at the entrance of a street where two policemen let nobody pass.

"What has happened?"

A woman turns round: "I don't know, but people say there's been a murder, two old ladies stabbed to death."

"Good Lord!"

A man intervenes: "Don't exaggerate, madam. It wasn't two ladies, only one."

"And isn't that enough for you?"

"No, ma'am, it's too much for me. But if it had been two, I'd find it even more."

A young lad joins the group.

"What's up?"

Another woman informs him: "They say there's been a murder, a young girl strangled with a turkish towel. They say she was an actress."

The two brothers Mauricio and Hermenegildo decide to go on a spree.

"I tell you what, tonight's just the night for having a bit of fun. If they give you that job, we'll have it celebrated in advance, and if they don't, it's just too bad. If we don't go on the town, all you'll do is turn things round and round in your head the whole night. You've done what you can, now all that's left is to wait and see what the others do."

Hermenegildo is preoccupied.

"I suppose you're right. Like this, thinking about the same thing all day long, the only result I get is that I'm a bundle of nerves. Let's go where you like, you know Madrid best."

"Do you feel like having a few glasses of sherry?"

"Yes, let's. But—just like this, on our own?"

"We'll find company, don't you worry. At this time of the night there's no shortage of girls."

Mauricio Segovia and his brother Hermenegildo go bar-hopping from one bar to the next in the Calle de Echegaray. Mauricio is the guide, Hermenegildo follows in his wake and pays.

"Let's take it that we're celebrating my getting the job. The drinks are on me."

"Agreed. And if you haven't enough left to get home, tell me, and I'll help you out."

In a cheap tavern in the Calle de Fernández y González, Hermenegildo jabs his elbow into his brother.

"Look at those two, they're having a petting party."

Mauricio turns round.

"Tut, tut! And poor Marguerite Gautier there doesn't seem too well, poor girl. Just look at the red camellia in her buttonhole! Really, brother mine, they've got a nice collection here."

From the other end of the room a mighty voice roars: "Don't be too greedy, Lady Photographer, leave something for later on!"

Pepe the Chip rises from his seat.

"Let's see if somebody wants to get slung out of this place."

Don Ibrahim explains to the judge-magistrate: "You see, Your Honor, we have been unable to throw any light on the matter. Every one of the tenants in this house has searched his own apartment, and none of us have found anything worth our attention."

A tenant from the first floor, Don Fernando Cazuela, solicitor, looks at the floor. He has indeed found something.

The magistrate puts Don Ibrahim through an interrogation: "Let's go step by step. Had the deceased any family?"

"Yes, Your Honor, a son."

"Where is he?"

"Pooh, how should anyone know? He's a man of bad habits, Your Honor."

"A womanizer?"

"Well, no, Your Honor, not that."

"A gambler, maybe?"

"Well, no, not to my knowledge."

The magistrate looks at Don Ibrahim. "A drinker?"

"No, no, not a drinker either."

The magistrate forces a little smile.

"Tell me, then, what do you call bad habits? Collecting stamps?"

Don Ibrahim is piqued.

"No, sir, I call a number of things bad habits, for instance, being a pansy."

"Ah, I see. The son of the deceased is a homosexual."

"Yes, Your Honor, a pansy through and through."

"I see. Well, gentlemen, thank you all very much. If you please, go back to your quarters. If I need you, I shall send for you."

Obediently the tenants go back to their apartments. When Don Fernando Cazuela enters his apartment, first floor on the right, he finds his wife in a flood of tears.

"Oh, Fernando, kill me if you like, but don't ever let our little boy know anything about it."

"My dear girl, I wouldn't dream of killing you with the whole Magistrate's Court milling about in this house. Come on, go to bed. The only thing it needs to make it all quite perfect would be for your lover to turn out to have murdered Doña Margot."

*   *   *   *

By now the crowd in the street is several hundred strong. For its amusement, a small gypsy boy of about six sings flamenco songs which he accompanies by clapping his hands. He is an attractive little gypsy, but we have seen rather a lot of him. . . .

"A master tailor was
Cutting a pair of trousers,
When a gypsy lad came past,
Who was a young shrimp seller."

When Doña Margot is carried out of the house on her way to the mortuary, the boy stops his singing reverently.

Chapter Three

AFTER lunch Don Pablo goes to a quiet café on the Calle de San Bernardo to have his game of chess with Don Francisco Robles y López-Patón, and leaves there between five and half past to fetch Doña Pura for the little walk that invariably leads them to Doña Rosa's café, where he drinks his cup of chocolate, though he always finds that it tastes a little watery.

At the next table, by the window, four men play dominoes: Don Roque, Don Emilio Rodríguez Ronda, Don Tesifonte Ovejero, and Señor Ramón.

Don Francisco Robles y López-Patón, a specialist in venereal diseases, has a daughter named Amparo who is married to Don Emilio Rodríguez, also a physician. Don Roque is the husband of Doña Visi, Doña Rosa's sister; and according to his sister-in-law, he is the worst man in the world. Don Tesifonte Ovejero y Solano, a captain in the Army Veterinary Corps, is a nice little country dandy, rather shy, who wears a ring with an emerald. And finally there is Señor Ramón, a baker who owns a biggish bakehouse not far away.

These six cronies who meet every afternoon are quiet, serious men, with their harmless peccadilloes; they get on well together, have no rows, and sometimes have talks with each other from table to table, apart from the patter belonging to the games, which do not always hold their interest.

Don Francisco has just lost a bishop.

"This doesn't look too good."

"Not too good? If I were you, I'd give up."

"Well, I won't."

Don Francisco looks at his son-in-law, who is paired with the vet.

"Tell me, Emilio, how's the girl?"

The girl is Amparo.

"She's well. She's really quite well now. Tomorrow I'll let her get up."

"Delighted to hear it. Her mother will be round at your place this evening."

"That's fine. Will you be coming?"

"I don't know yet. We'll see if I can."

Don Emilio's mother-in-law is called Doña Soledad, Doña Soledad Castro de Robles.

Señor Ramón has at long last laid down the double-five with which he had been stuck. Don Tesifonte produces the time-honored joke: "Lucky at games . . ."

"And the other way round, captain, if you get me."

Don Tesifonte makes a grimace while the others laugh. To tell the truth, Don Tesifonte is lucky neither with women nor at dominoes. He spends his whole day within his four walls and only comes to have his little game of dominoes.

Don Pablo, sure of his victory, is distrait and pays no attention to the chessboard.

"Say, Roque, your sister-in-law was in a foul temper last night."

Don Roque dismisses this with a gesture, as though to say that he is in possession of all the facts anyway.

"She always is. I think she was born with a foul temper. My dear sister-in-law is a nasty creature. If it hadn't been for my girls, I should have told her some juicy home truths long ago. But after all, you know: 'Patience, and shuffle the cards . . .' Fat, boozy old hags like her generally don't last long."

Don Roque is convinced that, if he only sits it out, the café La Delicia will belong to his daughters, and a good many other things. At bottom Don Roque isn't far wrong. The inheritance is certainly worth putting up with a lot, even the trouble of waiting fifty years. Paris is well worth a Mass.

Doña Matilde and Doña Asunción meet every afternoon immediately after lunch at a dairy in the Calle de Fuencarral, where they are friendly with the owner, Doña Ramona Bragado, a very entertaining old woman with dyed hair, who had been an actress 'way back in the days of General Prim. Doña Ramona was once the heroine of a major scandal when she was left a legacy of fifty thousand pesetas by the Marquis de Casa Peña Zurana, the well-known senator who was twice Undersecretary of Finance. He had been her lover for at least twenty years. As a woman of some common sense she did not waste the money, but bought the lease of the dairy, quite prosperous, with steady, faithful customers. In addition, Doña Ramona, being nobody's fool, makes money out of anything that comes along; she is the sort that draws blood out of a stone. One of her most profitable branches of commerce is to act as go-between and procuress under cover of her dairy. Here she whispers cleverly gilded lies into the ears of a young girl who is longing for a nice handbag; there she dips into the pockets of one of those idle young gentlemen who hate to bestir themselves and expect to get everything served on a silver tray. There are people who can turn their hand to anything.

This afternoon it is a gay little party at the dairy.

"Will you bring us some buns, Doña Ramona—on me?"

"But, my dear, what's this? Have you won at the lottery?"

"Well, there's lotteries and lotteries, Doña Ramona. I've had a letter from Bilbao, from Paquita. Look what she says here."

"Let's hear, what is it?"

"You read it, my sight's getting worse every day. Read the bit here down at the bottom."

Doña Ramona puts on her glasses and reads: " 'My friend's

wife has died of pernicious anemia.' Goodness, Doña Asunción, then it's no wonder—"

"Go on, go on."

" 'And my friend says we shall no longer take precautions, and if I get with child, he is going to marry me.' Well, my dear, you are a lucky woman!"

"Yes, God be praised, I've been pretty lucky with the girl."

"And her friend's that professor, isn't he?"

"That's right. Don José María de Samas, professor of psychology, logic, and ethics."

"Congratulations, my dear. You've placed her well in the world."

"Not too badly."

Doña Matilde, too, has her piece of good news; it is nothing definite such as the story with Paquita may turn out to be, but good news all the same. Her son, Florentino de Mare Nostrum, has been offered a very good contract for one of the halls of the Paralelo in Barcelona, in a high-class show entitled *Melodies of the Race*, for which official backing can be expected because of its patriotic background.

"It will be a great relief for me if he's working in a big city. People in small towns have no education, sometimes they even throw stones at artists of his kind. As if they were different from others! One day at Jadraque it was so bad the Civil Guards had to intervene. If they hadn't got there in time, my poor, poor boy would have been skinned alive by those soulless savages who love nothing better than a row and shouting vulgar things at the best artists. My poor angel—what a shock that was for him!"

Doña Ramona quite agrees.

"Oh, yes, in a large capital like Barcelona he'll be much better off. There his art will be more appreciated and they'll respect it more, and all that."

"Indeed they will. Why, if he tells me he's going on a tour in the provinces, it gives my heart quite a turn. Poor dear Florentino, being so sensitive and having to play to such ignorant audiences so full of prejudice, as he says. It's simply dreadful!"

"That's true, but after all, things are looking up now."
"Yes—if it lasts."

Laurita and Pablo usually have their coffee in an exclusive bar behind the Gran Vía where a casual passer-by would hardly dare to enter. To get to the tables—a mere half dozen, each with its tablecloth and a vase of flowers in the center—you have to walk past the bar counter, which is nearly deserted, except for a couple of young ladies sipping brandy and four or five scatter-brained youngsters gambling their fond parents' money away at dice.

"Hello, Pablo. Nowadays you don't speak to anybody any more. Of course, since you're in love. . . ."

"Hello, Mari Tere. Where's Alfonso?"

"With his family, dear. He's quite a reformed character these days."

Laurita wrinkles her nose. When they sit down at the table, she does not grasp Pablo's hands as usual. At bottom, Pablo feels something like relief.

"Tell me, who's that girl?"

"A friend of mine."

Laurita turns half sad, half captious. "A friend, just like I am now?"

"No, dear."

"But you did say a friend."

"An acquaintance, then."

"Oh, an acquaintance . . . Pablo, listen."

All at once Laurita's eyes are full of tears.

"What is it?"

"I'm so terribly unhappy."

"Why?"

"Because of that woman."

"Now listen, my child, stop it and don't be a nuisance."

Laurita heaves a sigh.

"There you are, you're scolding me on top of it all."

"No, pet, not on top and not at bottom. Don't be more tiresome than you can help."

"You see!"

"I see what?"

"Now you're scolding me."

Pablo changes tactics.

"No, darling, I'm not scolding you. It's just that these little displays of jealousy get on my nerves. There's nothing one can do about it. It's been the same all my life."

"The same with all your girl friends?"

"No, Laurita. With some more and with others less."

"And with me?"

"With you more than with the rest."

"Of course, because you don't love me. One's only jealous if one's very much in love, very, very much, like I am with you."

Pablo stares at Laurita with an expression on his face as though staring at a most peculiar insect. Laurita turns affectionate.

"Listen, Pablito."

"Don't call me Pablito. What is it?"

"Oh, Pablo, you're as prickly as a hedgehog."

"Maybe, but don't go on saying it; say it differently for a change. It's something I've been told by too many people already."

Laurita smiles.

"But I don't mind if you're prickly. I like you just as you are. Only I'm so frightfully jealous. Pablo, if you stop loving me one day, will you tell me?"

"Yes."

"The thing is, one can't really believe you. You're such liars, you men."

Drinking his coffee, Pablo begins to realize that he is getting bored with Laurita's company. Very pretty, very attractive, very affectionate, even very faithful; but not much variety to her.

At Doña Rosa's café, as in all cafés, the public that comes in to have coffee after lunch is by no means the same as the public that comes for refreshments in the early evening. They all are regular customers, they all sit on the same seats, drink from the same cups, take the same dose of bicarbonate, pay in the same currency of pesetas, put up with the same rude remarks from the proprietress. And yet—somebody might find an explanation for it—the public in the café at three o'clock has nothing to do with the public that comes in after half past seven. Perhaps the only thing to link them is the idea they all cherish at the bottom of their hearts, that they are the real Old Guard of the café. For the evening people, the others, the after-lunch people, are no better than intruders who may be tolerated but are not worth a thought, and the afternoon people feel the same about the evening people: not worth a thought. As individuals and as a whole, the two groups are incompatible, and if it occurs to one of the after-lunch customers to linger on and delay his departure for a while, the arriving evening customers give him angry looks, exactly the same sort of looks, neither more nor less angry, which the after-lunch-coffee people give to evening-snack people who drop in before their time. A well-organized café, a café somewhat on the lines of Plato's Republic, would no doubt establish a quarter of an hour's truce so that those who come would not have to meet those who are going at the revolving door.

In the after-lunch hour at Doña Rosa's café our only acquaintance apart from the proprietress herself and the waiters is Señorita Elvira, who has really come to be something like another piece of furniture.

"How are you, Elvira dear, did you have a good night's rest?"

"Oh, yes, Doña Rosa. And you?"

"Only so-so, dear, only just so-so. I spent the whole night trotting to the lavatory and back. I must have had something for supper that didn't agree with me, and my bowels were in a dreadful state."

"Oh, dear! And are you better now?"

"Well, in a way I am, but you know, it left me quite limp."

"I'm not surprised, diarrhea's very weakening."

"You're telling me! I've made up my mind, if I don't get

better tomorrow, I'm going to call the doctor. As it is I can't do any work or anything, and you know what it is, in a business like this, if one isn't after it all the time . . ."

"Of course."

Padilla, the cigarette boy, is trying to convince a gentleman that certain tipped cigarettes he has on sale are not filled with tobacco from cigarette butts.

"You know, sir, you can always recognize tobacco from stubs because it's got a funny taste even when it's been thoroughly washed. And then, stub tobacco smells of vinegar a mile off. Now, just take a sniff at these, sir, and you won't smell anything funny. I wouldn't like to swear that there's Gener tobacco in these cigarettes—I don't want to cheat my customers. But there's ordinary good tobacco in these butts, well sifted and free of stalks. You can see for yourself how they're made: nothing machine-made about them, all by hand. Feel them if you like."

Alfonsito, the messenger boy, is taking instructions from a gentleman who has left his car in front of the door.

"Now let's see if you've understood. We mustn't get it wrong. You go up to the apartment, ring the bell, and wait. If this young lady—have a good look at the photo, she's tall and blonde—if this young lady opens the door, you say, 'Napoleon Bonaparte.' Now get that into your head. And if she answers, '. . . was defeated at Waterloo,' you give her the letter. Have you got it all?"

"Yes, sir."

"Good. Write the bit about Napoleon down, and the other bit you'll get for an answer too, and learn it by heart while you're on the way. She'll first read the letter and then she'll tell you an hour, seven o'clock, or six, or whatever it may be. Don't forget it, mind. And then you come back, but hurry up, and tell me. D'you understand?"

"Yes, sir."

"Good. Then go right off. If you do the job well you'll get five pesetas."

"Yes, sir. But please, if somebody else opens the door, and not the young lady?"

"Yes, you're right! Well, if somebody else opens the door, you simply say you've made a mistake. You ask if Señor Pérez lives there, and when they tell you he doesn't, you clear out and that's that. Is everything clear now?"

"Yes, sir."

Consorcio López, the manager, gets a telephone call from none other than his old flame Marujita Ranero, the mother of the twins.

"But what are you doing in Madrid?"

"My husband's here for an operation."

López is a little taken aback; he is a resourceful man, but this telephone call has really caught him rather unprepared. "And the kids?"

"They're quite little men now. This year they take their entrance exam."

"How time does fly!"

"Yes, doesn't it?"

There is a faint tremor in Marujita's voice. "Tell me . . ."

"What is it?"

"Don't you want to see me?"

"Yes, but . . ."

"Of course, you think I'm a perfect wreck by now."

"No, my dear, don't be so silly. But just at the moment . . ."

"I don't mean at this moment. Tonight when you close up. My husband's at the nursing home and I'm staying in a boarding house."

"Which one?"

"It's called La Colladense, in the Calle de la Magdalena."

López feels as if little explosions are going off behind his temples. "Say, how could I get in?"

"Simply through the door. I've taken a room for you, number three."

"And say, how am I to find you?"

"Don't be a silly, I'll find you—no fear."

As López puts back the receiver and turns to the counter, his elbow knocks over a whole stand, the one with all the liqueur bottles: Cointreau, Calisay *anís*, Benedictine, curaçao, crème de café, crème de menthe. And hell breaks loose.

Petrita, Filo's maid, goes across to Celestino Ortiz's bar to fetch a siphon because little Javier has wind. The poor child gets it sometimes, and then the only thing that helps is to give him soda water.

"Say, Petrita, your lady's brother has become very rude."

"Leave him alone, Señor Celestino, he's having a very hard time, poor man. Does he owe you something?"

"Well, yes, he does. Twenty-two pesetas."

Petrita walks towards the back room.

"I've come for a siphon. Will you switch on the light for me?"

"But you know where the switch is."

"Yes, but sometimes one gets a shock. Do turn it on for me."

When Celestino Ortiz is in the back room to turn on the light, Petrita tackles him.

"Tell me, am I worth twenty-two pesetas?"

Celestino Ortiz fails to get her meaning.

"Eh?"

"I said, am I worth twenty-two pesetas?"

The blood rushes to Celestino Ortiz's head.

"You're worth an empire."

"And twenty-two pesetas?"

Celestino Ortiz throws himself at the girl.

"Cash in for Señorito Martin's coffees!"

It is as if an angel were passing through the back room of Celestino Ortiz's bar, raising a whirlwind with its wings.

"And you, why are you doing this for Señorito Martin?"

"Because I want to, and because I love him better than anything else in the world. If anybody wants to know, I'll tell him, and first of all my boy friend."

With her cheeks deeply flushed, her breast heaving, her voice husky, her hair disheveled, and her eyes shining, Petrita has a strange beauty, like that of a newly mated lioness.

"And does he feel the same as you do?"

"I don't let him."

At five o'clock the circle of friends at the café in the Calle de San Bernardo dissolves; at half past or even earlier every bird is back in its nest. Don Pablo and Don Roque are each at home, Don Francisco and his son-in-law in their consulting rooms, Don Tesifonte at his studies, and Señor Ramón is watching the opening of the shutters at his bakery, which is his gold mine.

Two men sit on in the café at a table apart, smoking and saying very little. One of them is called Ventura Aguado and is a law student who wants to become a notary.

"Let me have a butt."

"Here you are."

Martin Marco lights his cigarette.

"Her name's Purita. She's an enchanting woman, as gentle as a young girl and as dainty as a princess. What a foul life!"

At this hour Purita Bartolomé is having a snack in an eating house in the Calle de Cuchilleros together with a rich junk dealer. Martin remembers the last she said to him: "Bye-bye, Martin. You know I'm always at the boarding house in the afternoon, and you've only to give me a ring. But don't ring up this afternoon—I've a date with a friend."

"Right."

"Good-by, and give me a kiss."

"But—here?"

"Yes, silly. People will think we're man and wife."

Martin pulls at his cigarette with a lordly air. Then he takes a deep breath.

"Anyway . . . say, Ventura, could you let me have ten pesetas? I haven't had a square meal today."

"But my dear boy, that's no life for you!"

"Don't I know it?"

"And can't you pick up any job?"

"Nothing. The two commissioned articles, that's two hundred pesetas less nine per cent discount."

"That won't make you fat. All right, take this while the going's good. My father's drawn his purse strings tighter. Look, take twenty-five. Ten won't get you anywhere."

"Thanks a lot. Now let me stand you a treat with your money."

Martin Marco calls the waiter.

"Two coffees."

"Three pesetas."

"Give me the change."

The waiter puts his hand in his pocket and gives Martin the change for the bank note: twenty-two pesetas.

Martin Marco and Ventura Aguado are friends, real friends of long standing; they started their studies at the law school together, before the war.

"Shall we go?"

"Just as you like. There's nothing more for us to do here."

"The truth is, my friend, that I've got nothing to do anywhere else either. Where are you going?"

"I don't really know. I think I'll go for a little walk to kill time."

Martin Marco smiles.

"Then wait a moment till I've taken some bicarbonate. Nothing better for a tricky digestion."

Julián Suárez Sobrón, alias the Lady Photographer, aged fifty-three, born at Vegadeo in the province of Oviedo, and José Giménez Figueras, alias the Chip, aged forty-six, born at Puerto de Santa María in the province of Cádiz, hold hands in the basement of the Central Police Headquarters, waiting to be taken to the cells.

"Oh, Pepe, how I could do with a drop of coffee this moment!"

"Yes, and with a glass of strong *anís*. Ask for one—let's see if you get it."

Señor Suárez is more upset than Pepe the Chip; the Giménez Figueras creature is evidently more used to a crisis of this sort.

"Tell me, why d'you think they're keeping us here?"

"I've no idea. You haven't by any chance got some virtuous maiden with child and then left her, have you?"

"Oh, Pepe, what an imagination you have!"

"Well, we can't do anything about it, it's up to them."

"That's true enough. What hurts me most is that I couldn't let Mummy know about it."

"At it again?"

"No, no!"

The two friends had been detained last night in a bar in the Calle de la Vega. The police who picked them up came into the bar, took a short look round, and then pounced on them straight away. What fellows, and how used to that sort of job!

"Come along with us."

"Oh, what are you arresting me for? I'm a decent taxpayer, I don't interfere with anyone, and I've all my papers in order."

"Very good. You'll explain all that when you're asked. Take this flower out of your buttonhole."

"Oh, why? I've no reason to go with you, I've done nothing wrong."

"Don't make trouble, if you please. Look at this."

Señor Suárez looked. He saw the nickel-plated hoops of handcuffs sticking out of the policeman's pocket.

Pepe the Chip had already risen.

"Let's go with these gentlemen, Julián. Everything will be cleared up."

"Let's go, let's go, all right. But goodness me, what manners!"

At headquarters there had been no need for their descriptions to be entered in the files; they had them there anyway. All that was added was a date and four or five short words, which they did not manage to read.

"Why are we detained?"

"Don't you know?"

"No, I don't know anything at all. What should I know?"

"You'll hear in due course."

"Couldn't I send a message that I'm detained?"

"Tomorrow."

"But, you see, my mamma's a very old lady and she'll be so worried, poor dear."

"Your mother?"

"Yes, she's seventy-six."

"I see. Well, I can't do anything about it, or tell you anything either. Everything will be cleared up tomorrow."

In the cell in which they were shut up they couldn't see anything at first. It was an enormous room with a low ceiling, badly lit by a fifteen-watt lamp in a wire cage. After a little while, when their eyes got used to it, Señor Suárez and Pepe the Chip began to identify a few familiar faces: poor pansies, snatch thieves, pickpockets, professional spongers; people who have been drifting round, lurching like whipping tops and never striking it lucky.

"Oh, Pepe, how I could do with a drop of coffee right now!"

It smelled very bad inside the cell, a faint, rancid, insidious smell that tickled the nostrils.

"Oh, hello, you're back early today. Where've you been?"

"The usual place. I've had coffee with the boys."

Doña Visi gives her husband a kiss on the top of his bald head.

"If you only noticed how glad I am when you're back early!"

"Take it easy, it's a bit late in the day."

Doña Visi smiles. Doña Visi, poor woman, is always smiling.

"Do you know who's coming this evening?"

"Some old tabby, I bet."

Doña Visi never gets upset.

"No, my friend Montserrat."

"A good type, that!"

"That's what she is, she's very good."

"Hasn't she told of any new miracle that priest in Bilbao has worked?"

· 105 ·

"Hush, don't talk heresies. Why must you always say such things when you don't really feel them?"

"All right, all right."

With every day that passes Don Roque is more convinced that his wife is stupid.

"Will you stay here with us?"

"No."

"Oh, I'm so sorry."

The doorbell rings, and Doña Visi's friend enters the apartment just as the parrot on the third floor is screaming blasphemies.

"Listen, Roque, this is too much. If that parrot doesn't change its ways, I'm going to report it to the police."

"But my dear, do you realize what fun they'd make of you at the police station if they heard you reporting a parrot?"

The maid shows Doña Montserrat into the good parlor. "I'll go and tell the mistress you're here. Please sit down."

Doña Visi flies to welcome her friend, and Don Roque, after peeping out from behind the net curtains, sits down by the brazier and produces a pack of cards.

"If the knave of clubs turns up in the first five, it's a good sign, but if the ace does, it's too much. I'm no longer a callow boy."

Don Roque has his private rules of fortunetelling.

The knave of clubs turns up third.

"Poor Lola, what's in store for you. . . . I'm sorry for you, my girl. However . . ."

Lola is the sister of Josefa López, a former maid of the Robles family with whom Don Roque has had a certain amount to do, but who, now that she has run to flesh and advanced in years, has been supplanted by her younger sister. Lola is maid-of-all-work at Doña Matilde's, the widow with a pension who is the mother of the impersonator.

Doña Visi and Doña Montserrat are chattering like magpies. Doña Visi is delighted: on the last page of the *Missionary Cherub*, a fortnightly magazine, appear her name and those of her three daughters.

"You can see it with your own eyes, it's not something I've imagined, but it's the truth. Roque, Roque!"

From the other side of the apartment Don Roque shouts back: "What d'you want?"

"Give the girl the paper with that bit about the Chinese!"

"Eh?"

Doña Visi comments to her friend: "Oh, Lord, these men never hear anything." She raises her voice and calls out to her husband: "Give the girl . . . can you hear me?"

"Yes."

"Then give the girl the paper with the bit about the Chinese."

"What paper?"

"The one about the Chinese, you know, the one about the Chinese children at the missions!"

"Eh? I don't get you. What are you saying about the Chinese?"

Doña Visi smiles at Doña Montserrat: "This husband of mine's very kind, but he never knows what's going on. I'll go and get the paper myself, I won't be a minute. Excuse me just for a moment."

When Doña Visi comes into the room where Don Roque is playing solitaire, with the brazier alight under the table, she asks: "But, man, didn't you hear me?"

Don Roque never raises his eyes from the cards.

"What an idea to think that I'd get up for the sake of the Chinese!"

Doña Visi fumbles round in the sewing basket, finds the number of the *Missionary Cherub* she is looking for, and muttering under her breath, returns to the good parlor, which is so cold that it is hard to stay there.

The sewing basket gapes open after Doña Visi's search, and from between the mending cotton and the button box—a box that had held cough lozenges in the year one—timidly protrudes another of Doña Visi's magazines.

Don Roque leans back in his chair and picks it up.

"Here he is, that character!"

"That character" is the miracle-working priest from Bilbao. Don Roque begins to read in the magazine: "Rosario Quesada (Jaén), for recovery of her sister from acute colitis: 5 pesetas.

"Ramón Hermida (Lugo), for several favors granted to him in the course of his business: 10 pesetas.

"María Luisa del Valle (Madrid), for the disappearance of a small lump which she had on one of her eyes without her having to consult the oculist: 5 pesetas.

"Guadalupe Gutiérrez (Ciudad Real), for the cure of a nineteen-month-old baby from injuries caused by a fall from a first-floor balcony: 25 pesetas.

"Marina López Ortega (Madrid), for the taming of a domestic pet: 5 pesetas.

"A most pious widow (Bilbao), for the recovery of a package containing securities which had been mislaid by a servant of the house: 25 pesetas."

Don Roque falls into a brown study: "It's quite incredible. You can't take it seriously."

Doña Visi feels more or less obliged to apologize to her friend. "Aren't you cold, Montserrat? Some days this house is like an icebox."

"No, not at all, Visitación, it's very cozy here. Your apartment is most pleasant, with much comfort, as the English say."

"Thank you, Montserrat, you're always so sweet."

Doña Visi smiles and starts looking for her name in the list. Doña Montserrat—tall, mannish, bony, ungainly, with a mustache, somewhat slow in speech, and short-sighted—puts her lorgnette to her eyes.

True enough, as Doña Visi had claimed, the names of herself and her three daughters appear on the last page of the *Missionary Cherub*.

"Doña Visitación Leclerc de Moisés, for the baptism of two Chinese children with the names of Ignacio and Francisco Javier: 10 pesetas. Señorita Julita Moisés Leclerc, for the baptism of a Chinese child with the name of Ventura: 5 pesetas.

Señorita Visitación Moisés Leclerc, for the baptism of a Chinese child with the name of Manuel: 5 pesetas. Señorita Esperanza Moisés Leclerc, for the baptism of a Chinese child with the name of Agustín: 5 pesetas."

"Now, what do you think of this?"

Doña Montserrat expresses her agreement in flattering terms.

"I find it all excellent, excellent indeed. There is so much work to be done. It is shocking to think of the millions of infidels who are still to be converted. The heathen countries must be swarming like anthills."

"I should say so. And these tiny Chinese babies are so pretty! If we did not make some little sacrifices, depriving ourselves of this or that, they would all go straight to limbo. But in spite of our poor efforts, limbo must be chock-full of Chinese, don't you think?"

"Oh, yes."

"It gives me the creeps only to think of it. Just imagine the curse hanging over the Chinese. All of them walking round there, locked up and not knowing what to do. . . ."

"It's horrifying."

"And the little babies, dear, the toddlers who can't walk yet, will they be stuck there, too, like little worms, always in the same spot?"

"Indeed they will."

"We owe thanks and praise to the Lord that we were born Spanish women. Now, if we'd been born in China, our children might have to go to limbo without reprieve. Think of having children for that! With all one has to suffer before they're born, and with the trouble they give while they're small!"

Doña Visi sighs feelingly.

"My poor girls, they're quite unaware of the danger they escaped. It's all right for them, because they were born in Spain, but only think how it would have been if they'd been born in China. And it might have happened to them, don't you agree?"

All the neighbors of the deceased Doña Margot forgather in Don Ibrahim's apartment. The only ones missing are: Don Leoncio Maestre, arrested under the judge-magistrate's orders; Don Antonio Jareño, the tenant of apartment D, mezzanine, who works for the Wagons-Lits and is at present on a journey; Don Ignacio Galdácano, the tenant of apartment B, third floor, who is mad, poor man; and the son of the deceased, Don Julián Suárez, whose whereabouts are not known to anybody. Apartment A on the first floor is let to a commercial academy and nobody lives there. Of the rest, not one is missing; they are all greatly affected by what has happened and have at once followed Don Ibrahim's summons to an exchange of opinions.

Those convened scarcely find room in Don Ibrahim's flat, which is not very large, and the majority have to stand, leaning against a wall or against a piece of furniture, as if at a wake.

"Gentlemen," Don Ibrahim begins, "I have ventured to invoke your attendance at this meeting because in the house where we are residents something has occurred that is outside the normal orbit."

"Thank the Lord for it," interrupts Doña Teresa Corrales, the widow with a pension who lives in B on the fifth floor.

"Amen," several low voices chime in.

"Last night," Don Ibrahim de Ostolaza resumes, "when our neighbor Don Leoncio Maestre, whose innocence we all hope will soon blaze forth with the blinding intensity of the sun—"

"We mustn't obstruct the course of justice," shouts Don Antonio Pérez Palenzuela, a gentleman employed in the National Syndicates who lives in C, second floor. "We must abstain from premature opinions. I am the official responsible for this building, and it's my duty to prevent any possible pressure on the judiciary."

"Be quiet, man," Don Camilo Pérez, chiropodist, the tenant of D, first floor, intervenes. "Let Don Ibrahim continue."

"All right, Don Ibrahim, go on. I don't wish to interrupt the meeting. All I want is due respect for the proper legal authority and due consideration for its work on behalf of an order that . . ."

"Sh! Sh! Let him go on."

Don Antonio Pérez shuts up.

"As I was saying, last night, when Don Leoncio Maestre gave us the bad news of the accident that had befallen Doña Margot Sobrón de Suárez, I lost no time in asking our good personal friend the doctor Don Manuel Jorquera, here present, to give an exact and precise diagnosis of the state of our common neighbor. Don Manuel Jorquera, with a readiness that speaks well and highly for his sense of professional decorum, placed himself at my disposal, and together we entered the domicile of the victim."

Don Ibrahim's attitude as a champion and tribune reaches the highest level of refinement.

"I take the liberty of asking you to pass a vote of thanks to the eminent Doctor Jorquera, who, together with another eminent physician, Don Rafael Masasana, at this moment compelled by his modesty to seek shelter behind that curtain, honors us by dwelling as a resident in our midst."

"Hear, hear," exclaim, as though with one voice, Don Exuperio Estremera, the priest from C, fifth floor, and Don Lorenzo Sogueiro, the landlord of the Fonsagradino Bar, housed in one of the basements.

The admiring glances of all those present go from one doctor to the other. It is very much like a bullfight where the matador who pleased the public is called by applause into the center of the ring and takes with him a colleague who had less luck with his bulls and has not pleased the public so much.

"Well, then, gentlemen," Don Ibrahim proclaims, "as soon as I realized that the resources of science were unavailing in the face of the monstrous crime that had been committed, I had only two wishes, which, as a good Christian, I commended to the Lord: that none of us—and I beg my dear friend Señor Pérez Palenzuela not to read into my words even the faintest shadow of an intent to put pressure on anyone—that none of us, I say, should find himself implicated in this dastardly and shameful affair, and that Doña Margot should not go without those last honors that we all desire to have when the hour strikes, for ourselves, for our agnates, and for our cognates."

Don Fidel Utrera, the medical assistant of A on the mezzanine, who is very reckless, almost cries "Bravo!" He has it on the tip of his tongue, but fortunately manages to swallow it down.

"I propose, therefore, my esteemed neighbors, whose presence within my humble walls sheds so much luster and dignity upon them . . ."

Doña Juana Entrena de Sisemón, a widow with a pension and the tenant of B, second floor, gazes at Don Ibrahim. With what power, with what beauty and precision he expresses himself! Really, he talks like a book. On meeting Señor Ostolaza's glance, she turns her eyes to Francisco López, who has so often been confidant and comforter in her woes, and who is the owner of the ladies' hairdresser shop "Cristi and Quico" which is in C on the mezzanine.

As their glances cross, there is a mute dialogue, lightning-quick: "Well, what do you think?"

"Sublime, dear lady!"

Don Ibrahim continues unmoved: ". . . that we undertake, individually, to mention Doña Margot in our prayers and, collectively, to defray the funeral Mass for her soul."

"I'm in agreement," says Don José Leciñena, the tenant of D, third floor.

"In complete agreement," seconds Don José María Olvera, a captain in the Army Ordnance Corps who lives in A, second floor.

"Are you all of the same mind?"

Don Arturo Ricote, a clerk in the Banco Hispano Americano and tenant of D, fifth floor, says in his cracked little voice: "Yes, sir."

"Yes, yes," come the votes of Don Julio Maluenda, of C, third floor, a retired officer of the merchant navy, whose place is like a junk shop, full of maps, engravings, and ships' models, and of Don Rafael Sáez, the young surveyor from D, fourth floor.

"Señor Ostolaza is most emphatically right. We have to provide the offices for the soul of our departed neighbor," explains Don Carlos Luque, a shopkeeper, tenant of D, second floor.

"As for me, I agree with everything the others say," Pedro Tauste, the owner of a shoe-repair shop called "The Footwear Clinic," has no wish to swim against the current.

"It is a timely and convincing suggestion. Let's support it," says Don Fernando Cazuela, the solicitor from B, first floor, who last night, when he, like all the other tenants, searched for the murderer, found his wife's lover hiding in the dirty linen basket, all curled up.

"And I say the same," contributes as the last Don Luis Noalejo, the Madrid representative of "Casimiro Pons's Widow & Sons, Threads and Yarns" and tenant of Flat C, first floor.

"Thank you very much, gentlemen. I see that we are all agreed. We all have spoken and expressed identical points of view. I acknowledge your kind support and pass it on into the hands of our neighbor, the godly priest Don Exuperio Estremera, so that he may arrange the services according to his excellent knowledge of canons."

Don Exuperio's face has an expression of mystic wonder. "I accept your trust."

With this, the matter is concluded, and the meeting begins to disintegrate. Some of the tenants have things of their own to do, others, the minority, think that it is Don Ibrahim who is bound to have something to do, and still others—for it takes all kinds to make a world—troop off because they are tired of being on their feet for a full hour. Don Gumersindo López, a clerk of the Petrol Corporation, tenant of C on the mezzanine, and the only person present who has not said a word, wonders as he goes down the stairs in a thoughtful mood: "And that's what I asked some hours off for?"

Doña Matilde, back from Doña Ramona's dairy, talks with her maid.

"Tomorrow get some liver for lunch, Lola. Don Tesifonte says it's very good for one."

Don Tesifonte is Doña Matilde's oracle. He is also her boarder.

"A nice tender bit of liver so we can stew it with the kidneys, with a drop of wine and minced onion."

Lola says Yes to everything. Later in the market she gets whatever she happens to see first or feels like buying.

Seoane leaves his house. Every evening at half past six he starts playing the violin at Doña Rosa's café. His wife stays at home in the kitchen, mending socks and vests. The couple live in a damp, unhealthy basement in the Calle de Ruiz, for which they pay seventy-five pesetas a month; the best about it is that it is only a step from the café, and Seoane never has to spend a thing on trolley fares.

"Good-by, Sonsoles, see you soon."

His wife does not bother to lift her eyes from her sewing.

"Good-by, Alfonso, give me a kiss."

Sonsoles has weak eyes. Their lids are always red; she looks all the time as if she has just had a good cry. Poor thing, Madrid does not agree with her. As a bride she was handsome, plump, and glowing, a pleasure to look at, but now, though by no means old, she is a wreck. The poor woman's speculations have gone wrong; she had imagined that in Madrid the streets were paved with gold, married a Madrileño, and now, when there is nothing she can do about it, she realizes that it has all been a mistake. At home in Navarredondilla, in the province of Avila, she had been a young lady and had as much to eat as she wanted. In Madrid she is an unhappy wretch. Most days she goes to bed without any evening meal.

Macario and his fiancée sit close together holding hands on a bench in Señora Fructuosa's tiny porter's lodge. Señora Fructuosa is Matildita's aunt and a portress in the Calle de Fernando VI.

"For ever and ever . . ."

Marujita calls the waiter.

"A coffee, please."

"With milk?"

"No, black. Tell me, who's that lady who does all the shouting?"

"Oh, that's the mistress. I mean, our boss."

"Then ask her to be so kind and come over here."

The tray trembles in the poor waiter's hand. "But do you mean now, at once?"

"Yes. Tell her I've asked for her, would she please come here."

The waiter walks up to the counter with the expression of a criminal facing the gallows. "López, one black coffee. Madam, excuse me."

Doña Rosa turns round. "What do you want?"

"I, nothing, madam. It's that lady over there who's asking for you."

"Which one?"

"The one with the ring. The one who's looking this way."

"And she's asking for me?"

"Yes, for the proprietress, she said. I don't know what she wants, but she looks like somebody important, a lady with means. She said to me, she said, 'Ask the proprietress to be so kind and come over here.' "

Frowning, Doña Rosa goes up to Marujita's table. López puts his hand over his eyes.

"Good evening. You were looking for me?"

Matildita and Macario talk in whispers.

"Good-by, sweetheart, I must go to work now."

"Good-by, till tomorrow, my love. I shall be thinking of you all the time."

Macario squeezes his fiancée's hand for quite a while, and then gets up. A shiver runs down his spine.

"Good night, Señora Fructuosa, and many thanks."

"Good night, dear. Don't mention it."

Macario is a very courteous young man; he gives his thanks to Señora Fructuosa every day. Matildita's hair is reddish like the floss on a corncob, and she is a little short-sighted. She is tiny and graceful, even if she isn't pretty. When she can get them, she gives piano lessons. She teaches the little girls tangos from memory, which makes quite an impression.

At home she always lends a hand to her mother and her sister Juanita, who embroider on commission.

Matildita is thirty-nine.

As readers of the *Missionary Cherub* are aware, three daughters belong to Doña Visi and Don Roque; all three are young, all three very much alike, rather fresh and a little bit flighty.

The eldest is called Julita. She is twenty-two and has her hair bleached. When she wears it as a loose and wavy mane, she looks like Jean Harlow.

The middle one is called Visitación like her mother. She is twenty, has chestnut-brown hair and deep, dreamy eyes.

The youngest is called Esperanza. She has an official fiancé who comes to their house and talks politics with her father. Esperanza is already getting together her trousseau; she has just had her nineteenth birthday.

These days, Julita, the eldest, is head over heels in love with a young man who hopes to become a public notary and has turned her head. His name is Ventura Aguado, and for seven years—not counting the war years—he has taken exams to be appointed a public notary, and always without success.

His father, an almond grower at Riudecola in the district of Tarragona, tells him time and again: "Put in for the registrar's office at the same time, son."

"No, Dad, it's too much of a bore."

"But don't you see, boy, that you won't be made public notary ever, not even by a miracle?"

"You think I won't get appointed? Why, I can be any day I like. The point is, if I don't get posted to Madrid or Barcelona it isn't worth my while. I'd rather withdraw, that makes more sense. With a public notary, prestige counts for a lot, Dad."

"Yes, but all the same. . . . What about Valencia—or

Seville—or Saragossa? They aren't bad places either, I should think."

"No, Dad, you've got things out of focus. I've worked out my plan of action. If you want, I'll drop it. . . ."

"No, no, my boy. Don't upset things. You go on with it. After all, you've made a start. You know more about these things than I do."

"Thank you, Dad, you're a clever man. I've been very lucky to be born your son."

"Maybe. Any other father would have sent you to hell a long time ago. All right, but what I say is, 'Will you ever be a notary?' "

"Rome wasn't built in a day, Dad."

"No, son, but look here, in seven years or more they'd have had time to build a second town next to it, wouldn't they?"

Ventura smiles. "Don't you worry, Dad, I shall be public notary in Madrid. Have a Lucky?"

"Eh?"

"An American cigarette?"

"Phew, no. I prefer my own, thank you."

What Don Ventura Aguado Despojols thinks is that a son who smokes Virginian tobacco like a fine young lady will never come to be a public notary. All the notaries he knows are serious, severe, cautious, and weighty men, and all smoke black tobacco.

"D'you know your Castán by heart yet?"

"Not by heart, that doesn't make a good impression."

"And the Civil Code?"

"Yes—ask me anything you like from any section you like."

"I was only curious."

Ventura Aguado Sans can do what he likes with his father. He bewilders him with phrases like "plan of action" and "out of focus."

The second of Doña Visi's daughters, Visitación, has recently quarreled with the young man with whom she has been going for a year. His name is Manuel Cordel Estéban, and he is a medical student. For the last week the girl has been

· 117 ·

going out with another lad, also a medical student. The King is dead, long live the King!

Young Visi has an intuitive gift for love. The first day, she let her new escort press her hand, quite calmly, as they were saying good-by at the door of her house; they had been having tea and cakes at Garabay's. On the second day, she let him take her arm to cross the streets; they had been dancing and taking a light meal at the Casablanca. On the third day, she surrendered her hand and let him hold it the whole evening; they went to the Café María Cristina to listen to the music and gaze wordlessly at each other.

"That's the classic thing when a man and a woman are falling in love," he made bold to say, after much pondering.

On the fourth day, the girl did not object to his holding her arm; she pretended not to notice.

"No, not to the cinema. Tomorrow!"

On the fifth day, in the cinema, he kissed her hand, furtively. On the sixth, in the Retiro Park on an awfully cold day, she gave the excuse that is no excuse, the excuse of a woman who has lowered the drawbridge: "No, no, please. Let go of me, be good, I've forgotten my lipstick, people might see us . . ."

She was hot and flushed, and her nostrils quivered with every breath she took. It cost her an immense effort to refuse him, but she thought that it was better to leave it there, that it was more elegant.

On the seventh day, in a box at the Bilbao Cinema, he put his arm round her waist and whispered into her ear: "We're quite alone now, Visi . . . Visi darling . . . my love. . . ."

And she, letting her head droop on his shoulder, spoke in a small voice, a tiny broken voice heavy with emotion: "Yes, Alfredo. I'm so happy!"

Alfredo Angulo Echevarría felt his temples throbbing dizzily, as though with fever, and his heart beating at an unaccustomed rate. "The suprarenal glands; that's my suprarenal glands discharging their adrenaline."

The third of the girls, Esperanza, is light as a swallow and shy as a dove. There is more to her than meets the eye, as there is to anyone, but she knows that her role as future wife sits well on her, and she talks very little, always in a gentle voice, and says to everyone: "As you like, I'll do just as you like."

Her fiancé, Agustín Rodríguez Silva, is fifteen years older than she and owns a druggist's shop in the Calle Mayor.

The girl's father is delighted; he considers his future son-in-law an efficient man. So does her mother.

"Lagarto soap, prewar quality, think of it—nobody else has got it. But he brings me everything, absolutely everything I ask for, and in double-quick time."

Her friends regard her with a certain envy. What a lucky woman—Lagarto soap!

Doña Celia is ironing sheets when the telephone rings.

"Hello?"

"Doña Celia, is that you? Don Francisco speaking."

"Oh, Don Francisco! Have you any good news to tell?"

"Nothing very much, I'm afraid. Will you be at home?"

"Of course. You know I never stir from here."

"Right, then I'll be round about nine."

"Whenever you like, I'm always at your service. Shall I send for . . ."

"No, don't send for anybody."

"Very well."

Doña Celia hangs up the receiver, snaps her fingers, and goes to the kitchen to gulp a little glass of *anís*. There are days when everything works out well. The trouble is that there are other days when things go wrong, and you end without having earned enough for a box of matches.

As soon as Doña Matilde and Doña Asunción are out of the dairy, Doña Ramona Bragado puts on her coat and goes to the Calle de la Madera, where she is trying to enroll a young girl working as a packer at a printer's.

"Is Victorita about?"

"Yes, here she is."

Behind a large table Victoria is busy making book parcels.

"Hello, Victorita dear. Would you drop in at the dairy later? My nieces will be round, we're going to play cards, and I think we'll have a nice time and a bit of fun."

Victorita reddens.

"Well, yes. Yes, I'll come if you want me to."

Victorita is dangerously near to tears. She knows where she is heading. Victorita is not yet eighteen, but well developed for her age; she looks more like a woman between twenty and twenty-two.

The girl has a young man who was discharged from the army because of T.B. The poor fellow is unable to work and he spends the whole day in bed waiting for Victorita to drop in after work.

"How do you feel today?"

"Better."

When his mother left the bedroom, Victorita would go over to his bed and kiss him.

"Don't kiss me, or you'll catch it."

"I don't care, Paco. Don't you like kissing me?"

"Of course I do."

"Then that's the only thing that matters. For you I wouldn't mind doing anything. . . ."

One day Victorita looked so pale and haggard that he asked: "What's the matter with you?"

"Nothing. I've been thinking."

"Thinking what?"

"Well, I've been thinking that you could get rid of this trouble if you had medicine and plenty of food."

"Maybe, but there you are."

"I can get the money."

"You?"

Victoria's voice grew thick as if she had been drunk.

"Yes, I can. A young girl is always worth money—it doesn't matter if she isn't pretty."

"What do you mean?"

Victorita was quite calm.

"Just what I said. If it means that you get well again, I'll go with the first rich man who wants me as a mistress."

Paco went a little red, and his eyelids began to flutter. Victorita was slightly shocked when he answered: "All right." But at bottom, Victorita loved him all the more for it.

At the café Doña Rosa is fit to be tied. The scene she made with López because of the liqueur bottles was of epic proportions; you don't get rows like that every day.

"Don't go on like that, madam. I'll pay for the bottles."

"What? Of course you will, what else? A fine thing it would be if they had to come out of my own pocket, on top of it all. But it isn't only that. What about the terrible scandal? What about the shock to the customers? And the bad impression of all that stuff rolling on the floor and getting spilt? What about that, eh? How's that to be paid for? Who's going to pay me for that? You animal! That's what you are, an animal, and a dirty Red, and a rascal! It's my fault for not reporting the lot of you to the police. You may well say I'm kind! Where were your eyes? What hussy were you dreaming of? You and the rest, you're like oxen, you don't know where you put your clumsy feet."

White as a sheet, Consorcio López tries to pacify her: "But it was an unfortunate accident, it wasn't intentional."

"Whatever next, man? Of course! If you'd done it on purpose that would have been the limit. It would have been the last straw! What, have a little runt of a manager—for that's what you are—smash my thing here in my café, right under my nose, simply because he wants to and it suits him? No, it hasn't come to that yet, but one day it will, I can feel it in my bones. Only you and those others won't be here to see it. The day I get enough I'll send you straight to jail, one after the other, the whole pack of you. And you first, because you're a rascal. Lucky for you that I don't want to, because I would if I were as spiteful as you."

While the row is at its height and the whole café listens in silent awe to the shouts of the proprietress, a woman enters and sits down at a table facing the counter. She is tall, plump, not very young, but well preserved, handsome, and somewhat flashy. On seeing her, López loses what little color there is left in his face: after ten years, Marujita turns out to be a splendid, full-blooded, luxuriant woman, overflowing with health and vigor. Anyone who saw her in the street would put her down as what she is: a rich peasant, well settled in marriage, well dressed, well fed, accustomed to be the boss and to do as she pleases.

"Are you the owner of this café?"

"At your service."

"Then it was you I wanted to see. May I introduce myself: I'm Señora de Gutiérrez, Doña Maria Ranero de Gutiérrez. Here's my card with the address. My husband and I live in Tomelloso in the province of Ciudad Real. That's where we have our estate, a few farms that give us our income."

"I see."

"Yes, and now we've had enough of the country, we want to sell our property and come and live in Madrid. Down there things have gotten very bad since the war. There's always such a lot of envy and ill will and so on, you know."

"Oh, yes."

"Well, there it is. And then, the boys are getting big now, and all the rest of it, the worry about school and getting them started on a career, the usual thing. If we don't come to town with them, we shall lose them for good."

"Yes, that's quite true. Have you got so many sons, then?"

Señora Gutiérrez is not quite truthful. "There are five of them now. The two eldest are just on ten, they're quite grown up. They're twins, you know, the children from my first marriage. I was left a widow when I was very young. Here they are, look."

The faces of the two little boys dressed up for their first Communion remind Doña Rosa of somebody, but she can't think of whom.

"And of course, now we've come to Madrid we want to have a look round and see what's doing, more or less."

"Naturally."

Doña Rosa has calmed down, she seems a different woman. Like all those who like to shout their heads off, she can be smoothed out like a kid glove by anyone who shows that he or she might shout even louder.

"My husband's been thinking that it mightn't be a bad thing to have a café. One ought to do quite well out of it if one works hard."

"What's that?"

"Well, yes, we're thinking of buying a café if the owner's reasonable with the price."

"I'm not selling."

"Señora, nobody's said anything to you. Anyway, one can never tell. Everything depends. All I say to you is: think it over. At the moment my husband's ill, he's going to have an operation for an anal fistula, but in any case we intend to stay in Madrid for some time. As soon as he's better, he'll come and talk to you himself. The money belongs to both of us, jointly, but you understand, it's he who looks after everything. In the meantime think about it, if you like. Nobody's committed to anything, nothing's been signed, and so on."

Word that there is a lady who wants to buy the café runs from table to table like a train of gunpowder.

"Which one?"

"The one over there."

"She looks rich."

"My dear chap, if she wants to buy a café she can't be living on a pension."

When the news reaches the counter, López, who is in any case on his last legs, knocks over another bottle. Doña Rosa swings round, chair and all. Her voice resounds like a cannon shot: "You animal! You're an animal!"

Marujita grasps the opportunity to send López a little smile. She does it so discreetly that nobody notices. Probably not López either.

"Now look at that! If you end up with a café on your hands, you'd better be careful with this herd of cattle."

"They smash a lot, don't they?"

"Everything you let them touch. To my mind they do it on purpose. It's sheer sordid envy. They're rotten with it."

Martin is talking to Nati Robles, a girl who used to be his colleague in the days of the Republican Students' Association. He had met her a while ago in the Red de San Luis. Martin was staring at a jeweler's shop window, and she was in the shop to get the clasp of a bracelet repaired. Nati seemed a stranger; she had changed beyond recognition. Gone was the thin, lanky, slovenly girl of undergraduate days who looked rather like a suffragette, with her low heels and face innocent of make-up. This was a slender, elegant, well-dressed, well-shod young lady who used cosmetics with coquetry and considerable skill. It was she who recognized him.

"Marco!"

Martin looked at her timorously. Martin is always a little afraid of looking into faces that seem somehow familiar but which he cannot identify. He thinks the people are going to pounce on him and start saying unpleasant things. Probably, if he were better fed, he would not have this reaction.

"I'm Nati Robles, don't you remember? Nati Robles!" Martin was struck dumb, stupefied. "You?"

"Yes, dear, me."

A feeling of great happiness overcame Martin. "But how marvelous, Nati. How well you look! Like a duchess."

Nati laughed.

"I'm not, worse luck. And it isn't because I wouldn't want to. As you see me here I'm still unmarried and unengaged, as I used to be. Are you in a hurry?"

He hesitated a moment. "Not really. The truth is, you know, that I'm a man who never has anything worth while hurrying for."

Nati took his arm. "Still the same old silly."

Martin felt embarrassed and tried to slip away. "People might see us."

Nati burst into a peal of laughter, which made people turn

round and stare. Nati had a lovely voice, high, musical, ex-hilarating, full of gaiety—a voice like a clear, delicate little bell.

"Sorry, my dear, I didn't realize that it might put you in a spot."

Nati pressed her shoulder against Martin's and did not let go of his arm; on the contrary, she clung more tightly to him.

"Oh, you are the same as ever."

"No, worse I think, Nati."

The young girl began to walk.

"Come on, don't be such a slowpoke. The best thing for you would be if somebody woke you up, it seems to me. Are you still writing poems?"

Martin felt a little ashamed of still writing verse. "Well, yes, I'm afraid it's incurable."

Nati broke into fresh laughter. "You're a funny mixture, cocky, lazy, timid, and a hard worker, all at the same time."

"I don't understand you."

"Nor do I. Come, let's drop in someplace; we must celebrate our meeting."

"As you wish."

Nati and Martin went to the Café Gran Vía, which is lined with mirrors. In her high heels, Nati was slightly the taller of the two.

"Shall we sit here?"

"Yes, that's fine. Wherever you like."

"My dear, what gallantry! You sound as if I were your latest conquest."

And so they are sitting here. Nati's scent is wonderful.

In the Calle de Santa Engracia, on the left side near the Plaza de Chamberí, lives the widowed Doña Celia Vecino de Cortés. Her husband, Don Obdulio Cortés López, a shop-keeper, died after the end of the war and, according to a brief notice in the *A.B.C.*, because of the hardships he had suffered under the Red rule.

Don Obdulio had all his life been an exemplary, upright,

and honorable man, what is called "the model of a gentle-man." His great hobby was carrier pigeons, and when he died, the pigeon fanciers' own magazine devoted to him a deep-felt, affectionate obituary in the form of a photo, taken in his youth, with a caption that read: "Don Obdulio Cortés López, illustrious protagonist of Spanish pigeon fancying, author of the text of the anthem 'Fly without let or hindrance, dove of peace,' former president of the Royal Columbo-philic Society of Almería, founder and director of the—now extinct—excellent magazine *Doves and Dovecots* (monthly bulletin with reports from the whole world), to whom on the occasion of his demise we render the tribute of fervent admiration and lasting grief." The photo was published with a wide black band printed all round it. The author of the caption was Don Leonardo Cascajo, secondary-school teacher.

Don Obdulio's widow, poor woman, ekes out her existence by letting several small, shabby-genteel rooms in a "Cubist" style, painted orange and blue, to a few discreet men friends; here the not very abundant comfort is supplied within the limits of the possible, cheerfully, tactfully, and with a great desire to please and be of service.

In the front room, a sort of state room reserved for the best customers, there is Don Obdulio in a cheap, gaudy gilt frame. With bristling mustache and a gentle look in his eyes, Don Obdulio protects, like a malevolent yet roguish cupid, the clandestine affairs which make it possible for his widow to have something to eat.

Doña Celia's home oozes tenderness through every pore; a tenderness that is sometimes a little sour, and on certain occasions perhaps a tiny bit poisonous. Doña Celia has with her two little boys, the children of a young niece of hers who died four or five months ago, half of trouble and sorrow, half of avitaminosis. Every time a couple arrives, the little boys shout triumphantly down the passage: "Hurray, hurray, another gent's come!" The little cherubs know that the arrival of a gentleman with a young lady hanging on his arm means a cooked meal next day.

The first time Ventura appeared there with his girl friend,

Doña Celia told him: "Look here, the only thing I beg of you is that you behave decently, most decently, because there are little children about. For heaven's sake don't make too much noise and all that."

"Don't worry, Señora, don't be afraid, after all one *is* a gentleman."

As a rule Ventura and Julita shut themselves up in the room at half past three or four and do not leave till after eight. One never even hears them speak; it is a real pleasure.

The first time, Julita had been much less agitated than might have been expected; she took note of every detail in the room and commented on it.

"This lamp is too, too frightful. Look at it, isn't it exactly like an irrigator?"

Ventura failed to find it an exact resemblance.

"No, darling, I can't see that it looks like an irrigator. Come, stop being a little goose and sit down here with me."

"I'm coming."

In effigy, Don Obdulio gazes almost sternly down at the pair.

"I say, who d'you think this is?"

"How should I know? He's got a face like a corpse. He's probably dead by now."

Julita continued walking about. Possibly it was nerves that made her wander hither and thither in the room; in any case she showed no other sign of nerves.

"Nobody else would dream of putting up artificial flowers. I suppose they're stuck in sawdust because people believe it's pretty like this, don't you think?"

"Yes, you may be right."

But Julita wouldn't be stopped by anything.

"Look, look, that lamb there has only got one eye, poor thing."

Indeed, the lamb embroidered on one of the big cushions on the divan had one eye missing.

Ventura no longer took it as a joke. It looked too much as if it would never end.

"Will you keep still?"

· 127 ·

"Oh, darling, how rough you are!"

Inwardly, Julita thought: "But doesn't he understand how delightful it is to come to love on tiptoes?"

Julita was an artist, much more so, no doubt, than her young man.

Once out of the café, Marujita Ranero goes into a baker's shop to ring up the father of her twins.

"Did I please you?"

"Yes, you did. But listen, Maruja, you're quite crazy!"

"Not a bit of it. I went there so you should get a look at me. I didn't want you to get a surprise tonight, and perhaps be disappointed."

"No fear."

"Tell me, do I still please you, really and truly?"

"More than in the old days, I swear to it. And I liked you better than fried bread even then."

"Tell me, would you marry me if I were free?"

"My dear girl . . ."

"You know, I never had any children by him."

"But what about him?"

"Oh, he's got a cancer that's enormous. The doctor says he can't get over it."

"So that's how it is. Listen."

"What?"

"Do you really mean to buy the café?"

"If you'd like it, yes. As soon as he's dead and we can marry. Would you like it as a wedding present?"

"But, my dear!"

"Yes, my boy, I've learned a lot of things, I have. And what's more, I'm a rich woman and do what I like. He's left me everything in his will, he showed it to me. In a few months' time I'll be worth a cool five million."

"Eh?"

"I said, in a few months' time I'll be worth a cool five million. Can't you hear me?"

"Yes, yes . . ."

"D'you carry the kids' photos in your wallet?"

"Yes."

"And mine?"

"No, not yours. When you got married I burned the lot; I thought that was best."

"That's up to you. I'll give you a few new ones tonight. What time will you be round, more or less?"

"After closing, half past one or a quarter to two."

"Don't dawdle, do you hear? Come straight away."

"Yes."

"You remember where it is?"

"Yes, La Colladense, in the Calle de la Magdalena."

"That's right. Room number three."

"Yes. Listen, I'm going to hang up now, the old bear is heading this way."

"Good-by till later. Shall I blow you a kiss?"

"Yes."

"Here you are. Not one but many. Take them all, a thousand million of them. . . ."

The woman at the baker's shop is quite shocked, poor thing. When Marujita Ranero thanks her for the use of the telephone and says good-by, the woman cannot get out a word in answer.

Doña Montserrat is taking leave.

"Adieu, my dear Visitación. I should like to stay here the whole blessed day if I could. It's so pleasant to hear you talk."

"It's kind of you to say so."

"It's not flattery, it's the honest truth. But the fact is that today I don't want to miss the Adoration of the Blessed Sacrament. You understand."

"Oh, that's the reason?"

"Yes, you see, I missed it yesterday."

"I'm quite out of touch nowadays, like a real laywoman. I only hope God will not punish me for it."

When they are at the door, it occurs to Doña Visitación

that she would like to say to her friend: "Isn't it time we dropped formalities? I think we should say *tú* to each other, don't you agree?"

Doña Montserrat is a very nice woman; she would no doubt say Yes, with pleasure.

Doña Visitación would also like to add: "And if we do, I ought to call you Monse and you ought to call me Visi, don't you think?"

Doña Montserrat would agree to this, too. She is very obliging and, when you come to think of it, the two are almost veteran friends. But as things go in life, in face of the open door Doña Visitación lacks the courage to say more than: "Good-by, Montserrat, dear friend, and don't be so niggardly with your visits."

"No, no, in future I'll try to drop in here more often."

"I hope you will."

"Indeed I shall. By the way, Visitación, don't forget you promised me two cakes of Lagarto soap, and not too expensive."

"I shan't forget, don't worry."

When Doña Montserrat entered Doña Visi's flat, the parrot on the floor above was shrieking obscenities. Now she is taking leave under the same sign.

"How horrible! What's that?"

"Don't talk to me about it, dear. It's a parrot, and the bird's the devil in person."

"But how disgraceful. Such a thing shouldn't be allowed."

"You're quite right, but I simply don't know what to do about it."

Rabelais is a rascally, impudent parrot without the least moral principles, an outcast nobody is able to wean from his vices. He has periods when he is a little less noisy and says nothing but "chocolate" or "Portugal," and other words befitting a well-bred bird. But since he is an irrational creature, he will let himself go and screech obscenities and profanities in a cracked voice like an old spinster's just when you least expect it and in all probability while someone pays a formal call to his mistress. Angelito, a most pious-minded lad who lives near, has been trying to make Rabelais mend his ways, but his labors have come to nothing, his seed has fallen on stony ground. Now he has become disheartened and has practically given it up; Rabelais, once more without a tutor, has spent the last fortnight making anybody who listened to him blush with shame. It shows how bad things are that Don Pío Navas Pérez, a railway superintendent who lives on the first floor, found it necessary to comment about it to the parrot's mistress: "Look here, Señora, this parrot of yours is past a joke. I didn't mean to say anything to you, but it's really going too far. Remember I've got a young lassie at home who's at the stage of having suitors, and it isn't right for her to hear such things. At least, that's what I say."

"It's gospel truth what you say, Don Pío, and I do beg your pardon. I'm going to explain it to him. Only, that Rabelais is incorrigible!"

Alfredo Angulo Echevarría tells his aunt, Doña Lolita Echevarría de Cazuela: "Visi's a perfect charmer, you'll see. She's a modern girl, smart-looking, intelligent, pretty, anything you want. I really believe I'm very fond of her."

Aunt Lolita seems absent-minded. Alfredo suspects her of not having paid the slightest attention to his story.

"It looks to me as if you didn't care a bit about my affairs and what I've been telling you, Aunt Lolita."

"Don't be so silly. Of course I do—why wouldn't I?"

At this point, Señora de Cazuela begins to wring her hands and make odd faces, and ends by bursting into tears, violently, dramatically, ostentatiously. Alfredo is scared stiff.

"What's the matter with you?"

"Nothing, nothing, go away!"

Alfredo tries to comfort her.

"But what is wrong, Aunt Lolita dear? Have I put my foot in it?"

"No, no, go away and let me cry."

Alfredo tries to tease her, hoping that it will cheer her.

"All right, auntie, don't get hysterical. You aren't exactly eighteen any more. Anyone would think, to look at you, that you've been crossed in love."

It was the wrong thing to say. Señora de Cazuela turns pale, shows the whites of her eyes, and flops on the floor, face downward. Uncle Fernando is out; he is at a tenants' meeting. They want to discuss a murder that had been committed in the house last night and to agree on certain measures. Alfredo deposits his aunt in an easy chair and throws water into her face. As soon as she comes to, he asks the maids to prepare a cup of lime-blossom tea for her.

When Doña Lolita is again able to speak, she looks at Alfredo and asks him: "Do you know who might buy a dirty-linen basket from me?"

The question rather startles Alfredo.

"I don't know, any junk dealer, I suppose."

"If you see to it that it's got out of the house, you can have it. I never want to set eyes on it again. Keep whatever they pay for it."

"Right."

Alfredo feels somewhat worried. When his uncle comes in, he takes him aside and says: "Look here, Uncle Fernando, I think you ought to take Aunt Lolita to a doctor. It seems to me she suffers badly from weak nerves. Anyway, she's got queer ideas in her head. She's just asked me to get the dirty-linen basket out of the house because she doesn't want to set eyes on it again."

Don Fernando Cazuela's face does not change, he stays as cheerful as if there were nothing wrong. Seeing him so impassive, Alfredo decides that it is their own business and he'd best not interfere.

"Now look here," he tells himself, "if she's going mad, let her. I've told him about it in so many words. If they don't listen to me, it's their funeral. Later they're going to cry to Heaven and tear their hair, I'm sure."

On the table lies a letter. Its printed head reads: "AGROSIL, Perfumery and Pharmacy. 20, Calle Mayor, Madrid." The letter is written in a fine penman's hand, with a wealth of flourishes, curlicues, and arabesques. The text, now completed, reads:

"Dear Mother,

I am writing you these few lines to give you a piece of news which I know will please you. But before doing so, I want to express my wish that this may find you in the same state of perfect health as I am in at this moment, for which God be praised, and that you may continue to enjoy it for many years to come, in company of my good sister Paquita, her husband, and the children.

Mother, what I have to tell you is that I am no longer alone in the world, except for all of you, and that I have met the woman who will help me to found a family and set up a home, who will be my helpmate at my work and who, the Lord permitting, will make me a happy man thanks to her good Christian virtues. Now see you take heart this summer and come here to visit your son, who misses you exceedingly, and meet her on that occasion. Also, Mother, I want to ask you not to be worried about the costs of such a journey, since I shall be only too happy to pay them, and much more, for the sake of the joy of seeing you again, as you are well aware. You will see, my fiancée is an angel. She is good and industrious, and as good-looking as she is modest. Even her Christian name, which is Esperanza, is a good sign and a message of hope that all will turn out well. Please pray often to the Lord for our future happiness, which shall also be the torch that will bring light into your old age.

I finish now for today and send you, dear Mother, an affectionate kiss from your son who loves you dearly and never forgets you.

Tinín"

This letter finished, its author gets up, lights a cigarette, and reads it aloud to himself.

"It's come out rather nicely, I think. That bit at the end about the torch is pretty good."

He walks across to the night table and kisses, as gallantly

and devotedly as any knight of the Round Table, a leather-framed photograph with an inscription: "To my beloved Agustín with a thousand kisses, his Esperanza."

"Good. If my mother comes here I'll put it away."

There had been an afternoon, at about six, when Ventura opened the door and called softly to the mistress of the house: "Señora!"

Doña Celia left the pan in which she was brewing coffee for her evening snack.

"Coming! Is there anything you wish?"

Doña Celia turned down the gas so that the coffee should not come to the boil and appeared before him in a hurry, throwing her apron over one shoulder and wiping her hands on her smock.

"You were calling, Señor Aguado?"

"Yes, I wonder if you could lend us the ludo?"

Doña Celia took the ludo from the side table in the dining room, handed it to the two lovers, and began to ponder. It pained Doña Celia, and it also made her tremble for her purse, to think that the tenderness of the two turtledoves might be waning, that things might begin to go wrong.

"No, perhaps it isn't that," Doña Celia told herself, trying as usual to see the bright side. "Maybe it's only that the girl's not well."

Doña Celia is, business apart, a woman who gets attached to people once she knows them. Doña Celia is a sentimentalist—a highly sentimental keeper of a house of assignation.

Martin and his friend from student days have been talking for the last hour.

"And you've never thought of getting married, Nati?"

"Well, no, not for the moment at least. I'll marry, no doubt, if and when a good match turns up. You must admit there wouldn't be any point in marrying and staying poor. I shall

· 134 ·

marry one day, but in the meanwhile I think there's time for everything."

"You're lucky. I believe there is no time for anything. I believe that, if there's time to spare, it's only because we have so little time that we don't know what to do with it."

Charmingly, Nati wrinkles her nose. "Oh, Marco dear! Don't assault me with profound statements!"

Martin laughs. "Don't you pull my leg, Nati."

The girl looks at him with a slightly provocative expression, opens her bag, and takes out an enameled cigarette case.

"Want a cigarette?"

"Yes, please. I'm out of tobacco. What a pretty case!"

"Yes, not so bad. A present."

Marco fumbles in his pockets.

"I did have matches . . ."

"Here's a light. The present included a lighter."

Nati smokes with a thoroughly European air, with deft, elegant movements of her hands. Martin cannot take his eyes off her.

"Say, Nati, we must make an odd pair: you perfectly turned out, with not a single detail wrong, and I the complete rag bag, stains all over and with my elbows sticking through . . ."

The girl shrugs. "Never mind. All the better, silly. As it is, we leave people guessing."

Slowly and by almost imperceptible stages, Martin is getting sad, while Nati observes him with an infinite tenderness, a tenderness she would not for anything in the world let be noticed.

"What's the matter with you?"

"Nothing. Do you remember when we used to call you Natasha?"

"Yes."

"Do you remember when Gassón chucked you out of the course in administrative law?"

Nati, too, turns a little sad. "Yes."

"Do you remember the afternoon in the Parque del Oeste when I kissed you?"

"I knew you were going to ask me that. Yes, I remember. I've thought of that afternoon many times. You were the first man who kissed me on the lips. . . . It's a long time since. Marco, listen—"

"Yes?"

"I swear to you, I'm not a tart."

Martin feels a faint inclination to tears. "But, my dear, why tell me this?"

"I know why, Marco. You see, I'll always owe you a tiny bit of faithfulness, at least enough to tell you things."

With his cigarette in his mouth and his hands clasped over his knees, Martin watches a fly crawling round and round the rim of a glass. Nati goes on talking.

"I've thought a great deal about that afternoon. At the time I believed I would never need a man at my side because politics and the philosophy of law would be enough to fill my life. How stupid I was! But that afternoon didn't teach me anything. I kissed you, but it didn't teach me a thing. On the contrary, I thought things were always as they'd been between you and me. Later I saw that I'd been wrong, that things weren't like that . . ."

Nati's voice trembles slightly.

". . . that they were different, much worse . . ."

Martin makes an effort. "Forgive me, Nati, I must go now. It's gotten late. But frankly, I haven't even the five pesetas to treat you. Could you let me have five pesetas—to treat you?"

Nati searches in her bag and feels for Marco's hand under the table.

"Here, that's fifty. Use the change to get me a present."

Chapter Four

THE policeman Julio García Morrazo has been patrolling the Calle de Ibiza for a full hour. The light of the street lamp shows him walking up and down, never going very far away. The man walks slowly, as though in deep thought, and seems to be counting his steps, forty down, forty up, and then the same again. Occasionally he adds a few steps and goes as far as the corner.

The policeman Julio García Morrazo is from Galicia. Before the war he did nothing; he spent his time taking his blind father from one saint's fair to the other, singing songs in praise of St. Sibrán and playing the small guitar. Sometimes, when there was wine to help, Julio played the bagpipes for a short while, but on the whole he preferred to dance while someone else played the bagpipes.

When the war broke out and he was called up, Julio García Morrazo—the policeman—was a young man bursting with life like a yearling steer. He had an urge to leap and buck like a wild colt, and was much given to fat sardines, full-bosomed girls, and Ribero wine. One unlucky day on the Asturian front he got a shot in the ribs, and from that time Julio García Morrazo began to lose weight and would not get well; the worst was that his injury was not serious enough to get him dismissed from the service as unfit. He had to go back to the front and never had a chance to recover his health.

After the end of the war, Julio García Morrazo found someone to recommend him and joined the police.

"You're no longer fit for working on the land," said his father, "and anyway you don't like working. Now, if they took you on for the Customs Police . . ."

Julio García Morrazo's father felt too old and tired to like the idea of going back to saints' fairs.

"I'm going to stay at home. I can get along on what I've put by, but it's not enough for the two of us."

For some days Julio pondered, turning the matter over in his mind, and finally, when he saw that his father remained firm, he came to a decision.

"The Customs Police won't do, it's too difficult because all the corporals and sergeants put in for it. But I wouldn't mind the ordinary police."

"All right, that wouldn't be so bad either. All I say is that there isn't enough here for both of us. I wish there were!"

"Oh, well . . ."

The policeman Julio García Morrazo's health improved somewhat, and with time he put on nearly fourteen pounds. True, he was never again the man he had been, but he did not complain: others next to him in the battle line had been left there, stretched on their backs. No need to look further than his cousin Santaguiño, who got a shot in the knapsack where he carried his hand grenades; the biggest piece they found of him was not four inches long.

The policeman Julio García Morrazo is happy in his job. Being able to have free rides on the trolley greatly impressed him from the start. "Of course," he tells himself, "it's because I'm part of the authorities now."

In the barracks he is well liked by all his superiors because he is obedient and disciplined and has never been too big for his shoes like certain of his comrades, who fancy themselves lieutenant generals. The man does what he is told, never sulks, and finds everything all right; he realizes that this is the only thing to do, and it never occurs to him to have ideas beyond it.

"As long as I carry out orders," he says to himself, "they can't ever tell me off. Anyway, the one in command has got to command. That's why they have stripes and stars, and I haven't."

The man is most adaptable and wants no complications.

"As long as they give me hot meals every day and all I've got to do is to amble behind black marketeers . . ."

At suppertime Victorita has a quarrel with her mother.

"When will you give up that consumptive of yours? Look here, what do you get out of it anyhow?"

"I get out of it what I want."

"Yes, germs—and one day a big belly."

"I know what I'm doing. What happens to me is my own business."

"You? A fine lot you know. You're a little sniveler, that's all, and don't know half of what's what."

"I know as much as I need to."

"All right, but don't forget one thing: if he gets you in the family way, you won't set foot in this house again."

Victorita turns white.

"Is that what Grandmother said to you?"

Her mother gets up and slaps her face twice with great gusto. Victorita never even moves.

"You hussy! You bad girl! You're a common slut, that's what you are. That's no way to speak to your mother!"

With her handkerchief, Victorita wipes a few drops of blood from her gums.

"And no way to speak to your daughter either! If my fiancé is ill, that's bad enough, without your calling him a consumptive all the time."

Victorita jumps up and leaves the kitchen. So far her father has not spoken a word. Now he says: "Let the girl go to bed. It isn't right to talk to her like that. What about it if she's in love with the lad? Let her. The more you say, the worse you make it. Anyway, the poor chap won't last long."

In the kitchen they can just hear the half-choked sobs of the girl, who has thrown herself face down on her bed.

"Turn off the light, kid. You don't need it for sleeping."

Victorita fumbles for the bulb and turns it out.

Don Roberto rings the bell at the door of his apartment. He had left his keys in his other pair of trousers. This always happened to him, although he constantly tells himself: "Take the keys from the other trousers, take the keys from the other trousers." His wife comes to open the door to him.

"Hello, Roberto."

"Hello."

The woman does her best to be kind and pleasant with him. He works like a black to keep them afloat.

"You must be frozen stiff. Put on your slippers, I've kept them warm for you next to the gas ring."

Don Roberto puts on his slippers and the old jacket he wears at home, a frayed coat of a suit which had once been dark brown with a thin white stripe that made it look smart and in very good taste.

"How are the children?"

"Fine. They're in bed now, the darlings. The baby didn't want to go to sleep. I don't know, perhaps he isn't quite well."

The couple go to the kitchen; it is the only room where they can stay in winter.

"Has that scatterbrain been round?"

His wife avoids giving an answer. The two may have met in the doorway, and then she would put her foot in her mouth. It happens sometimes that one puts one's foot in one's mouth precisely when one tries to make things go straight and avoid complications, and then there is the devil to pay.

"I've got fried pilchards for supper."

Don Roberto is highly pleased. Fried pilchards is one of his favorite dishes.

"Excellent!"

· 140 ·

His wife smiles at him indulgently.

"And with a little money I saved by shopping in the market, I've bought you half a bottle of wine. You work so hard, and a drop of wine now and then is so good for you!"

That "beast" González, as his brother-in-law calls him, is a poor little man, a decent father of a family with the worst luck in the world, who is very prone to tenderness.

"How good you are, darling! I've thought it so often. Some days I wouldn't know what to do, if it weren't for you. Well, we've got to be patient. These first few years till I've made my way are the worst. The first ten years. After that it will be smooth going, you'll see."

Don Roberto gives his wife a kiss on her cheek.

"Do you love me a lot?"

"A lot, Roberto—you know I do."

The pair of them have a supper of soup, fried pilchards, and one banana. After the dessert, Don Roberto fixes his gaze on his wife.

"What would you like me to give you tomorrow?"

The woman smiles, full of joy and gratitude.

"Oh, Roberto! I'm so happy! I thought you wouldn't remember it this year either."

"Hush, you silly. Why shouldn't I remember? Never mind about last year, but this year . . ."

"But you see, I don't think I matter very much."

If she were to go on for another moment reflecting on her own insignificance, her eyes would fill with tears.

"Now, tell me, what shall I give you?"

"But, dear, when we're so badly off . . ."

Don Roberto stares at his plate and lowers his voice.

"I asked for a small advance at the bakery."

His wife looks tenderly at him, with a touch of sadness.

"How silly of me! In talking I've forgotten to give you your glass of milk."

While she goes to the larder, Don Roberto continues: "They also gave me ten pesetas to buy a little something for the children."

"You're so kind, Roberto!"

"No, dear, that's just your way of talking. I'm no better than the rest and no worse."

Don Roberto drinks his milk; his wife always has a glass of milk for him, to keep him well nourished.

"I've been thinking of getting a ball for the kids. If there's something left, I'll have a vermouth. I didn't mean to tell you anything about it. But there you are. I can't keep a secret."

Don Mario de la Vega, the owner of a printing works, rings up Doña Ramona Bragado. The man wants some news about a matter she has been pursuing for the last few days.

"Besides, you're in the same trade. The girl works at a printer's, I believe she's still an apprentice."

"Oh, yes? In what firm?"

"It's called Tipografía El Porvenir, on the Calle de la Madera."

"I know. Good, excellent, so it all stays in the profession. Listen, you really think that . . . ? Well, you know what?"

"Oh, yes, don't you worry, that's my business. Tomorrow when you close, come round to the dairy and call on me with some excuse or other."

"All right."

"Very well. I'll have her there for you—we'll think up some reason. It looks to me as if she's just about ripe and ready to fall. The young thing's up to her neck in trouble and fed up with it and she won't hold out any longer than we wish to leave her alone. She has a young man who's ill, and wants to buy medicines for him. Those young girls in love are the easiest of all, you'll see. It's a sure thing."

"I hope it is."

"You'll see for yourself. But listen, Don Mario, I'm not coming down a single penny. D'you get me? I've been reasonable enough."

"All right, we'll talk it over."

"No, we won't talk it over. Everything's been said. Look to it, or I'll back out."

"All right, all right."

Don Mario laughs, as though to show that he is a man of wide experience. Doña Ramona does not want to leave any loose ends.

"Agreed?"

"Yes, by all means agreed."

Returning to his table in the café, Don Mario says to the other man: "You start at sixteen pesetas a day, but I won't hear of a labor contract, is that understood?"

And the other replies: "I understand, sir."

This other man is a poor lad who has studied a bit but never managed to fit in anywhere. He has neither good luck nor good health. There is a streak of tuberculosis in his family. One of his brothers, by the name of Paco, had been sent back from the barracks because he was done for.

By now the front doors of the houses have been shut for some time, but the world of night birds continues to send a trickle, ever more slowly, towards the buses.

When night has fallen, the street assumes a half-hungry, half-mysterious air, while a little wind, prowling like a wolf, whistles between the houses.

The men and women who make their way in Madrid at this hour are the real night strollers, who go out for the sake of going out and are possessed by an inertia that makes them stay out the whole night: the moneyed patrons of cabarets and cafés on the Gran Vía, places crowded with perfumed, provocative women who sport dyed hair and impressive fur coats, black with a few white hairs here and there; or the night wanderers with a meager purse who stay at a table chatting with old cronies or go boozing from bar to bar.

The others, the occasional night birds, who frequent cinemas and only go out at night for a set purpose, never at random, have disappeared some time ago, before the front doors are locked. First to go are the patrons of the cinemas in the center of the town; they are in a hurry, they are well dressed and try to get a taxi: the regulars of the Callao, the Capitol, the Palacio de la Música, who pronounce the actresses' names almost correctly, and some of whom even receive an occasional invitation to see films at the British Embassy in that place in the Calle de Orfila. They know a lot about the cinema, and instead of saying, like the public of the cinemas in the outlying districts, "It's a marvelous film with Joan Crawford," they say, as though talking only to initiates, "It's a pleasing comedy by René Clair, extremely French"; or, "It's a brilliant drama by Frank Capra." Not one knows exactly what is so "extremely French" about it, but it does not matter. We live, up to a point, in the age of effrontery, a spectacle which a few pure-hearted people contemplate from the ringside with amazement, without quite understanding what is being played—though it is clear enough.

The patrons of the outer-district cinemas, the people who never know the film producer's name, go home somewhat later, when the front doors are already locked; they are in no hurry, are less well dressed and also less harassed, at least at these hours. They walk the whole way, as though on a stroll, to the Narváez, the Alcalá, the Tivoli, the Salamanca, where they see films that are famous, even if their fame may be somewhat fly-blown after running for several weeks in the Gran Vía; films with beautiful, poetic names, posing tremendous human riddles which they do not always solve.

The public of these cinemas will have to wait for some time before they see *Suspicion* or *The Adventures of Marco Polo* or *If the Dawn Never Comes*.

On one of the occasions on which the policeman Julio García Morrazo gets as far as the street corner, he remembers Celestino, the owner of the bar.

"That Celestino is the very devil. The things he thinks of! But he's nobody's fool; he's a man who's read a hell of a lot of books."

Celestino Ortiz, after recalling that passage about blind anger and the animal state, took the book, his only book, from on top of the vermouth bottles and put it away in the drawer. Strange things do happen. If Marco Martin left the bar without getting his head split open, it was thanks to Nietzsche. If Nietzsche were to come to life again . . . !

Behind the net curtains of her mezzanine apartment, Doña María Morales de Sierra—sister of Doña Clarita Morales de Pérez, the wife of Don Camilo, the chiropodist, who lives in the same house as Don Ignacio Galdácano, the gentleman who would never be able to attend a meeting in Don Ibrahim's apartment because he is mad—says to her husband, Don José Sierra, technical assistant at the Ministry of Public Works: "Have you noticed that policeman? He does nothing but walk up and down, just as if he were waiting for somebody."

Her husband does not even answer. He is reading the newspaper, as completely out of reach as if he were living in a mute, foreign world far away from his wife. If Don José Sierra had not attained this perfect state of abstraction, he would never have been able to read the newspaper at home.

"Now he's coming back here again. I'd give a lot to know what he's up to. And this is such a quiet neighborhood, with everybody so respectable. Now, if it were over there, near the building sites in the Plaza de Toros, where it's all as black as the wolf's gullet . . ."

The building sites in the former bullring are no farther than a few dozen steps from Doña María's mezzanine.

"Over there it would be another story; over there they're quite capable of assaulting you. But here? Goodness me, it's as calm as a pond. There isn't even a mouse stirring."

Doña María turns round, smiling. Her husband misses her smile, for he is still reading his paper.

Victorita has been a long time weeping. In her head, plans and projects crowd helter-skelter: taking the veil or going on the streets—anything seems better than to stay at home. She would propose to her fiancé that they should go off together if only he were fit to work; with both of them in a job, it would be odd if they didn't scrape together enough money to keep themselves fed. But it is only too clear that her fiancé is unfit for anything but to lie in bed, doing nothing at all and hardly speaking. It is fate. Everybody says that his kind of illness is sometimes cured with the help of plenty of food and injections; if people are not cured completely, they at least recover sufficiently to live on for many years, to marry, and to lead a normal life. But Victorita does not know where to get the money. Or rather, she does know, but has not made up her mind; if Paco were to find out, he, with his temper, would chuck her at once. And yet, if Victorita were to make up her mind to do something indecent, it would be for Paco's sake, not for anything or anybody else. Victorita has moments in which she thinks that Paco would say: "All right, do as you like, I don't mind." But she soon realizes that this is untrue, that Paco could not say such a thing.

By now she is convinced that she cannot stay at home. Her mother makes life impossible for her by preaching the same sermon all the time. Yet to take the plunge, just like this, blindly, without anyone to give her a helping hand, is very dangerous. Victorita has been thinking it out before—she sees all the pros and cons. If everything goes well it is like a smooth glide, but things hardly ever go altogether well, and sometimes they go very badly. It all depends on luck, and on having someone to turn to. But to whom could Victorita turn? Of the people she knows, not one has saved as much as fifty pesetas, not one lives on anything but a daily wage. Victorita is bitterly tired. At the printer's she has to be on her feet all day long; in the evenings she finds her fiancé worse every time; her mother is like a cavalry sergeant who does nothing but shout; her father is a spineless little man, always half drunk, on whom it is useless to count.

Pirula has had good luck. Pirula used to work at the printer's with Victorita, also as a packer; then she was taken away by a gentleman. He not only keeps her like a queen, giving her whatever she fancies, but he also is fond of her and respects her. Pirula would not say No if Victorita asked her for money. But while she might give her a hundred pesetas, she naturally had no reason to give her more. Nowadays Pirula lives like a duchess. Everybody calls her Señorita; she is well dressed and has a little apartment with a radio set. One day Victorita saw her in the street. In one year of living with her gentleman-friend the girl had changed beyond belief; she did not look the same woman, she even seemed to have grown, and so forth.

Victorita would not ask for so much . . .

The policeman Julio García Morrazo has a talk with the night watchman, Gumersindo Vega Calvo, who comes from the same region.

"A lousy night."

"I've seen worse."

For the last few months, the policeman and the night watch-man have been pursuing a subject of conversation which gives them both pleasure, and to which they return night after night with tenacious enjoyment.

"So you say you come from the Porreño district?"

"That's right, from near there; I'm from Mos, I am."

"Well, I've got a sister who's married in Salvatierra, her name's Rosalía."

"The wife of Burelo, the nail maker?"

"That's her."

"She's in clover, isn't she?"

"Yes, she is. That one's made a good marriage."

The lady in the mezzanine continues with her conjectures; she is something of a gossip.

"Now he's with the night watchman. He must be asking him for information about someone who lives here, don't you think?"

Don José Sierra goes on reading with exemplary stoicism and resignation.

"Night watchmen always know everything there is to know, don't they? Things people like us have no idea about are old stories to them."

Don José Sierra has finished reading an editorial on social insurance and embarks on another, dealing with the proce-dures and prerogatives of the traditional Spanish Chamber of Deputies.

· 147 ·

"Perhaps there's a secret Freemason in one of these houses. After all, you never know by looking at people."

Don José Sierra makes a strange sound in his throat, a sound that may mean "Yes" or "No," or "Who knows?" Don José is a man who, by dint of having to bear with his wife, has learned to live through many hours, and sometimes through days on end, without saying more than an occasional "H'm!" followed by a further "H'm!" after a certain interval, and so on. This is an extremely discreet way of indicating to his wife that she is a fool, without telling her in so many words.

The night watchman is happy about his sister Rosalía's marriage; the Burelos are people with a good name in the whole district.

"She's got nine brats already, and the tenth coming."

"Did she marry a long time ago?"

"Yes, quite a long time. She married ten years ago."

The policeman takes some time working it out, but the watchman does not let him finish his arithmetic; he resumes the thread of their conversation.

"Our family comes more from over La Cañiza way. We're from Covelo. Haven't you heard of the 'Baldies'?"

"No, I haven't."

"Well, that's us."

The policeman Julio García Morrazo feels bound to reciprocate.

"They call my father and me the Foxes."

"Do they, now?"

"We don't mind it at all, everybody calls us that."

"Do they?"

"The guy who kicked up a storm was my brother Telmo, the one who died of typhoid. They used to call him the Mangy Whistler."

"Did they, now? Some people have a nasty character, haven't they?"

"And how! Some people are the very devil. My brother Telmo couldn't stand being kicked."

"People like that always come to a bad end."

"That's what I say."

The policeman and the watchman converse in Castilian; they want to prove to each other that they are no yokels.

At this hour the policeman Julio García Morrazo always begins to feel sentimental.

"It's a good country, ours, isn't it?"

The night watchman Gumersindo Vega Calvo is a Galician of the other kind, rather skeptical and shy of admitting that things are plentiful.

"It's not so bad."

"Of course it isn't. There's a good life for you, what?"

"That's right."

From a bar on the other side of the road that is still open at this hour, there drifts into the cold street the sounds of a slow fox trot meant to be heard, or danced to, in private.

Somebody comes up and calls for the night watchman: "*Sereno!*"

The night watchman is intent on his memories.

"The best things at home are the potatoes and the sweet corn, and then there's wine, too, in the part we come from."

The man who has turned up calls him again, this time with more familiarity: "*Sindo!*"

"Coming!"

At the entrance to the underground station Narváez, a few steps from the corner of the Calle de Alcalá, Martin comes across his friend the "Uruguayan" out with another man. At first he pretends not to see her.

"Hello, Martin, you frightened mouse."

Martin turns his head, since he cannot escape.

"Hello, Trinidad, I didn't see you."

"Now, come here, I want to introduce you."

Martin goes up to them.

"Here you've a good friend of mine, and this is Martin—he's a writer."

They call her the Uruguayan because she comes from Buenos Aires.

"This chap you see here," she tells her friend, "actually writes poetry. Come on, for goodness' sake, shake hands now I've introduced you."

Obediently, the two men shake hands.

"It's a pleasure. How are you?"

"Well dined and well wined, thank you."

The Uruguayan's companion is one of those men who like to be funny. The couple burst into loud laughter. The Uruguayan's front teeth are blackish and decaying.

"Come, have a coffee with us."

Martin hesitates because it seems to him that the other fellow might not like it.

"Really . . . I don't think . . ."

"Yes, sure, come and join us, do. Of course you must!"

"It's very nice of you. Just for a few minutes."

"Don't be in a hurry, stay as long as you like. The night's young! Do stay with us, I think poets are great fun."

They sit down in a café on the corner, and the sucker orders coffee and brandy for three.

"Send me the cigarette boy."

"Yes, sir."

Martin has placed himself opposite the couple. The Uruguayan is slightly tipsy.

The cigarette boy comes up. "Good evening, Señor Flores. It's quite a time since we last saw you here. . . . Do you wish anything?"

"Yes, give us two cigars, good ones. Say, Uruguaya, have you got anything to smoke?"

"I've very little tobacco left. Get me a packet."

"All right, a packet of Virginians for her."

Celestino Ortiz's bar is empty. It is a tiny bar with a dark-green signboard that reads "Aurora—Wines and Meals." At present there are no meals to be had. Celestino intends to start serving meals once things go better for him; you can't do everything in one day.

The last customer, a policeman, is drinking his wretched glass of *anís* at the counter.

"That's just what I'm telling you. I'm not swallowing their fairy tales."

As soon as the policeman is gone, Celestino means to close down, pull out his mattress, and go to sleep. Celestino does not like late hours, he prefers to go to bed early and lead a healthy life, at least as healthy a life as he can.

"It doesn't matter a damn to me, I tell you."

Celestino sleeps in his bar for two reasons: because it is cheaper, and because this way he will not be robbed the night he least expects it.

"The seat of the evil is higher up. Not over there, I assure you."

Celestino soon became proficient in making up an excellent bed—though he sometimes tumbles off it—by stretching his horsehair mattress over eight or ten chairs placed together.

"It doesn't seem fair to me to arrest the black-market women in the underground. People have got to eat, and if they can't get work, they must fend for themselves as best they can. The cost of living has gone up sky-high, you know it as well as I do, and what they issue on ration is nothing, it isn't even a start. I don't want to offend anyone, but I do think if a few poor women sell cigarettes and bread it's wrong for you of the police to be after them."

The policeman drinking his *anís* is no dialectician.

"I do as I'm told."

"I know. Don't think I can't appreciate the difference."

After the policeman's departure, Celestino rigs up the contraption on which he sleeps, lies down, and reads for a short while. He likes to cheer himself up a bit by reading before he turns off the light and falls asleep. In bed, Celestino usually reads ballads and broadsheets; he keeps Nietzsche for the daytime. He has a whole pile of them and knows some of the sheets by heart from A to Z. They all are lovely, but the ones he likes best are two ballads entitled "The Insurrection in Cuba" and "An Account of the Murders committed by the two True Lovers, Don Jacinto del Castillo and Doña Leonor de la Rosa, so as to attain the Fulfillment of their Vows of Love." The second of the two is a ballad in the classic style, one of those that open in the good old way:

"Holy Virgin Mary, Our Lady,
Light of the Vaults of Heaven,
Daughter of the Eternal Father,
Mother of the All-Highest Son,
And Spouse of the Holy Spirit,
For, through virtue and power,
The most gracious of Beings,
In your Virgin Womb conceived,
After nine months was born,
The Author most divine
Of the Redemption of Man,
Clothed in human flesh,
While your intact womb remained
Chaste, clean, unspotted and pure."

These old-fashioned ballads are Celestino's favorites. To justify his taste, he sometimes talks about the wisdom of the common people and other gibberish of the same kind. He is also very fond of the last words of Corporal Pérez when facing the firing squad:

"Soldiers, now that my fate
Has brought me to such a pass,
I shall give you four duros,
So that you give me a good death.
Pérez asks of you only
To see that your aim be straight,
Although he has done no evil
To make this slaughter right.
Let two of you aim at his temples
And two of you at his heart."

"There was a fellow! They were real men in the old days!" Celestino says, aloud, before switching off the light.

· 152 ·

    ✻   ✻   ✻   ✻

At the back of a dimly lit room a long-haired violinist, brimful of literary reminiscences, plays Monti's czardas with great passion.

The guests are drinking. The men, whiskey; the women, champagne or, if they had sat in a porter's lodge until a fortnight ago, crème de menthe. There are plenty of unoccupied tables in the place; it is still rather early.

"Oh, Pablo, I love this stuff."

"Then drink as much as you can, Laurita, that's all you have to do."

"Tell me, is it true that it makes one get excited?"

The night watchman goes to the house where they call him.

"Good evening, Señorito."

"Hello."

The watchman takes out his key and pushes the door open. Then, as though it were of no importance, he holds out his open hand.

"Thank you very much."

The watchman turns on the light in the staircase, closes the front door, and ambles off, knocking on the pavement with his pointed stick, to resume his talk with the policeman.

"That fellow comes every night round about this hour and doesn't leave till four. He's got a young lady in an attic flat. She's a fair marvel. Her name's Señorita Pirula."

"That's the way to live."

The lady in the mezzanine never takes her eyes off them.

"They must be talking about something, because they stay together all the time. Just think, when the watchman has to open a door to somebody, the policeman waits for him."

The husband puts down his paper. "You do love to stick your nose in other people's business. I expect he's waiting for some servant girl to come out."

"Of course, you've always got a quick answer to everything."

*   *   *   *

The gentleman who keeps his mistress in the attic flat takes off his overcoat and drops it on the sofa in the hall. It is a minute hall, with no more furniture than a sofa with room for two and a wooden shelf under a gilt-framed mirror.

"What news, Pirula?"

Señorita Pirula has come to the door on hearing his key in the lock.

"Nothing, Javier darling, for me there's no news except you."

Señorita Pirula is a young girl with a very refined and very educated manner, although it is scarcely more than a year since she used to use slangy expressions.

From an inner room, softly lit by a low-placed lamp, comes the discreet sound of a radio.

"Would you dance, Señorita?"

"Thank you, no, kind sir. I'm rather tired. I've been dancing the whole evening."

The couple bursts into laughter, though not—of course—into loud laughter like the Uruguayan and Señor Flores, and then they kiss.

"Pirula, you're a little girl."

"And you a big schoolboy, Javier."

The pair walks to the inner room, arms tightly enlaced round each other's waists, as though going down an avenue of acacias in bloom.

"A cigarette?"

The ritual is the same every night, and the words they speak are more or less the same, too. Señorita Pirula has a shrewd conservative instinct; she will probably get on well in her career. Anyhow, for the time being she cannot complain: Javier treats her like a queen, he is fond of her, he respects her. . . .

Victorita does not ask for so much. All that Victorita asks for is to have enough to eat and to go on loving her young man in case he ever gets well. Victorita has no desire for a loose life, but needs must when the devil drives. She has never yet behaved like a slut; she had never slept with anyone except her young man. Victorita has strength of character, and though she is sensuous enough, she knows how to keep herself in hand. She has always behaved well to Paco and has never once deceived him.

Once, before he fell ill, she had told him: "I like all men, that's why I don't go to bed with anybody except you. If I started at all, there wouldn't be an end to it."

The girl was blushing and choking with laughter while she made this confession, but her young man failed to appreciate the joke.

"If I'm the same to you as any other man, do as you like, go and do whatever you feel like."

One day, when he was already ill, a smartly dressed man followed her in the street.

"Where to in such a hurry, Señorita?"

The girl liked the man's appearance; he was a fine man with an elegant air who knew how to introduce himself.

"Please leave me alone. I'm going to work."

"But, my dear young lady, why should I leave you alone? It's good to hear that you're going to work. It's a sign that you're a decent girl, young and pretty as you are. But what harm is there in our exchanging a few words?"

"None, as long as there isn't more to it."

"And what more could it be?"

The girl felt the words escaping her. "It could be what I'd like . . ."

The well-dressed man remained impassive.

"Of course. Remember, a man isn't a cripple either, he does what he can."

"And what they let him do."

"Well, yes, and what they let him do."

The gentleman walked a little way with Victorita. Shortly before they came to the Calle de la Madera, Victorita dismissed him: "Good-by, leave me alone now. Anyone from the printing works might see us."

The gentleman frowned.

"So you work at a printer's hereabouts?"

"Yes, right on the Calle de la Madera. That's why I asked you to go. We can meet another day."

"Wait a moment." Smiling, the gentleman took the girl's hand. "Would you like us to?"

Victorita, too, was smiling. "And you?"

The gentleman looked straight into her eyes. "What time do you finish work this afternoon?"

Victorita dropped her gaze. "At seven. But don't come to fetch me. I've got a fiancé."

"And he comes to fetch you?"

Victorita's voice had a sad tinge. "No, he doesn't. Good-by."

"Till we meet again."

"Well, if you like. Till we meet again."

At seven, when Victorita came from her work at El Porvenir, she found the gentleman waiting for her on the corner of the Calle del Escorial.

"It's just for a moment, Señorita, I quite realize that you have to go and see your fiancé."

Victorita was surprised that he had returned to a formal mode of address.

"I shouldn't like to cast the slightest shadow between you and your fiancé. Please understand that I've not the least interest in doing so."

The couple walked down the street to the Calle de San Bernardo. The gentleman was correctness itself; he did not take her arm, not even on crossing a street.

"I'm very pleased to think that you will be happy with your fiancé. If it depended on me, you and he would marry tomorrow."

Victorita looked askance at the gentleman. He was talking to her without giving her a glance, as if he were talking to himself.

"What better thing could anyone wish for a person he esteems than happiness?"

Victorita walked as on a cloud. She was remotely happy, with a vague happiness of which she was barely conscious, a happiness that was at the same time a little wistful, a little distant and unreal.

"We'll go in here. It's too cold to go for a walk."

"All right."

Victorita and the gentleman went into the Café San Bernardo and sat down at one of the tables farthest back, face to face with each other.

"What would you like to order?"

"A cup of hot coffee."

When the waiter came, the gentleman said: "Bring a *café exprès* with milk for the young lady, and a jam tart. Black coffee for me."

The gentleman took out a packet of Virginian cigarettes.

"You smoke?"

"No, I hardly ever smoke."

"What does 'hardly ever' mean?"

"Well, I only smoke now and then, on Christmas Eve for instance. . . ."

The gentleman did not insist. He lit his cigarette and stowed away the packet.

"Well, yes, as I was saying, Señorita, if it depended on me, you and your fiancé would marry tomorrow, without fail."

Victorita looked at him. "And why is it that you want to get us married? What would you get out of it?"

"I get nothing out of it, Señorita. You can well imagine that it is all the same to me whether you marry or stay single. If I mentioned it to you, it was only because I thought you'd be glad to get married to your fiancé."

"Of course I should be glad. Why should I tell you a lie?"

"You're quite right. By talking, people get to understand one another. For the matter I want to discuss with you, it's all the same whether you're a married woman or single."

The gentleman gave a little cough. "We're in a public place, with people all round us and this table between us."

The gentleman brushed Victorita's knees with his legs. "May I speak to you with complete frankness?"

"Yes, do. As long as you don't go too far."

"It's impossible to go too far, Señorita, if one speaks frankly. What I'm going to tell you is a sort of business proposition. You can take it or leave it, you aren't committed to anything."

The girl felt somewhat perplexed.

"May I speak, then?"

"Do."

The gentleman changed his position.

"Well, look here, Señorita, let's get to the point. At least you'll agree that I'm not trying to deceive you and that I put things to you quite openly."

The café was stuffy, it was very hot, and Victorita pushed her light cotton overcoat from her shoulders.

"The trouble is that I don't know how to begin. . . . You've made a great impression on me, Señorita."

"So it's just what I thought you were going to tell me."

"I believe you're mistaken. Please don't interrupt now, you'll have your say at the end."

"All right, go on."

"Good. As I said before, Señorita, you've made a great impression on me. Your walk, your face, your legs, your waist, your breasts . . ."

"I understand—everything." The girl smiled for a fleeting moment, with a certain air of superiority.

"Exactly. Everything. But don't smile, I'm talking to you seriously."

Once more the gentleman brushed her knees and took one of her hands, which Victorita let him hold, well pleased and almost with deliberation.

"I give you my word, I'm speaking to you in utter seriousness. Everything about you pleases me. I visualize your body, firm and warm and softly tinted . . ."

The gentleman squeezed Victorita's hand.

"I'm not rich and can offer you very little. . . ."

The gentleman was amazed that Victorita did not withdraw her hand.

"But what I'm going to ask of you is not much either."

The gentleman gave another little cough.

"I should like to see you naked. To see you, no more."

Victorita squeezed the gentleman's hand.

"I must go now, it's getting late for me."

"You're right. But do give me an answer before you go. I

want to see you naked. I promise you that I won't touch one of your fingers, I won't brush so much as a thread of your clothes. I know you're a respectable girl and not a cocotte. . . . I beg you to keep this. Whatever your decision turns out to be, please accept this from me, to buy something as a souvenir."

Under cover of the table the girl took the bank note which the gentleman handed her. Her pulse did not beat faster as she took it.

Victorita rose and walked out of the café. From one of the near-by tables a man hailed her.

"Good night, Victorita, proud girl that you are! Since you've started hobnobbing with a marquis, you don't see us poor people any more."

"Good night, Pepe."

Pepe was one of the printers who worked at El Porvenir.

Victorita has been weeping for some time; in her head, plans are jostling one another like people coming out of the underground. Anything, from taking the veil to going on the streets, seems better to her than to stay at home and put up with her mother.

Don Roberto raises his voice. "Petrita! Bring me the tobacco that's in the pocket of my coat."

His wife intervenes. "Not so loud, dear, or you'll wake the children."

"Nonsense, why should they wake up? They're little angels; once they're asleep nothing on earth will wake them."

"I'll get you what you want. Don't go on calling Petrita. The poor kid must be worn out."

"Never mind about her, her kind don't even notice it. You've more reason to be worn out."

"Yes, and more years on my shoulders."

Don Roberto smiles. "Come now, Filo, don't show off. So far they don't exactly weigh you down yet."

The maid comes into the kitchen with the tobacco.

"Bring me the newspaper, it's in the hall."

"Yes, sir."

"And listen, put a glass of water on the night table for me."

"Yes, sir."

Again Filo intervenes. "I'll put out everything for you, dear. Let her go to bed."

"To bed, you say? If you give her permission, she'd go out now, and not be back till two or three in the morning, you'll see."

"Yes, that's quite true, but . . ."

Señorita Elvira is tossing and turning in her bed. She is uneasy and restless, and one nightmare chases the other. Señorita Elvira's bedroom smells of worn clothing and of woman; women do not smell of perfume, they smell like stale fish. Señorita Elvira's breath comes in pants and gasps, and her strained, unquiet sleep, the sleep of a hot head and a cold belly, makes her ancient mattress creak plaintively.

A black, partly bald cat, with an enigmatic smile that is quite human and a frightening glint in its eyes, leaps upon Señorita Elvira from an enormous distance. The woman wards it off with kicks and blows. The cat falls on a piece of furniture and rebounds like a rubber ball, once more to assault the bed. The cat's belly gapes open, red as a pomegranate, and from the hole in its behind there grows something like a poisonous, pestilentious, many-colored flower similar to a plume of fireworks. Señorita Elvira covers her head with the sheet. Inside the bed, a great number of dwarfs swarm round mad with fear, showing the whites of their eyes. The cat slips in like a ghost, seizes Señorita Elvira by the belly and licks her stomach, while it laughs in great guffaws that frighten the very soul. Señorita Elvira is terrified, she throws it out of the room; it costs her a colossal effort, for the cat is very heavy, it seems made of iron. Señorita Elvira takes care not to squash the dwarfs. One of them shouts at her, "Saint Mary! Saint Mary!"

The cat comes back, passing under the door, stretching its

body to the shape of a slice of dried cod. It has a baleful stare, like an executioner's. It climbs on the night table and fixes its eyes on Señorita Elvira with a bloodthirsty expression. Señorita Elvira dares not even breathe. The cat jumps down on the pillow and licks her mouth and eyelids, gently, like a slobbery old man. Its tongue is warm like the inside of the groin, and as soft as velvet. It unties the ribbons of her nightdress with its teeth. The cat shows its gaping underbelly, which palpitates in a regular beat, like a vein. With every moment the flower sticking out of its backside grows more lovely, more luxuriant. The cat has an infinitely soft skin. A blinding light begins to flood the bedroom. The cat grows to the size of a slim tiger. The dwarfs continue to mill about in despair. Señorita Elvira's entire body is shaking. She gasps for breath, as she feels the cat's tongue licking her lips. The cat goes on stretching and stretching to greater length. Señorita Elvira can no longer breathe, her mouth has gone dry. Her thighs open, first cautiously, then unashamedly.

Suddenly Señorita Elvira wakes, and switches on the light. Her nightdress is soaked with sweat. She feels cold, gets up, and throws her coat over her feet. There is a slight hum in her ears, and her nipples rise rebelliously, almost haughtily, as in her good days.

She goes to sleep with the light on, does Señorita Elvira.

"Well, yes. So what? I let him have fifteen pesetas on account. Tomorrow is his wife's birthday."

Señor Ramón never manages to show sufficient firmness; however hard he tries, he never manages to be firm enough.

"What d'you mean by 'so what'? You know very well. Haven't you got eyes in your head? It's up to you. If I've told you once, I've told you a dozen times: like this we'll never be anything but poor. Is that what we've been scraping and saving for?"

"But my dear, it's just an advance, I deduct it next time. What difference does it make to me? It isn't as if I'd given it to him as a present."

· 161 ·

"Oh, yes, I know: you deduct it—unless you forget!"

"I haven't forgotten ever."

"Not ever? And what about those seven pesetas of Señora Josefa's? Where have those seven pesetas gone to?"

"Now listen, that was because she needed some medicine. Even at that, look what a state she's in now."

"And what about us? Can you tell me what it matters to us if other people are ill?"

Señor Ramón stamps out his stub.

"Look, Paulina, I'll tell you something."

"What?"

"That I'm the boss when it comes to my money. Make a note of that. I know exactly what I'm doing, so let's have no more of this."

Señora Paulina mutters the rest of her arguments under her breath.

Victorita cannot go to sleep. She is beset by memories of her mother, who is a scold.

"When will you give up that consumptive of yours?"

"I shall never give him up. Consumptives are better company than drunkards."

Victorita would never have dared to say anything of that sort to her mother. If only her fiancé could be cured . . . To get her fiancé cured, Victorita would be capable of doing anything, of doing everything she was asked to do.

Twisting round in her bed, Victorita goes on weeping. A handful of pesetas would be enough to cure her young man. It's an old story: poor people with T.B. die; rich people with T.B. either get cured, or they can at least take care of themselves and struggle along. Money is not easy to come by. Victorita knows it only too well. It needs luck. Everything else can be arranged for, but one can't arrange for luck; luck comes if and when it chooses, and the fact is that it chooses almost never.

The thirty thousand pesetas that gentleman had offered her were lost because Victorita's fiancé had been full of scruples.

"No, no. At that price I don't want anything, not thirty thousand pesetas and not five times as much."

"But what does it matter to us?" the girl had asked him. "It doesn't leave any trace, and no one will ever know."

"Would you risk it?"

"For you, yes. And you know it."

The gentleman who offered those thirty thousand pesetas was a moneylender of whom Victorita had heard.

"He'll lend you three thousand pesetas quickly enough," they had told her. "You'll have to go on paying them back for the rest of your life, but he'll lend you them easily enough."

Victorita went to see him; on three thousand pesetas they would have been able to marry. Her fiancé was not yet ill. He caught colds, coughed, got easily tired, but he was not ill yet; he had not yet taken to his bed.

"So, young woman, you want three thousand pesetas?"

"Yes, sir."

"And what do you want them for?"

"Well, you see, for getting married."

"Ah, so you're in love, eh?"

"Well, yes . . ."

"And you're very fond of your fiancé?"

"Yes."

"Very, very fond?"

"Yes, sir, very fond."

"Fonder of him than of anyone else?"

"Yes, sir, more than of anyone else."

The moneylender twisted his green velvet cap two times. His head was pointed, like a pear, and his hair was colorless, lanky and greasy.

"Tell me, my girl, are you a virgin?"

Victorita grew angry.

"What the hell has that got to do with you?"

"Nothing, baby, nothing at all. Curiosity, you know. . . . But your manners! D'you know that you're rude?"

"Look who's talking."

The moneylender smiled. "Really, there's no reason to be

· 163 ·

so cross. After all, whether your virginity is intact or not is your own affair, and your fiancé's."

"That's just what I think."

"There you are."

The moneylender's small eyes shone like an owl's. "Listen."

"What is it?"

"If I gave you not three thousand pesetas, but thirty thousand, what would you do for me?"

Victorita went red and hot. "Anything you asked me to."

"Everything I'd ask you?"

"Yes, sir, everything."

"Everything?"

"Yes, everything, sir."

"And your fiancé, what would he do to me?"

"I don't know. If you wish, I'll ask him."

Two blush-pink patches flowered on the moneylender's pallid cheeks.

"And you, my pretty, d'you know what I want of you?"

"No, sir, you tell me."

There was a slight quiver in the moneylender's voice. "Listen, show me your breasts."

The girl lifted her breasts out of the low neck of her dress.

"You know what that is—thirty thousand pesetas?"

"Yes, sir."

"Have you ever seen so much money in a heap together?"

"No, sir, never."

"Well, I'll show it to you. It's all up to you, to you and your fiancé."

A listless breeze drifted sluggishly through the room, butting against one piece of furniture after the other like a dying butterfly.

"Agreed?"

Victorita felt her cheeks flush in shame.

"For myself, yes. For thirty thousand pesetas I'm willing to spend the rest of my life doing what you want. And any other life I may have, too."

"And your fiancé?"

"I'm going to ask him if he agrees."

✻   ✻   ✻   ✻

The front door of Doña María's house opens. The girl who comes out and crosses the street is almost a child.

"Look here, look here, I think somebody's come out of our house."

The policeman Julio García parts from the watchman Gumersindo Vega.

"Good luck!"

"That's what I need."

Left alone, the night watchman first thinks about the policeman. Then he remembers Señorita Pirula. And then the way in which he had dealt with an importunate loafer last summer: a sharp prick in the small of the back with his pointed stick. The watchman has to grin: "How that beggar did run!"

Doña María lowers the blind. "Goodness, what times we live in! The way people carry on!"

For a few moments she keeps quiet. "What's the time now?"

"Going on twelve. Come, let's go to bed, that's the best."

"Shall we go to bed?"

"Yes, that's the best."

Filo makes the round of her children's cots and blesses each of them with the sign of the Cross. This is—how shall we put it?—a precaution she never fails to take every night.

Don Roberto cleans his denture and puts it in a glass of water, which he covers with a sheet of toilet paper. But first he manufactures little frills along the edge of the paper, like on the cornets in which almonds are sold at fairs. Then he smokes his last cigarette. Don Roberto enjoys a cigarette when he is in bed and has taken out his denture, and he smokes it every night.

"Don't burn a hole in my sheets."

"No, my dear."

The policeman goes up to the girl and takes her by the arm. "I thought you were never coming."

"Well, here I am."

· 165 ·

"Why are you so late?"

"Now listen. The kids wouldn't go to sleep. And then it was the master with his things: 'Petrita, bring me some water . . . Petrita, bring me the tobacco that's in my coat pocket . . . Petrita, bring me the paper from the hall' . . . I thought he'd go on all night sending me to fetch things for him."

Petrita and the policeman disappear in the mouth of an alley leading to the building plots in the Plaza de Toros.

A breath of cold air blows up the girl's warm legs.

Javier and Pirula are smoking, both from the same cigarette. It is their third this night. They do not speak. Every now and then they kiss, voluptuously and sparingly.

Lying on the couch, with their faces very close, their eyes half shut, they take pleasure in thinking about nothing, or next to nothing, lazily adrift.

Then comes the moment when they exchange a longer, deeper, more abandoned kiss. The girl breathes deeply as though complaining. Javier picks her up in his arms like a child and carries her to the bedroom.

The bedspread of moiré throws back the outline of a porcelain chandelier, pale violet in color, which hangs from the ceiling. A small electric heater burns by the bedside.

A breath of tepid air wafts along the girl's warm legs.

"Is that thing on the night table?"

"Yes . . . don't speak. . . ."

From the building plots on the Plaza de Toros, the uncomfortable refuge of poor couples who accept what comes, like those fierce, utterly honest lovers in the Old Testament, it is possible to hear the trolley cars passing not far away, on their run to the sheds. They are old, decrepit, and loose-jointed, with rattling coachwork and harsh, grinding brakes.

The waste plot that is the morning playground of noisy, quarrelsome boys who throw stones at each other all day long is, from the time the front doors are locked, a rather grubby

Garden of Eden where one cannot dance smoothly to the music of a concealed, almost unnoticed radio set; where one cannot smoke a scented, delightful cigarette as a prelude; where no easy, candid endearments may be whispered in security, in complete security. After lunchtime the waste ground is the resort of old people who come there to feed on the sunshine like lizards. But after the hour when the children and the middle-aged couples go to bed, to sleep and dream, it is an uninhibited paradise with no room for evasion or subterfuge, where all know what they are after, where they make love nobly, almost harshly, on the soft ground which still retains the lines scratched in by the little girl who spent the morning playing hopscotch, and the neat, perfectly round holes dug by the boy who greedily used all his spare time to play at marbles.

"Are you cold, Petrita?"

"No, Julio. I feel so good next to you!"

"Do you love me very much?"

"Very much. As if you didn't know it."

Martin Marco wanders through the city, unwilling to go to bed. He hasn't so much as a brass farthing on him, and prefers to wait until the underground has stopped and the last, sickly, yellow trolleys of the night go into hiding. Then the city seems more his, more the place of those who, like him, go walking without a fixed course, their hands in their empty pockets—which sometimes are not even warm—their heads empty and their eyes empty and their hearts, for no intelligible reason, empty with a yawning, remorseless emptiness.

Martin Marco goes up the Calle de Torrijos as far as the Calle de Diego de León, slowly and almost unconsciously; then he goes down the Calle del Príncipe de Vergara, through the Calle General Mola to the Plaza de Salamanca, where the Marquis of Salamanca stands in the middle, dressed in a frock coat and surrounded by carefully tended green lawn. Martin Marco loves lonely walks, long, weary tramps through the wide streets of the city, the same streets which in daytime, by something like a miracle, fill to overflowing—like an honest breakfast cup—with the cries of street vendors, the ingenuous, un-restrained songs of servant girls, the sounds of motor horns and the wails of babies, tender, violent, citified, tamed wolf cubs.

Martin Marco sits down on a wooden bench and lights a cigarette stub he has been carrying, with several others, in an envelope with a printed head saying: "City Council of Madrid. Identity Cards Department."

Street benches are a sort of anthology of every form of trouble and of nearly every form of good fortune: the old man seeking to ease his asthma, the priest reading his breviary, the beggar delousing himself, the bricklayer lunching together with his wife, the consumptive panting for breath, the madman with huge, dreaming eyes, the street musician resting his horn on his knees—each one of them with his urge, great or small, impregnates the planks of the seat with the stale smell of flesh totally unaware of the mystery of blood circulation. And the young girl recovering from fatigue after her deep moan of pleasure, and the lady reading a long novel about love, and the blind woman waiting for the hours to pass, and the little typist gulping her sandwich of sausage and coarse bread, and the woman with cancer fighting her pain, and the moron with her gaping mouth dribbling softly, and the woman who sells miniature packets of cards, her tray on her lap, and the little girl who likes nothing so much as to watch men peeing . . .

The envelope Martin Marco uses for his stubs has come from his sister's place. Really, the envelope is no longer good for anything but to carry cigarette stubs, or tacks, or bicarbonate. It is some months since they withdrew the old identity cards. Now there is talk of issuing a new kind of identity paper with a photograph and even with fingerprints, but in all probability this is a long way off. Official affairs have a very slow pace.

So then Celestino turns to his unit and says: "Courage, my lads! Forward to victory! Anyone who's afraid can stay behind. I won't have any with me but real men who're willing to let themselves be killed in the service of an idea."

The unit stays silent, deeply moved, and hanging on his lips. The soldiers' eyes glitter furiously with the lust for battle. "We're fighting for a better mankind. What does it matter if we sacrifice ourselves, as long as we know that it is not in vain and that our children shall reap the harvest of what we are sowing today?"

Enemy planes are flying overhead. Not one in the unit stirs.

"Against our enemies' tanks, we shall pitch the courage of our hearts!"

The unit breaks its silence: "We're with you!"

"Perish the weak, the cowards, and the sick!"

"We're with you!"

"Perish the exploiters, the speculators, and the rich!"

"We're with you!"

"And those who play with the hunger of the working men!"

"We're with you!"

"We shall share out the gold of the Bank of Spain!"

"We're with you!"

"But if we want to reach the goal of final victory, our great ambition, we must make our sacrifice on the altar of liberty!"

"We're with you!"

Celestino is more verbose than ever. "Forward then, without dismay, without a single doubt!"

"Forward!"

"We fight for bread and freedom!"

"We're with you!"

"No more words! Let every man do his duty! Forward!"

Celestino suddenly feels the urge to perform a small physical necessity. "One moment!"

The unit is somewhat taken aback. Celestino turns round. His mouth is parched. The unit begins to lose outline, to get blurred. Celestino Ortiz rises from his mattress, turns on the light in the bar, drinks a sip of soda water, and goes to the lavatory.

Laurita has finished her crème de menthe. Pablo has finished his whiskey. Presumably the long-haired violinist is still scraping, with a dramatic flourish, that fiddle of his which oozes czardas and Viennese waltzes.

Pablo and Laurita are already alone.

"Will you never leave me?"

"Never, Laurita."

The girl is happy, indeed, very happy. And yet, at the bottom of her heart there rises the faintest insubstantial shadow of a doubt.

The girl is slowly undressing, and as she does so she watches the man with sorrowful eyes, like a boarding-school girl.

"Never, really and truly?"

"Never. You'll see."

The girl wears a white slip embroidered with small pink flowers.

"Do you love me a lot?"

"An enormous lot."

The two kiss, standing in front of the wardrobe mirror. Laurita's breasts are flattened against the man's jacket.

"It makes me feel ashamed, Pablo."

Pablo laughs. "Poor little girl!"

The girl wears a diminutive brassiere.

"Undo it for me."

Pablo kisses her on the back, starting from the top.

"Ooh!"

"What's the matter?"

Laurita smiles but lets her head droop. "You're so naughty!"

The man kisses her again, on the mouth. "Don't you like it?"

The girl feels a profound gratitude towards Pablo. "Yes, I do, Pablo. I like it very much, very, very much. . . ."

Martin feels cold and decides to make the rounds of the small houses in the Calle de Alcántara, the Calle de Montesa, and the Calle de las Naciones, which is a short alley, full of mystery, with trees growing from its broken pavements. Passersby who are poor and of a pensive turn of mind get fun out of watching people come and go in the houses of assignation and of imagining all that may happen inside, behind the somber red brick walls.

It is not really an amusing spectacle, not even for Martin, who sees it from inside, but it helps to pass the time. Also, between one house and another, one always gathers a little warmth.

And a little affection, too. Some of the girls are very nice, those in the fifteen-peseta class; they are not exactly pretty, to be honest, but they are very kind and pleasant. They usually have a boy at school with the Augustinians or the Jesuits, a son for whom the mother does everything within her power, and beyond it, so that he should not turn out a "son of a bitch," and whom she goes to see now and then on a Sunday afternoon, with a little veil over her hair and no make-up at all. The others, the high-class tarts, are quite unbearable with their pretensions and their sham-aristocratic manners; admittedly they are lovely women, but they also are capricious and overbearing, and none of them has a son hidden away anywhere. Expensive whores get an abortion or, when this is not practicable, they choke the newborn baby by putting a pillow over its head and sitting on it.

Martin is deep in thought while he walks on; sometimes he mumbles to himself.

"I can't understand," he says, "how there is still such a thing as a little servant girl of twenty earning sixty pesetas a month."

Martin imagines Petrita, with her firm body, her clean-scrubbed face, her straight legs, and her breasts that swell beneath her thin blouse or sweater.

"She's an enchanting creature. She would make her career and even save money. However, the longer she goes on being a decent girl, the better for her. The trouble will start when she's tumbled by some fishmonger or policeman. Then she'll discover that she's been wasting her time. And that will be that."

Martin turns off through the Calle de Lista, and when he comes to the corner of the Calle de General Pardinas a policeman stops him, searches him, and asks for his papers.

Martin had been dragging his feet, making a clip-clop on the pavement stones. It always amuses him to do so.

Don Mario de la Vega has gone to bed early. He wants to be fresh tomorrow, in case Doña Ramona's strategy comes off.

The man who starts tomorrow at sixteen pesetas a day would by now be the brother-in-law of a girl who works as a packer at the El Porvenir printing works on the Calle de la Madera if his brother Paco had not fallen ill with T.B. in its most virulent form.

"Good, my lad, see you tomorrow then."

"Good night, sir, and keep well. I'll be here tomorrow. And good luck to you, please God. I'm deeply grateful to you."

"That's quite all right, man. The point is whether you're a good worker."

"I'll try my best, sir."

Out in the night air, Petrita is groaning with pleasure; all the blood in her body has mounted to her face.

Petrita is very fond of her policeman. He is her first boy friend, the first man who ever took her. At home, in the village, she had an admirer shortly before she left, but it was not serious.

"Oh, Julio, oh, oh! Oh, you're hurting me so! You beast! You greedy beast! Oh! Oh!"

The man is biting her on her rosy throat, where the warm little pulse of life is beating.

For a short while the two lovers stay silent, motionless. Petrita seems thoughtful.

"Julio?"

"Yes?"

"Do you love me?"

＊　　＊　　＊　　＊

The night watchman of the Calle de Ibiza takes shelter inside a doorway, leaving the front door ajar in case someone calls for him.

The watchman turns on the staircase light. Then he blows on his fingers, left exposed by the woolen mittens, so as to get rid of their numbness. The light in the staircase goes out quickly. The man rubs his hands, and switches it on again, after which he takes out his pouch and rolls himself a cigarette.

Martin speaks in a pleading, frightened voice, and the words tumble out. Martin is trembling, his face has turned greenish.

"I haven't any papers on me, I left them at home. I'm a writer, and my name's Martin Marco."

Martin has a spell of coughing. Then he laughs.

"He, he. Excuse me, but I've got a slight cold, that's it, a slight cold, he, he."

It astonishes Martin that the policeman fails to recognize him.

"But I'm a contributor to the press of our movement, you can ask about it at the Vice-Secretariat here in the Calle de Génova. My last article came out a couple of days ago in several provincial papers: in the *Odiel* at Huelva, the *Proa* at León, the *Ofensiva* at Cuenca. Its title is 'Reasons for the Spiritual Permanence of Isabella the Catholic.' "

The policeman takes a pull at his cigarette.

"Right, you can go. Go home to bed, it's cold."

"Thank you, thank you."

"Nothing to thank me for. Hi, you!"

Martin feels he is dying. "Yes, please?"

"May your inspiration never dry up!"

"Thank you, thank you. Good night."

Martin hurries off without once turning his head; he dares not. There is a terrible fear in his very bones, a fear which is past understanding.

✻   ✻   ✻   ✻

While Don Roberto is finishing his paper, he pets—partly out of politeness—his wife, who lets her head rest on his shoulder. At this time of the year they always put an old greatcoat over their feet.

"What d'you think tomorrow will be, Roberto, a very sad day or very happy day?"

"A very happy day, my dear."

Filo smiles. In one of her front teeth there is a deep, round, blackish little hole.

"Yes, if one looks at it the right way."

When she smiles with sincerity and feeling, the woman forgets about that black spot and shows her teeth.

"You're right, Roberto. It will be a happy day tomorrow."

"Of course it will, Filo. You know what I'm always saying: 'As long as we're all in good health . . .' "

"Our health is good enough, thank God."

"Yes, the fact is that we've no right to complain. So many people are worse off. We're pulling through, one way or another. And I don't ask for more."

"Nor do I, Roberto. Really, we've got much to be thankful for, don't you think?"

Filo is affectionate with her husband. She is most grateful to him; it makes her happy if she is given a little attention.

In a changed tone, Filo says: "Listen, Roberto."

"What?"

"Oh, let the paper be, dear."

"If you wish . . ."

Filo clutches Don Roberto's arm. "Listen."

"What?"

She talks like a girl in love. "Do you love me very much?"

"Yes, of course, my dear girl. Naturally I love you very much. What a thing to ask!"

"Very, very much?"

Don Roberto pronounces his words as if he were preaching a sermon; when he deepens his voice to say something solemn, he sounds like a priestly orator.

"Much more than you imagine."

*   *   *   *

Martin rushes on, with heaving chest and burning temples, his tongue cleaving to his palate, his throat constricted, legs shaky, his stomach like a music box with a broken spring, his ears buzzing, his eyes more short-sighted than ever.

As he runs, Martin tries to think. Ideas jostle, collide, push, fall, and rise again in his head, which is now the size of a train that, for no good reason, just fails to bump into the rows of houses on either side of the street.

Cold as it is, Martin feels a stifling heat in his body, a heat which chokes his breath and is moist; perhaps it is even kindly, for it is linked by a thousand invisible threads to other waves of heat, full of tenderness and brimming with sweet memories.

"Oh, Mother, Mother, those eucalyptus fumes, the eucalyptus fumes—more eucalyptus fumes, please—don't be like that . . ."

Martin's forehead aches, it throbs in a strictly regular beat, with sharp, ominous stabs.

"Oh!"

Two steps.

"Oh!"

Two steps.

"Oh!"

Two steps.

Martin touches his forehead with his hand. He is sweating like a bull calf, like a gladiator in the circus, like a pig in the slaughter house.

"Oh!"

Two steps more.

Martin begins to think at great speed.

"What is it I'm afraid of? He, he! What am I afraid of? What of, what of? He had a gold tooth. He, he! I'd look nice with a gold tooth. How elegant! He, he! I'm not involved in anything. Not in anything. What can they do to me if I don't get myself involved in anything? He, he! What a fellow! And what a gold tooth. Why is it that I'm afraid? One scare after another! He, he! Suddenly—like this—a gold tooth. 'Halt, your papers.' I haven't got any papers. He, he! Nor a gold tooth. I'm Martin Marco. With or without a gold tooth. He, he! In this country nobody knows us writers, not even God Almighty. Paco now, if Paco had a gold tooth . . . He, he! 'Yes, write for their papers, write for their papers, don't be a fool, they'll catch you out, you'll see . . .' What a joke. He, he! It's enough to drive one mad. This is a world of madmen. Of madmen ripe for the straitjacket. Of dangerous madmen. He, he! My sister could do with a gold tooth. He, he! No Isabella the Catholic, and no Vice-Secretariat, and no spiritual permanence of anyone. Is that clear? All I want is to eat. To eat. Am I talking Latin? He, he! Or Chinese? You there, bring me a gold tooth. Everybody understands that. He, he! Everybody. To eat. What? To eat? And I want to buy a whole packet of cigarettes and not smoke the stubs that beast left. What? This world is rotten muck. Here everybody looks after Number One. What? Everybody. The ones who shout loudest shut up as soon as they get a thousand pesetas a month. Or a gold tooth. He, he! And we poor devils who go about abandoned and undernourished, we have to face the music and do all the dirty jobs. That's fine. That's excellent. It makes you feel like sending everything to hell, to stinking hell."

Martin spits vigorously and stops, his body sagging against the gray wall of a house. He sees everything blurred and for several moments he does not know whether he is alive or dead.

Martin is exhausted.

The Gonzálezes' bedroom has furniture made from plywood which once was aggressively brilliant, but now is faded and discolored: the bed, two night tables, a small chest of drawers, and a wardrobe. They have never been able to afford a looking glass for the wardrobe. In its place, the plywood looks bare, raw, pale, and accusing.

The ceiling lamp with its green glass globes seems to have

been switched off. But the ceiling lamp with its green glass globes is innocent of light bulbs, it is ornamental. The room is lighted by a small lamp without a shade that stands on Don Roberto's night table.

On the wall over the head of the bed, a chromolithograph of Our Lady of Perpetual Help, a wedding present from Don Roberto's colleagues in the Council offices, has already presided over five successful deliveries.

Don Roberto puts down the paper.

The couple kiss with a certain skill. In the course of the years Don Roberto and Filo have discovered an almost limitless world.

"But, Filo, have you looked at the calendar?"

"What do we care about the calendar, Roberto! If you only knew how much I love you. Every day more!"

"All right, but shall we do it . . . like this?"

"Yes, Roberto, like this."

Filo's cheeks are rosy, almost flushed.

Don Roberto argues like a philosopher.

"Well, after all, where five kids can eat there will be something for six. Agreed?"

"Yes, of course, dear, of course. God grant us our health, and as for the rest. . . . Now look here: if we won't have more room we'll have a little less room, and that's that."

Don Roberto takes off his spectacles, puts them in their case and places it on the night table next to the glass of water in which his denture floats like a mysterious fish.

"Don't take off your nightdress, you'll get cold."

"I don't mind, all I want is that you like me."

Filo smiles with a touch of roguery.

"All I want is that my darling likes me very much."

Naked, Filo retains a certain beauty.

"Do you like me still?"

"Very much, every day more."

"What's the matter?"

"I thought I heard one of the children crying."

"No, dear, they're all asleep. Go on. . . ."

Martin pulls out his handkerchief and wipes his mouth. At a water spout he crouches down and drinks. He thought he would go on drinking for an hour, but his thirst is soon quenched. The water is cold, almost freezing, with a little white-frost rim round it.

A watchman comes up, his head wrapped tight in a muffler.

"Having a drink, what?"

"Well, yes. That's it. . . . Having a little drink. . . ."

"What a beauty of a night, isn't it?"

The night watchman walks on, and Martin searches his envelope by the light of the street lamp to find another stub in fairly good condition.

"The policeman was a very pleasant man, really. He asked me for my papers just under a street lamp, and that must have been because he didn't want to give me a scare. What's more, he let me go quickly. No doubt he noticed that I don't look like somebody who gets involved in things, and that I'm all against sticking my nose into things that don't concern me. Those people are trained to spot such differences. He had a gold tooth and a marvelous greatcoat. Yes, I'm sure he's a grand fellow, a very pleasant man. . . ."

Martin feels his whole body atremble and notes that his heart again beats more violently in his breast.

"I could get over all this for fifteen pesetas."

The master baker calls his wife. "Paulina!"

"What is it?"

"Bring me the basin."

"What, again?"

"Yes. Be quiet now, and come here."

"Coming, coming! Any one would think you were twenty!"

Their bedroom is filled with pieces of sturdy furniture in sound, solid walnut, strong and straightforward as their owners. From the wall there shine, resplendent in three matching gilt frames, a reproduction of *The Last Supper* on white metal, a lithograph of one of Murillo's Immaculate Conceptions, and a wedding portrait with Paulina in a white veil, a black dress, and a smile, and Señor Ramón in a trilby hat, with his mustache erect, and a golden watch chain.

Martin walks down the Calle de Alcántara to the chalets, turns into the Calle de Ayala, and calls the night watchman.

"Good evening, sir."

"What's that? No, not this place."

By the light of an electric bulb he sees the name of the little house: "Villa Filo." Martin still has a vague, imprecise shadowy feeling of respect for his family. What happened with his sister . . . Well, what's done is done, and water that has flowed past can't drive the mill. His sister is no slut. Affection is a thing that ends goodness knows where. And one doesn't know where it begins either. This business of his sister's . . . Bah, when all's said and done, a man isn't fussy when he's in heat. In this we human beings are still just like the animals.

The letters that spell "Villa Filo" are black, uncouth, chilling, all too straight, and without any charm.

"I beg your pardon, but I think I'll go round to the Calle de Montesa."

"Just as you wish, sir."

Martin thinks: "This night watchman is a wretch. They're all wretches, these night watchmen. They never give a smile and never lose their tempers without first having made their calculations. If this one knew that I haven't a bean, he would have kicked me out of here and given me a thrashing with his stick."

Already in bed, Doña María, the lady who lives on the mezzanine, is talking to her husband. Doña María is a woman of forty or a couple of years more; her husband appears to be some six years older than she.

"Listen, Pepe."

"What?"

"You're a bit cross with me."

"Not at all."

"Yes, I think you are."

"Don't be absurd."

Don José Sierra treats his wife neither well nor badly. He treats her as if she were a piece of furniture to which—out of one of those fixed ideas people have—one sometimes speaks as to a person.

"Listen, Pepe."

"What?"

"Who's going to win the war?"

"What does it matter to you? Now come, forget about it and go to sleep."

Doña María fixes her eyes on the ceiling. After a short while, she addresses her husband again.

"Listen, Pepe?"

"What?"

"Would you like me to fetch the towel?"

"All right, fetch whatever you like."

On the Calle de Montesa all you have to do is to push open the garden gate and knock with your knuckles on the front door. The bell has lost its push button and the iron shaft that is left may give you an electric shock. Martin knows this from previous occasions.

"Hello, Doña Jesusa, how are you?"

"All right. And you, dearie?"

"As you can see! Tell me, is Marujita about?"

"No, dearie. Tonight she hasn't come, I can't think why. Perhaps she'll turn up later. Would you like to wait for her?"

"All right, I'll wait. It isn't as if I had anything else to do."

Doña Jesusa is a fat, amiable, servile woman, a peroxide blonde who looks as if she once had been very handsome; she is quick and resourceful.

"Come along, sit with us in the kitchen. You're like one of the family."

"Ye-es. . . ."

Around the kitchen range, on which several pots of water are boiling away, sit five or six girls, wearily dozing, looking neither happy nor sad.

"How cold it is!"

"Yes, indeed. It's good in here, isn't it?"

"I should say so. It's very good in here."

Doña Jesusa comes close to Martin.

"Here, come near the fire, you're frozen. Haven't you got an overcoat?"

"No."

"You poor thing!"

Martin is not amused by kindness. Fundamentally, Martin, too, is a follower of Nietzsche.

"Tell me, Doña Jesusa, isn't the Uruguayan here either?"

"Yes, but she's engaged. She came in with a gentleman and shut herself up with him. They're staying here overnight."

"Really!"

"Tell me, if it isn't indiscreet to ask, what did you want Marujita for? Did you want to stay with her for a while?"

"No, it's just that I wanted to give her a message."

"Now look here, don't be daft. Is it because you're badly off just now?"

Martin Marco smiles. He is beginning to feel warm.

"Not badly, Doña Jesusa—worse."

"You're foolish, dearie. After all this time you might really trust me better, seeing how fond I was of your poor mother, God rest her soul."

Doña Jesusa taps on her shoulder one of the girls sitting near the fire. She is a thin little thing who has been reading a novel.

"Listen, Pura, go with this fellow. Weren't you feeling unwell? Go to bed, you two—and don't come down again, Pura. Don't worry, tomorrow I'll arrange things for you."

Pura, the girl who is unwell, looks at Martin and smiles. She is a very pretty young woman, small, thin, and rather pale, with deep shadows under her eyes and with something about her that suggests a virgin going in for vices.

Martin takes Doña Jesusa's hand.

"Thank you, Doña Jesusa, thank you. You're always so kind to me."

"Nonsense, you flatterer. Anyway, you know you're like a son in this place."

Three flights of stairs, and a garretlike room. A bed, a washstand, a small white-framed mirror, a clothes rack, and a chair. A man and a woman.

Where tenderness is absent, you try to find warmth. Pura and Martin throw all their clothing on the bed to be warmer. They put out the light ("No, no, keep still, my girl, quite still . . .") and go to sleep in each other's arms like two newlyweds.

Out in the street, the night watchman cries from time to time: "Coming!"

Through the matchboard partition sounds the creaking of a mattress, as meaningless and as frank as the chirping of a cricket.

About half past one or two in the morning, night closes down on the strange heart of the city.

Thousands of men are sleeping with their arms round their wives, forgetful of the harsh and cruel day that may be lying in wait for them a few hours hence, crouched like a wild cat.

Hundreds and hundreds of bachelors lapse into the intimate, exalted, utterly refined vice of the solitary.

And several dozens of girls are hoping—what are they hoping for, O God? Why do You let them be thus deceived?—with their minds full of golden dreams. . . .

Chapter Five

JULITA is usually back home by half past eight in the evening
or even earlier.

"Hello, Julita darling."

"Hello, Mamma!"

Her mother looks her over, from top to toe, with a foolish
pride.

"Where have you been?"

The girl puts her hat on the piano and smoothes her hair
in front of the looking glass. She chatters at random, without
glancing at her mother.

"Oh, you know, I've been about."

Her mother assumes a tender tone, as if trying to please.

"About . . . about . . . you spend the whole day out, and
then, when you come home, you don't tell me anything. And
you know how I love to hear about what you're doing! You
don't tell anything to your mother who loves you so. . . ."

The young girl puts on lipstick, looking at her face in the
polished back of the powder compact.

"And where's Papa?"

"I don't know. Why? He went out a while ago and it's early
for him to be back. Why do you ask?"

"Oh, for no special reason. I thought of him because I saw
him in the street."

"That's funny in such a big city as Madrid."

Julita goes on talking.

"Big? It isn't bigger than a hankie. I saw him in the Calle de Santa Engracia when I was coming out of a house where I got myself photographed."

"You didn't tell me that."

"I wanted to give you a surprise. . . . He was going into the same house; apparently he's got a sick friend there."

The girl looks at her mother's reflection in the glass. Sometimes she thinks that her mother looks stupid.

"He didn't tell me a word about it either." Doña Visi looks sad. "None of you ever tells me anything."

Julita smiles and goes to her mother to give her a kiss. "How sweet my old lady is!"

Doña Visi kisses her, leans away, and raises her eyebrows. "Pooh, you smell of tobacco."

Julita pouts. "Well, I haven't been smoking. You know I don't smoke because I think it just isn't feminine."

Her mother attempts to look stern. "Then—somebody must have kissed you."

"Good Lord, Mamma, who do you take me for?"

The poor woman grasps both her daughter's hands. "Forgive me, darling, you're quite right. I do talk nonsense."

For a few moments she remains thoughtful and talks quietly, as if to herself. "You see, a mother imagines everywhere dangers for her eldest daughter."

Julita sheds two tears. "You say such awful things . . ."

The mother forces a smile and strokes the girl's hair. "Come, don't be a baby, don't take any notice of me, I was only teasing."

Julita is absent-minded, she seems not to hear her. "Mamma . . ."

"Yes?"

Don Pablo considers that his wife's nephew and niece have come specially to spoil things for him; their visit has wasted his whole afternoon. At this time of the day, he is always at Doña Rosa's café, drinking his cup of chocolate.

His wife's niece is called Anita, her nephew-by-marriage, Fidel. Anita is the daughter of one of Doña Pura's brothers who is a clerk at the City Council of Saragossa and was awarded a Cross of Merit for having rescued a lady from drowning in the Ebro; it turned out that this lady was first cousin to the President of the Provincial Assembly. Anita's husband Fidel owns a confectioner's shop in Huesca. They are spending a few days in Madrid on their honeymoon.

Fidel is a young lad with a tiny mustache who wears a pale green tie. Six or seven months back he won a tango competition in Saragossa, and on that night he was introduced to the girl who is now his wife.

Fidel's father, also a confectioner, had been a rough fellow who took sand as a purgative and talked of nothing else but Aragonese dances and Our Lady of the Pillar. He prided himself on his culture and enterprise, and used two different visiting cards. One read *Joaquín Bustamante, Tradesman*, while the other, in Gothic type, read *Joaquín Bustamante Valls. Author of the Plan to Double the Agricultural Output of Spain.* At his death he left an enormous amount of deckle-edged paper covered with figures and drawings. He wanted to double the crops by a scheme of his own invention: huge terraced mounds packed with fertile soil were to be irrigated from artesian wells and to enjoy constant sunshine through a system of mirrors.

Fidel's father had changed the name of the cake shop when he inherited it from his eldest brother, who died in the Philippines in 1898. Formerly it had been called "The Sweetener," but this name did not seem meaningful enough to him and he called it instead "The Site of Our Forefathers." It took him more than six months to decide on a new name, and in the end he had listed at least three hundred of them, nearly all in the same style.

During the Republic, Fidel took advantage of his father's death and changed the name of the shop once more, to "The Golden Sorbet."

"Confectioner's shops ought not to have political names," he said. With rare intuition, Fidel associated the name "The Site of Our Forefathers" with certain currents of thought.

"What we've got to do is to serve our buns and éclairs to whoever comes. The Republicans pay with the same sort of pesetas as the Traditionalists."

The young people, as you heard, have come to Madrid to spend their honeymoon, and felt obliged to pay a long visit to their uncle and aunt. Now Don Pablo does not know how to get rid of them.

"So you like Madrid, do you?"

"Yes, we do . . ."

Don Pablo waits a few seconds before he says: "Good."

Doña Pura is quite put out. The young couple, however, do not seem to be very observant.

Victorita goes to the Calle de Fuencarral, to Doña Ramona Bragado's dairy: the dairy of the former mistress of that gentleman who was twice Undersecretary of Finance.

"Hullo, Victorita, I'm so pleased to see you."

"Hullo, Doña Ramona."

Doña Ramona gives her a honeyed, obsequious smile. "I knew my little girl wouldn't miss her date."

Victorita tries to return the smile. "Yes, one can see you're used to it."

"What d'you mean?"

"Oh, nothing."

"My dear, how suspicious you are!"

Victorita takes off her coat. The neck of her blouse is unbuttoned; her eyes have a strange look that might be imploring, humiliated, or cruel.

"Do I look all right like this?"

"But, my dear, what's the matter with you?"

"Nothing, nothing at all."

Looking in the other direction, Doña Ramona tries to marshal her old skill at procuring.

"Now, come, come, don't be childish. Go in there and play cards with my nieces."

Victorita refuses to budge.

"No, Doña Ramona, I haven't got time. My fiancé's waiting for me. You know, I'm fed up with beating about the bush. I don't want to go round and round like a donkey at a water wheel. You and I, we aren't interested in anything but getting to the point. Do you understand me?"

"No, my girl, I don't."

Victorita's hair is rather tousled.

"Well, then, I'll tell you in so many words. Where's the old billy goat?"

Doña Ramona is shocked. "What?"

"I said, where's the old billy goat? D'you understand me? Where is he?"

"My goodness, girl, you're a slut!"

"All right, I'm whatever you like. I don't care. I've got to throw myself at one man to buy medicine for another. Bring in the old man."

"But, my dear, why talk like this?"

Victorita raises her voice. "Because I don't feel like talking any other way, you old bawd! Is that clear? Because I don't want to."

On hearing the loud voices, Doña Ramona's nieces peep in. Behind them Don Mario shows his ugly mug.

"What's the matter, aunt?"

"This wicked hussy, this ungrateful little bitch wanted to hit me."

Victorita is perfectly calm. The moment before doing something enormous one is always completely calm. And also the moment before deciding not to do it.

"Look, Señora, I'll come back another day when you've got fewer lady customers."

The girl opens the door and goes out. Before the next street corner Don Mario catches up with her. He raises his hand to his hat brim.

"Excuse me, Señorita. It seems to me—why should we talk

in riddles?—that I am to blame for all this, to a certain extent. I . . ."

Victorita cuts him short. "Well, I'm certainly glad to meet you. Here I am. Weren't you looking for me? I give you my word, I haven't ever slept with anyone except my fiancé. For the last three months, or nearly four, I haven't had anything to do with a man. I love my fiancé very much. I'll never love you, but so long as you pay me, I'll sleep with you. I'm fed up. My fiancé will be saved by a few pesetas. I don't mind being unfaithful to him. What I do mind about is getting him well. If you can get him well for me, I'll live with you or sleep with you until you get tired of it."

The girl's voice has begun to quiver. At the end she bursts into tears. "Forgive me . . ."

Don Mario, who is a troublemaker with a sentimental streak, feels a little knot in his throat. "Calm down, young lady. We'll have coffee together, that will do you good."

In the café, Don Mario says to Victorita: "I would give you money for your fiancé, but whatever we may do or not do, he is going to believe what he wants to. Don't you think so too?"

"Yes. Let him think what he likes. Come on, take me to bed."

Julita is absent-minded, she seems not to hear, as if she were far away in the clouds.

"Mamma . . ."

"Yes?"

"I must confess something to you."

"You? Oh, darling, don't make me laugh."

"No, Mamma, I mean it seriously, I've got to confess something to you."

Her mother's lips tremble very faintly; one would have to look closely to notice it.

"Tell me, dear, tell me."

"Well . . . I don't know if I dare to."

"Yes, child, do tell me. Don't be cruel to me. Remember the saying that a mother is her daughter's best friend."

· 188 ·

"Well, if it's like that . . ."

"Come on, tell me."

"Mamma . . ."

"Yes?"

Julita suddenly bursts out: "Do you know why I smell of tobacco?"

"Why?"

Her mother is gasping, a single hair would be enough to choke her.

"Because I was very close to a man, and that man was smoking a cigar."

Doña Visi breathes again, yet her conscience still exacts seriousness. "You?"

"Yes, I."

"But . . ."

"Don't be afraid, Mamma, he's very nice."

The girl strikes a dreamy posture; she might be a poetess. "Very, very nice . . ."

"But is he a decent person, dear, which is the main thing?"

"Yes, Mamma, he's decent as well."

That last, drowsy little worm of desire which lives on in the aged changes position in Doña Visi's heart. "Good, darling, I don't know what to say. God bless you . . ."

Julita's eyelids tremble very faintly, so little that no watch could measure their movement in a fraction of time.

On the following day, Doña Visi is sewing when somebody rings at the door.

"Tica, go and open the door."

Escolástica, the grubby old maid they all used to call Tica for short, goes down to open the front door.

"Madam, a registered letter."

"What, a registered letter?"

"Yes."

"But how odd!"

Doña Visi signs for it on the postman's block of slips.

"Here, give him a little tip."

The envelope of the registered letter says: "Señorita Julita Moisés. Calle de Hartzenbusch 57, Madrid."

"What can it be? It feels like cardboard."

Doña Visi looks at it against the light and sees nothing.

"I am so curious! A registered letter for Julita. How very odd!"

Doña Visi remembers that Julita can't be long now, so that she will soon be relieved of her doubts. Doña Visi goes on sewing.

"What can it be?"

Again Doña Visi picks up the envelope, which is pale yellow and rather bigger than the usual size; again she looks at it from every angle, again she feels it.

"How silly of me! A photo! The girl's photo. But that's pretty quick."

Doña Visi slits open the envelope, and a gentleman with a mustache drops onto the work table.

"Goodness, what a face!"

The more she looks at it, and the more she turns it round in her mind . . .

The man with the mustache was in his lifetime called Don Obdulio. Doña Visi does not know him. Doña Visi is ignorant of nearly everything that goes on in the world.

"Who can this man be?"

When Julita comes home, her mother goes to meet her.

"Look, Julita, my pet, you've had a letter. I've opened it because I saw it was a photo and I thought it must be yours. I'm so looking forward to seeing it!"

Julita makes a face. Julita is at times somewhat high-handed with her mother.

"Where is it?"

"Here—I suppose it's a joke."

As Julita sees the photo she goes white.

"Yes, a joke in very bad taste."

With every moment that passes, her mother understands less of what is going on.

"Do you know him?"

"No, how should I?"

Julita puts away Don Obdulio's photo and a slip of paper that came with it. It says, in a clumsy servant girl's hand: "Do you know him, dearie?"

When Julita meets her young man, she says to him: "Look what I've had through the post."

"The deceased!"

"Yes, the deceased."

For a moment Ventura stays silent, with a conspiratorial face.

"Give it to me. I know what to do with it."

"Here."

Ventura gives Julita's arm a little squeeze.

"Do you know what I think?"

"What?"

"I think it will be better for us to change our nest and find another hideaway. This whole thing smells bad to me."

"And me, too. Yesterday I met my father on the stairs."

"Did he see you?"

"Of course he did."

"And what did you say to him?"

"Oh, nothing. That I was coming from the photographer's."

Ventura thinks it over.

"Have you noticed anything odd at home?"

"No, so far I haven't noticed anything."

Shortly before meeting Julita, Ventura came across Doña Celia in the Calle de Luchana.

"Good afternoon, Doña Celia."

"Oh, Señor Aguado, just the man I was looking for. I'm so glad I've met you, I wanted to tell you something rather important."

"To tell me something?"

"Something that will interest you. It means that I'll lose a good client, but it can't be helped. You know, needs must . . . I must tell it to you, because I don't want complications.

You'll have to watch out, you and your young lady—her father's coming to my place."

"What?"

"Yes, it's quite true."

"But . . ."

"Nothing. I told you, it's quite true."

"Oh, well . . . All right. Thank you so much."

People have had their evening meal.

Ventura has just written a short note; now he is addressing the envelope to: "Sr. Don Roque Moisés, Calle de Hartzenbusch 57, Back Entrance."

The note, which is typewritten, reads as follows:

"Dear Sir,

Enclosed I send you the photograph which may testify against you in the Valley of Jehoshaphat. Watch your step and do not try any tricks, it might be dangerous. A hundred eyes are watching you, and more than one hand would not hesitate to twist your neck. Take care, we know very well what way you voted in 1936."

The letter went unsigned.

Later, when Don Roque receives it, it will leave him agasp. He will not be able to identify Don Obdulio, but the letter will certainly put the fear of God into him.

"This must be the work of the Freemasons," he will think. "It has all the characteristics of their doings, and the photo's only meant to put me off the track. But who may this wretched man be, who looks as if he's been dead thirty years?"

Doña Asunción, Paquita's fond mother, tells the story of her daughter's good luck to Doña Juana Entrena de Sisemón, the widow with a pension who is a neighbor of Don Ibrahim's and of poor Doña Margot's.

In return, Doña Juana tells Doña Asunción all sorts of details about the tragic death of the mamma of Señor Suárez, who bears the unpleasant nickname of "Lady Photographer."

Doña Asunción and Doña Juana are very nearly old friends; they first met when they were being evacuated to Valencia in the same lorry, at the beginning of the Civil War.

"Oh, yes, my dear, I'm delighted. When I got the news that the wife of my Paquita's friend had died, I went nearly mad with joy. God forgive me, I've never wished anybody any harm, but that woman was the shadow that hung over my daughter's happiness."

With her eyes fixed on the floor, Doña Juana returns to her subject: the murder of Doña Margot.

"With a towel! Do you think that's right? With a towel! such a lack of respect for an old lady! The murderer strangled her with a towel as if she'd been a pullet. He stuck a flower in her hand. The poor dear had her eyes still open, they tell me she looked like an owl. I didn't have the courage to go and look at her. That sort of thing affects me so. I don't want to make a mistake, but my nose tells me that her boy must be mixed up in all this. The son of Doña Margot, God rest her soul, is a pansy—did you know?—and keeps very bad company. My poor husband always used to say: 'He that lives ill comes to a bad end.' "

Doña Juana's late husband, Don Gonzalo Sisemón, had breathed his last in a third-rate bawdy house where he died of heart failure one fine evening. His friends had to take him away by night, in a taxi, to avoid complications. They told Doña Juana that he had died while queueing before the image of the Christ of Medinaceli, and Doña Juana believed them. The corpse arrived without suspenders, but Doña Juana did not guess the truth.

"Poor Gonzalo," she said. "Poor Gonzalo! The only thought that comforts me is that he must have gone straight to heaven and is now much better off than we down here. Poor Gonzalo!"

With no more attention for Doña Juana than for the patter of raindrops, Doña Asunción pursues the subject of her Paquita.

"Now I pray God that she gets in the family way. That

· 193 ·

would be a piece of good luck. Her friend is very highly thought of everywhere, he isn't a Mr. Nobody, he's a real professor with a chair. I've made a vow to walk barefoot to the Cross on the Cerro de los Angeles if the girl gets pregnant. Don't you think that's the right thing to do? In my opinion no sacrifice is too great for one's daughter's happiness, don't you agree? What a joy it must have been to Paquita to hear that her friend was free at last!"

Between a quarter and half past five Don Francisco comes home for his consulting hours. In his waiting room he always finds a few patients sitting, silent and grave-faced. Don Francisco is accompanied by his son-in-law, with whom he shares the practice.

Don Francisco has set up a popular clinic which brings him a nice income every month. Across its four balcony windows it displays a notice that says: "Pasteur-Koch Institute, Director-Owner, Dr. Francisco Robles. Tuberculosis, Lung and Heart Complaints. X Rays. Skin, Venereal Diseases, Syphilis. Hemorrhoids treated by Electrocoagulation. Consultation Fee: 5 pts." The poorer patients from the Glorieta de Quevedo, from Bravo Murillo, San Bernardo, and the Calle de Fuencarral have great faith in Don Francisco.

"He's a wizard," they say, "a regular wizard, a doctor who puts his finger on the right spot and has great experience."

Don Francisco usually cuts them short.

"It takes more than faith to cure you, my dear friend," he would say gently, in a confidential tone. "Faith without works is a dead faith, a faith that leads to nothing. You will have to do something for yourself as well; you need obedience and perseverance, plenty of perseverance. You mustn't let yourself go or stop coming here as soon as you notice a slight improvement. . . . It isn't the same thing to feel well as to be cured, far from it. Unfortunately, the viruses that produce an illness are as cunning as they are treacherous and deceitful."

Don Francisco is a bit of a trickster. The man has to shoulder the burden of an extremely large family. If a patient asks to be given sulfonamides, and asks it timidly, full of apologies, Don Francisco talks him out of it almost peevishly. Don Francisco views the progress of pharmaceutical science with a heavy heart.

"One day," he thinks, "we doctors won't be needed any more, and the chemists will put up a list of pills so that the patients will be able to make out their own prescription."

If someone speaks to him of, say, sulfa drugs, Don Francisco generally replies: "Do just as you like, but don't come back to me. I cannot undertake to look after the health of a man who deliberately weakens his own blood."

Usually, Don Francisco's words have a great effect.

"No, no, it's for you to say, I won't do anything except what you tell me."

In an inner room of the apartment, his wife, Doña Soledad, darns socks and lets her imagination wander. Her imagination is slow, motherly, and limited as a hen's flight. Doña Soledad is not happy. She invested her whole life in her children, but they neither knew nor cared about making her happy. She bore eleven, and all of them are living, mostly far away, and one or the other has disappeared from her view. The two eldest daughters, Soledad and Piedad, became nuns years ago, at the time of Primo de Rivera's fall from power; it is only a few months since they dragged one of their younger sisters, María Auxiliadora, to the convent in their wake. The third of the children and the elder of her two sons, Francisco, has always been the apple of her eye; at present he is an army doctor at Carabanchel and comes occasionally to spend a night at home. Amparo and Asunción are the only two married daughters. Amparo has married her father's assistant, Don Emilio Rodríguez Ronda; Asunción is married to Don Fadrique Méndez who is medical assistant at Guadalajara, a hard-working and skillful man equally capable of giving a small child an injection and a distinguished old lady a clyster, of repairing a radio set and of patching up a rubber bag. Poor Amparo has no children and will never have any; she is always in bad health, always troubled by tantrums and ailments; first she had a miscarriage, then a long series of disorders, and finally they had to remove her ovaries and clean out all that was causing her trouble, which must have been quite a lot. Asunción, on the other hand, is stronger and has three splendid children: Pilarín, Fadrique, and Saturnino, of whom the eldest is five years old and already going to school.

Next in Don Francisco and Doña Soledad's family comes Trini, unmarried and quite plain, who borrowed money and set up a draper's shop in the Calle de Apodaca.

Her shop is tiny, but clean and painstakingly looked after. It has a minute show window which displays skeins of wool, children's clothes, and silk stockings, and a pale blue shop sign with "Trini" painted on it in angular letters, and underneath, in still smaller letters, the word "Draper." A young man living nearby, who regards the girl with profound tenderness and is a poet, often tries in vain to explain to his family across the lunch table: "You aren't aware of it, but those tiny, secluded shops that have the name 'Trini' over their doors make me feel nostalgic."

"The boy's a fool," says his father. "Goodness knows what will become of him the day I'm gone."

The local poet is a pale young lad with long hair who in his mind is always somewhere else, not noticing what is going on so as not to lose his inspiration—the inspiration which is something like a butterfly, blind and deaf but luminous, a little butterfly flying at random, at times butting against the walls and at times drifting above the stars. The local poet has two pink spots on his checks. Occasionally, when he is in the mood, the local poet faints in a café and has to be carried to the lavatory, where he is brought round by the smell of the disinfectant that sleeps in its wire cage like a cricket's.

After Trini comes Nati, Martín's former fellow-student, a girl who dresses very well, perhaps only too well; and after her comes María Auxiliadora, the one who entered a nunnery a short while ago to join her two sisters. The list of the children ends with three calamities: the three youngest. Socorrito ran away with a friend of her brother Paco's, by the name of Bartolomé Anguera, a painter; the two lead a bohemian life in a studio on the Calle de los Caños, where they must be freezing to death and will one morning be found as stiff as icicles. The girl assures her girl friends that she is happy and that she doesn't mind anything as long as she can be with her Bartolo, helping him to carry out his work. She pronounces the word "work" with enormous emphasis, as though it were spelled in capital letters; she sounds like a member of the jury that decides on the selection for National Exhibitions.

"There is no critical standard at the National Exhibitions," says Socorrito. "They have no idea what they're about. Never mind, sooner or later they can't help awarding a medal to my Bartolo."

When Socorrito went away, it caused a serious upset in her home.

"She might at least have left Madrid," repeated her brother Paco, who has a geographical concept of honor.

Shortly afterwards her sister María Angustias began to talk of becoming a singer and adopted the name of Carmen del Oro. She had also considered calling herself Rosario Giralda or Esperanza de Granado, but a journalist friend of hers said No, the most suitable name was Carmen del Oro. At that stage, and before her mother had time to get over her shock about Socorrito, María Angustias threw caution to the winds and eloped with a banker from Murcia, called Don Estanislao Ramírez. Her poor mother no longer had any tears left.

The youngest, Juan Ramón, has turned out a bit of a pansy, and spends his days admiring himself in the mirror and rubbing beauty creams on his face.

At about seven, between two patients, Don Francisco goes to the telephone. What he says is almost inaudible.

"Are you going to be at home? . . . Good, then I'll be there towards nine. . . . No, don't send for anybody."

The girl seems in a trance, with a dreamy expression, a faraway look in her eyes, and a smile of bliss on her lips.

"He's so good, Mamma, so good, so good! He took my hand, looked straight into my eyes . . ."

"Nothing more?"

"Oh, yes. He came very close to me and said: 'Julita, my heart is aflame with passion, I can no longer live without you. If you scorn me, my life will no longer have any meaning, I will be like a body drifting aimlessly, at the mercy of fate.' "

Doña Visi smiles, deeply touched. "Just like your father, pet, just like your father."

Doña Visi turns her eyes to heaven and stays in blissful thought, in sweet and perhaps rather wistful repose. "Of course . . . time passes. . . . You make me feel quite old, Julita."

Doña Visi is silent for a few seconds. Then she puts her handkerchief to her eyes and dries two tears that have welled up timidly.

"But, Mamma!"

"It's nothing, darling, just emotion. To think that one day you will belong to a man! Let's pray to God, my darling, that He may grant you a good husband and make you the wife of a man worthy of you."

"Yes, Mamma."

"And be very careful, Julita, for the love of God. I implore you, don't trust him in any way. Men are crafty, they're out for what they can get. Don't you ever trust fine words. Remember, men like to have their fun with forward girls, but in the end they marry the respectable ones."

"Yes, Mamma."

"Of course, yes, my dear. You must guard what I guarded till my twenty-third year for your father to take. It's the only thing we decent women without a fortune have to offer our husbands."

Doña Visi dissolves into tears. Julita comforts her: "Don't worry yourself, Mamma."

At the café, Doña Rosa goes on explaining to Señorita Elvira that her bowels are upset, and that she spent the whole night going backwards and forwards between bedrooms and lavatory.

"Something must have disagreed with me. Food isn't always nice and fresh. If it isn't that, I don't know."

"Of course, that's what it must have been."

Señorita Elvira, who by now is just like a piece of furniture in Doña Rosa's café, says amen to everything. It seems extremely important to her to have Doña Rosa for her friend.

"And did you have cramps?"

"Oh, my dear girl, did I not! My stomach felt like the box they keep the thunder in. I think I must have had too much for supper. As the saying goes: big suppers—full graves."

Señorita Elvira again agrees. "Yes, they say it's bad to eat a large supper because one doesn't digest it well."

"I should say so. Not well but very badly."

Doña Rosa lowers her voice. "Are you sleeping well?"

Doña Rosa treats Señorita Elvira as the spirit moves her, at times familiarly and at times formally. "Well, yes, I usually do."

Doña Rosa jumps to a conclusion. "Then you take very little supper, I'm sure."

Señorita Elvira feels embarrassed. "Yes, well, to tell you the truth, I don't take much for supper. In fact, I eat very little for supper."

Doña Rosa leans on the back of a chair. "What did you have last night, for instance?"

"Last night? Oh, well, not very much, you see. Some spinach and two small pieces of hake."

Señorita Elvira's supper had consisted of a peseta's worth of roast chestnuts, twenty roast chestnuts, and an orange for dessert.

"There you are, that's the secret. To my mind, all that stuffing yourself can't be healthy."

Señorita Elvira thinks exactly the opposite, but she keeps it to herself.

Don Pablo Tauste, the neighbor of Don Ibrahim de Ostolaza and owner of the shoe-repair shop called "The Footwear Clinic," sees Don Ricardo Sorbedo come into his wretched little shop. The poor man is an utter wreck.

"Good evening, Don Pedro. May I come in?"

"Come right in, Don Ricardo. What piece of good luck sends you to me?"

Don Ricardo Sorbedo, with his unkempt mane, his faded scarf thrown on haphazardly, his tattered suit, shapeless and full of stains, his limp spotted cravat, and his greasy, broad-brimmed green hat, is a strange type, half beggar, half artist, who lives, badly enough, on cadging, and on exploiting other people's kindness and compassion. Don Pedro feels a certain admiration for him and occasionally gives him a peseta. Don Ricardo Sorbedo is a short little man, with a jaunty walk, high-falutin and formal manners, a precise, ponderous way of talking, and a habit of turning out neat, well-sounding phrases.

"No good luck, my dear friend Don Pedro, since goodness is rare in this base world. It is, rather, misfortune that brings me into your presence."

Don Pedro is familiar with this start, it never varies. Like the gunners, Don Ricardo fires his shots at a high angle of elevation.

"Do you want a peseta?"

"Even did I not stand in need of it, my noble friend, I should always accept it in response to your generous gesture."

"Here you are."

Don Pedro Tauste takes a peseta out of his till and hands it to Don Ricardo Sorbedo.

"It's little enough."

"Yes, Don Pedro, little enough, but your unselfishness in offering it to me is as a gem of many carats."

"Well, if it's like that . . ."

Don Ricardo Sorbedo is quite friendly with Martin Marco; when they meet, they sometimes sit down on a bench in a park and embark on a discussion of art and literature.

Until recently, Don Ricardo had a girl friend, whom he dropped because he was tired and bored with her. Don Ricardo Sorbedo's girl friend was a half-starved, sentimental, and somewhat pretentious little tart called Maribel Pérez. Whenever Don Ricardo complained that everything was going to the dogs, Maribel tried to console him with philosophical statements.

"Don't worry," she would tell him, "the Mayor of Cork held out more than a month before he died."

Maribel was fond of flowers, children, and animals. She was a fairly well-educated girl and had refined manners.

"Look at that little boy with the fair hair, what a pet!" she said to her lover one day when they wandered round the Plaza del Progreso.

"Just like the rest," answered Don Ricardo Sorbedo. "The boy isn't any different from the others. When he's grown up, that's to say, if he doesn't die before, he will be a shopkeeper or a little clerk at the Ministry of Agriculture, or he may even become a dentist—who knows? He might, at that, go in for art and turn out a painter or a bullfighter, and have his sexual complexes, and all that."

Maribel did not always understand what her friend told her.

"He's a very brainy fellow, is my Ricardo," she would tell the other girls. "There isn't much he doesn't know."

"Are you going to get married?"

"Yes, when we can. But first he says he wants me to keep on the straight and narrow, because this business of being married has got to be tried and sampled, it seems, like a melon you want to buy. I think he's right about it."

"Maybe. Tell me, what's your friend doing?"

"Well, as for doing, what you might call a job, my dear, he doesn't do anything, but he'll find something, don't you think?"

"Yes, something always turns up."

Quite a number of years ago, Maribel's father used to have a modest corsetry on the Calle de la Colegiata, until he sold it because his wife Eulogia got it into her head that it would be better to set up a bar with female service in the Calle de la Aduana. Eulogia's bar was called "The Earthly Paradise," and did fairly well until its mistress lost her head and ran off with a guitar player who was always half drunk.

"It's a shame," Maribel's papa, Don Braulio, used to say. "There's the missus tied up with that wretch who'll let her starve!"

Poor Don Braulio died a little later, of pneumonia, and his funeral was attended by Pepe the Sardine, in deep mourning and full of compunction, who was living with Eulogia in Carabanchel Bajo.

"Do you think we're of no account, eh?" said the Sardine at the funeral to a brother of Don Braulio's who had come from Astorga to be present at the burial.

"Oh, well . . ."

"Life is like that, don't you agree?"

"Yes, that's a fact, life is like that," answered Don Bruno, Don Braulio's brother, while they were in the bus going to the East Cemetery.

"He was a good man, your brother, God rest his soul."

"Of course he was. If he hadn't been so good he would have taken the hide off you."

"That's true enough, too."

"Of course it's true too. But what I say is that in this life you've got to be tolerant."

The Sardine gave no answer. He was thinking to himself that Don Bruno was a man with modern ideas.

"I'll say he is. He's a hell of a modern guy. Whether we like it or not, that's the modern idea, and no mistake about it."

Don Ricardo Sorbedo was not very impressed by his girl friend's arguments.

"Yes, dear, but the hunger strike of the Mayor of Cork doesn't fill my stomach, I promise you."

"But don't you worry, my dear, don't get all excited, it isn't worth it. Anyway, you know, we'll all be dead in a hundred years."

Don Ricardo Sorbedo and Maribel had this conversation sitting in front of two glasses of white wine in a low bar in the Calle Mayor, opposite the Civil Governor's offices. Maribel was the proud possessor of a peseta and had said to Don Ricardo: "Let's have a glass of wine somewhere. I've had enough of wandering round the streets and getting frozen."

"All right, let's go where you like."

The two were waiting for a friend of Don Ricardo's who was a poet and sometimes treated them to a light coffee with a bun thrown in. This friend of Don Ricardo's was a young man by the name of Ramón Maello; he wasn't exactly swimming in wealth himself, but he couldn't be said to go hungry. Being the son of a good family, he always managed to have a few pesetas in his pocket. This young man lived on the Calle de Apodaca, above Trini's drapery, and even though he was not on very good terms with his father, he had not been forced to leave home. Ramón Maello was not at all strong, and if he had left home, it would have cost him his life.

"Say, d'you think he'll come?"

"Yes, my dear, Ramón is a serious lad. His head's a bit in the clouds, but all the same, he's reliable and helpful. He'll come all right, you'll see."

Don Ricardo Sorbedo took a sip and looked thoughtful. "Tell me, Maribel, what does this taste of?"

Maribel also took a sip. "I don't know, I think it tastes of wine."

For a couple of seconds, Don Ricardo felt sick to death of his girl friend. "The woman is like a chattering magpie," he thought.

Maribel did not notice. The poor thing hardly noticed anything.

"Look what a beautiful cat! This cat must be very happy, don't you think?"

The cat—a black, glossy, well-fed, and well-slept cat—was walking, careful and wise like an abbot, along the ledge of the plinth, a noble, old-fashioned ledge at least the width of a palm.

"In my opinion this wine tastes of tea, it tastes exactly like tea."

At the counter, some taxi drivers also were drinking wine.

"Look, look, it's amazing it doesn't fall."

In a corner, another couple were adoring one another in silence, hand in hand, gazing into each other's eyes.

"I believe if one's stomach is empty, everything tastes of tea."

A blind man went from table to table, offering tickets for the lottery in benefit of the blind.

"What a lovely black cat! It looks nearly blue. What a cat!"

The door opened, and from the street came a gust of cold air together with the even colder sound of the trolleys.

"It tastes of tea without sugar, the sort of tea people take when they have stomach trouble."

Stridently, the telephone began to ring.

"That cat's an acrobat; it could get a job in a circus."

The bartender wiped his hands on his green-and-black-striped apron and picked up the receiver.

"Tea without sugar seems more suitable to bathe in than to swallow down."

The bartender hung up the telephone and shouted: "Don Ricardo Sorbedo!"

Don Ricardo waved to him. "What is it?"

"Are you Don Ricardo Sorbedo?"

"Yes. Is there a message for me?"

"Yes, it's from Ramón: he can't come, his mother's been taken ill."

At the bakery on the Calle de San Bernardo, in the tiny office where the books are kept, Señor Ramón has a talk with his wife Paulina and with Don Roberto González, who has come back today in gratitude for the twenty-five pesetas his boss gave him, to add a few finishing touches to the accounts and clear up a few entries.

The baker, his wife, and Don Roberto are chatting round a stove burning sawdust, which gives off considerable heat. On the top of the stove a few bay leaves are boiling in an old tunnyfish tin.

Don Roberto feels happy today; he is telling the baker and his wife funny stories.

"And then the thin one goes and says to the fat one: 'You're a pig!' And the fat one turns round and answers: 'Now listen, you, d'you believe I always smell like this?' "

Señor Ramón's wife is dying with laughter; she has the hiccups, puts both hands over her eyes, and cries: "Stop it, stop it, for God's sake!"

Don Roberto wants to clinch his victory. "And all that—inside an elevator!"

The woman weeps between guffaws and throws herself back in the chair. "Stop it, stop it!"

Don Roberto has to laugh himself.

"The thin man looked as if he had very few friends."

Señor Ramón, with his hands folded over his stomach and a cigarette stub hanging from his lips, looks from Don Roberto to Paulina.

"Don Roberto does come out with funny things when he's in form."

Don Roberto is tireless. "And I've still got another one ready, Señora Paulina."

"Stop, stop, for heaven's sake!"

"All right, I'll wait till you've recovered, I'm in no hurry."

Slapping her stout thighs with her palms, Señora Paulina goes on thinking of the bad smell of the fat man.

The man was sick and penniless, but he killed himself because of a smell of onions.

"There's a foul smell of onions. The smell of onions is horrible."

"Oh, do shut up. I can't smell anything. Would you like me to open the window?"

"No, it makes no difference. The smell wouldn't go; it's the walls that smell of onions. My hands smell of onions."

His wife was a model of patience.

"Do you want to wash your hands?"

"No, I don't want to. Even my heart smells of onions."

"Now calm down, do."

"I can't. It smells of onions."

"Please, try to sleep for a bit."

"I couldn't possibly, everything smells of onions to me."

"Would you like a glass of milk?"

"No, I don't want a glass of milk, all I want is to die. To die, and to die quickly. The smell of onions is getting stronger all the time."

"Don't talk nonsense."

"I shall talk as I like. It does smell of onions."

The man burst out crying.

"It smells of onions."

"All right, dear, all right, it smells of onions."

"Of course it smells of onions. It stinks."

The woman opened the window. The man, his eyes full of tears, began to shout: "Shut the window. I don't want the smell of onions to go."

"As you like."

The woman shut the window.

"I want water, but in a cup, not in a glass."

The woman went into the kitchen to get a cup full of water for her husband.

The woman was just washing out the cup when she heard a hideous bellow, as if a man had suddenly burst both his lungs.

She did not hear the fall of the body on the flagstones in the courtyard. Instead she felt a pain in her temples, an icy, stabbing pain as though a very long needle had pierced them.

"Oooh!"

The woman's cry went out by the open window. No one answered her. The bed was empty.

A few neighbors looked out of their courtyard windows.

"What's the matter?"

The woman could not speak. Had she been able to speak, she would have said: "Nothing, there was a slight smell of onions."

Before going to Doña Rosa's café to play the violin, Seoane drops in at an optician's shop. He wants to find out about the price of dark glasses because his wife's eyes are getting worse and worse.

"Have a look at these, with fancy frame and Zeiss lenses: two hundred and fifty pesetas."

Seoane smiles politely.

"Oh, no, I should like a less expensive pair."

"Very well, sir. Perhaps this model suits you. A hundred and seventy-five pesetas."

Seoane keeps smiling.

"No, perhaps I haven't made myself clear. I should like to see something at fifteen or twenty pesetas."

The assistant gives him a look of profound scorn. He wears a white overall and ridiculous pince-nez; his hair is parted in the middle; when he walks he waggles his bottom.

"You'll find that type at a druggist's. I'm sorry I can't help you, sir."

"All right. Good-by. Sorry to have troubled you."

Seoane stops on his way at the show windows of druggist's shops. The better ones, the kind that also develop films, have in fact colored glasses in their windows.

"Have you any sunglasses at fifteen pesetas?"

The assistant is a pretty and obliging girl.

"We have, but I wouldn't recommend them, sir, they're very brittle. At a slightly higher price, we could offer you a fairly good model."

The girl searches in the drawers of the counter and brings out a few trays.

"Here you see, twenty-five pesetas, twenty-two, thirty, fifty, eighteen—these aren't so good—twenty-seven . . ."

Seoane knows that all he has in his pocket is fifteen pesetas.

"Now these at eighteen, would you say they are really bad?"

"Yes, they are. The difference in price isn't worth it. These here, at twenty-two, are quite another thing."

Seoane smiles at the girl.

"Thank you, Señorita, thank you very much. I'll think it over and come back. I'm sorry to have troubled you."

"Not at all, sir, that's what we're here for."

At the bottom of her heart, Julita's conscience pricks her a little. Those afternoons at Doña Celia's suddenly appear to her edged with the flames of eternal damnation.

This is only for a moment, a bad moment—then she is herself again. The little tear that very nearly trickled down her cheek is blinked away.

The girl shuts herself in her room and takes from her chest of drawers a notebook of black American cloth, in which she enters certain strange accounts. She finds a pencil, notes down a few figures, and smiles at herself in the mirror, her lips pursed, her eyes half closed, her hands on the nape of her neck, and the buttons of her blouse undone.

Julita is lovely, very lovely, as she winks at the mirror.

"Today Ventura came up to his record."

Julita smiles and her lower lip quivers; even her chin begins faintly to tremble.

She puts away her notebook, after breathing on the covers to remove the dust.

"The truth is, I'm going at a pace that's . . . that's . . ."

While she turns the key, which she has adorned with a pink ribbon, she reflects almost with compunction: "That Ventura is insatiable!"

All the same, that's how things are—a gush of optimism floods her mind as she leaves the bedroom.

Martin takes leave of Nati and makes for the café where he was thrown out the day before for not paying.

"I've forty-odd pesetas left," he argues. "I don't think it would be stealing if I bought myself cigarettes and gave a lesson to that repulsive old woman at the café. I can make Nati a present of a couple of small engravings, which will cost me twenty-five to thirty."

He takes trolley No. 17 and gets out at the Glorieta de Bilbao. Before the mirror of a barber's window he smoothes down his hair and straightens his tie.

"I think I look pretty good . . ."

Martin enters the café by the same door through which he came out yesterday. He wants to get the same waiter and if possible the same table.

There is a sticky, dense heat in the café. The musicians are

· 208 ·

playing "La comparsita," a tango that has some vague, sweet, remote memories for Martin. So as to keep in practice, the proprietress is shouting away amid the general indifference, raising her arms to heaven and letting them fall heavily on her belly with studied effect. Martin sits down at a table adjoining that of yesterday's scene. The waiter comes up to him.

"She's in an awful temper today. If she sees you, she'll sure kick."

"Let her. Here's five pesetas, and bring me a coffee. One-twenty for yesterday's and one-twenty for today's is two-forty. You can keep the change. I'm not a down-and-out."

The waiter is taken aback; he looks even more foolish than usual. Before he is out of reach Martin calls him back.

"Send me the bootblack."

"Right."

Martin persists. "And the cigarette boy."

"Right."

It has cost Martin an enormous effort. His head aches a little, but he does not have the courage to ask for an aspirin.

Doña Rosa is talking to the waiter and throwing stupefied glances at Martin. Martin pretends not to see.

He gets his coffee, takes a couple of sips, and rises to go to the lavatory. Later he will not be certain whether or not it was there he had taken his handkerchief from the pocket in which he had put the money.

Back at the table he has his shoes cleaned and spends five pesetas on a packet of cigarettes.

"Give this dishwater to your mistress, she can drink it herself, d'you hear? It's a filthy malt brew."

He rises haughtily, almost with solemnity, and pushes the door open with a restrained movement.

Out in the street, Martin notes that his whole body is trembling, but he considers that everything has been worth his while: at least he has behaved like a man.

Ventura Aguado Sans says to his fellow boarder, Don Tesifonte Ovejero, captain in the Veterinary Corps: "Make no mistake, Captain, in Madrid there is a positive glut of love affairs. And now, since the war, more than ever. Nowadays every woman is more or less out for what she can get. All you've got to do is to spend a short while with them every day! You can't catch trout without getting your trousers wet."

"Yes, yes, I'm aware of that."

"Of course you are, of course you are. How can you have fun if you don't do something about it yourself? You may be sure, the women won't come and seek you out. We haven't got to that stage yet, not here in this country."

"That's true enough."

"So there you are. You've got to be quick on the uptake, Captain, you've got to have enterprise and guts, a lot of guts. And above all you mustn't be put off by failures. Suppose you fail once with a woman—what of it? There's more than one fish in the sea."

Don Roque sends a note to Lola, the maid of Doña Matilde, the widow with a pension: "Come at eight to Santa Engracia. Your R."

Lola's sister, Josefa López, was for many years maid in the house of Doña Soledad Castro de Robles. From time to time she said that she had to go home to her village on a visit, and went into the Maternity Hospital for a few days. In the end she had five children who were brought up on charity by nuns at Chamartín de la Rosa: the eldest three were by Don Roque, the fourth by Don Francisco's eldest son, and the fifth by Don Francisco himself, who was the last to discover the lay of the land. In each case, the paternity was beyond doubt.

"I may be whatever you like," Josefa would say, "but as long as a man pleases me, I wouldn't deceive him. When a girl has had enough of a man she shows him the door, and that's that. But till then it's like the turtledoves, one male, one female."

Josefa used to be a handsome woman, rather on the big side. Now she keeps a boarding house for students in the Calle de Atocha, where she lives with her five offspring. Gossipmongers among her neighbors maintain that she has an understanding with the gasman, and that one day she made the grocer's boy, a lad of fourteen, go red like a turkeycock. It is very difficult to find out what is true in all this.

Her sister Lola is younger, but she too is large and full-breasted. Don Roque buys her cheap trinkets, such as bracelets, and treats her to cakes, and she is delighted. Less decent than Josefa, she apparently goes in for affairs with one or the other of the young bucks as well. One day Doña Matilde caught her in bed with Ventura, but preferred not to say anything about it.

As soon as the girl gets Don Roque's note, she dresses up and makes for Doña Celia's place.

"Hasn't he come yet?"

"No, not yet, but go in there."

Lola goes into the bedroom, undresses, and sits down on the bed. She wants to give Don Roque the surprise of opening the door to him, mother-naked.

Doña Celia looks through the keyhole; she likes to watch girls undressing. Sometimes, when she feels very flushed, she calls her lap dog: "Pierrot, Pierrot, come to your mistress, pet."

Ventura cautiously opens the door of the room he is using. "Señora!"

"Coming."

Ventura puts fifteen pesetas in Doña Celia's hand. "Please let the young lady go out first."

Doña Celia agrees to everything: "Just as you wish."

Ventura goes into a lumber room, to light a cigarette and let some moments pass while the girl gets away; she walks down the stairs with downcast eyes.

"Good-by, dear."

"Good-by."

Doña Celia raps on the door of the room where Lola is waiting.

"Do you want to go to the big bedroom? It's no longer occupied."

"Thanks."

· 211 ·

On the landing of the mezzanine Julita meets Don Roque.

"Hello, my girl, where have you come from?"

Julita is embarrassed.

"From . . . from the photographer's. And you, where are you going to?"

"Well . . . to see a sick friend. The poor man's in a very bad way."

It costs the daughter an effort to think that her father is going to Doña Celia's, and her father feels the same about her.

"No, it's too silly of me. What an idea!" thinks Don Roque.

"The story about his friend must be true," thinks the girl. "Papa's bound to have affairs, but it would be frightfully bad luck if he came here, of all places."

As Ventura is on his way out, Doña Celia stops him.

"Just wait half a moment, there's someone at the door."

Don Roque enters, looking rather pale.

"Hello. Has Lola come?"

"Yes, she's in the front bedroom."

Don Roque gives two light taps on the door.

"Who is it?"

"Me."

"Come in."

Ventura goes on talking to the captain, almost eloquently.

"Look here, at the present moment I've a little affair, quite a regular one, with a young girl whose name doesn't matter. The first time I saw her I thought 'nothing doing.' I went up to her because it would have been a pity to let her out of sight without having a go at her; I said a few nice things, bought her two vermouths and shrimps—and now, you see, now I've got her on a string like a pet lamb. She does everything I ask for, and dare not even say a loud word. I met her at the Barceló towards the end of last August, and within the week, just on my birthday, I had her in bed with me. But if I'd kept away like a silly fool, watching others flirt with her and paw her, I should now be in the same state as you."

"Yes, that's all very well, but I can't help thinking that things are just a matter of luck."

Ventura leaps in his seat.

"Luck? That's precisely where you're wrong. There is no such thing as luck, my dear chap. Luck is like a woman, it falls to the man who goes after it, and not to somebody who sees it walk past in the street and doesn't drop it a single word. Anyway, one thing is absolutely wrong: to stay in here all the blessed day long, as you do, looking after that bloodsucker, the mamma of the sissy, and studying the diseases of cows. I tell you, that's no way to get anywhere."

Seoane puts his violin on the piano, after having finished playing "La comparsita," and says to Macario: "I'm going to the W.C. for a moment."

Seoane threads his way between the tables. The prices of spectacles are still going round in his head.

"It's really worth while to wait a bit longer. Those for twenty-two are rather good, it seems to me."

He kicks open the door marked "Gentlemen": two pans fixed to the wall, and a weak fifteen-watt bulb screened by a few wires. A cake of disinfectant presides over the scene.

Seoane is alone. He walks up to the wall, looks at the floor and exclaims: "What?"

Saliva sticks in his throat, his heart leaps, a long-drawn hum fills his ears. Seoane focuses his glance on the floor; the door is closed. Seoane stoops quickly. Yes, it's twenty-five pesetas. A bit wet, but that doesn't matter. Seoane dries the note with his handkerchief.

Next day he goes back to the druggist's shop.

"The ones for thirty, miss, please give me the ones for thirty."

Lola and Don Roque have a talk sitting side by side on the couch. Don Roque is still in his overcoat and holds his hat on his knees. Lola is naked, with her legs crossed. An oilstove burns in the room; it is fairly warm. The wardrobe mirror throws back the image of their two figures, a truly strange pair: Don Roque muffled up and looking worried, Lola naked and in a bad temper. Don Roque has finished talking.

"That's all."

Lola scratches her navel, after which she smells her finger.

"D'you know what I think?"

"What?"

"That your daughter and I are birds of a feather and could shake hands."

Don Roque shouts at her: "Shut up, I tell you. Shut up!"

"All right, I can shut up."

Both are smoking. Lola, plump, naked, and puffing smoke, looks like a performing seal.

"Your girl's story about the photographer is the same as yours about your sick friend—"

"Will you shut up?"

"Now that's enough of your 'shut ups' and your silly rubbish. It's just as if you hadn't got any eyes in your head."

In another place we have already said the following: "With bristling mustache and a gentle look in his eyes, Don Obdulio protects, like a malevolent yet roguish cupid, the clandestine affairs which make it possible for his widow to have something to eat."

Don Obdulio is on the right-hand side of the wardrobe, behind a flower stand. On the left hangs a portrait of the mistress of the house in her youth, surrounded by lap dogs.

"Come on, get dressed. I'm no good for anything now."

"All right."

Lola thinks: "That girl is going to pay me for this, as sure as God's in heaven. She's going to pay for it, and how!"

Don Roque asks her: "Will you go out first?"

"No, you go, I'll get dressed in the meantime."

Don Roque leaves, and Lola bolts the door.

"Nobody will miss him if he isn't here," she thinks.

She unhooks Don Obdulio and puts him in her bag. Then she damps down her hair at the basin and lights a cigarette.

·   ·   ·   ·

Captain Tesifonte seems to respond at last. "Right . . . we'll try our luck. . . ."

"You don't really mean it?"

"Yes, certainly, you'll see. One day when you're going on a spree, call for me and we'll go together. Agreed?"

"Yes, sir, agreed. Next time I go on the prowl, I'll let you know."

The junk dealer's name is José Sanz Madrid. He has two pawnshops where he buys and sells secondhand clothes and "*objets d'art*," and where he hires out dress suits to students and morning coats to penniless bridegrooms.

"Go in there and try some on, there's plenty to choose from."

Indeed there is plenty to choose from: hung on hundreds of clothes-hangers, hundreds of suits are waiting for the customer who will give them an airing.

One of the pawnshops is in the Calle de los Estudios and the other, the more important one, in the Calle de la Magdalena, about halfway up.

After his evening snack, Señor José takes Purita to the pictures; he likes to relax before going to bed. They go to the Ideal Cinema, opposite the Calderón, where they are showing *His Brother and He* with Antonio Vico and *A Family Affair* with Mercedes Vecino, both "passed by the censor." The Ideal has the advantage that the performance is continuous and that it is so large that there are always some seats.

The usher shows them the way with his flashlight.

"Which seats?"

"These will do. We'll be all right here."

Purita and Señor José sit down in the back row. Señor José puts his arm round the girl's neck.

"Well, what news?"

"Nothing at all."

Purita stares at the screen. Señor José takes both her hands.

"You're cold."

"Yes, it's very cold."

For a few moments they stay silent. Señor José is not comfortable in his seat, he shifts round continually.

"Listen."

"Yes?"

"What are you thinking about?"

"Psh . . ."

"Don't rack your brains, I'm going to settle that thing with Paquito for you. I've got a friend with a lot of influence in the Social Aid organization—he's first cousin of the Civil Governor of thingumajig."

Señor José lets his hand slide down to the open neck of the girl's blouse.

"Ooh, that's cold!"

"Never mind, it will get warm."

The man puts his hand into Purita's armpit, outside the blouse.

"How warm you are here under the arm!"

"Yes."

Purita's armpit is hot, as if she were not well.

"So you think they'll take on Paquito?"

"I should say so, my dear. Even if my friend hadn't so much influence, he'd get him in."

"And will your friend do it?"

Señor José has his other hand on one of Purita's garters. In the winter Purita wears a garter belt: the circular garters don't keep up her stockings properly because she is rather thin. In the summer she goes without stockings. Though it may not sound like it, it saves quite a lot of money.

"My friend does what I tell him to; he owes it to me for all the favors I've done him."

"I hope you're right, God grant it."

"You'll see."

The girl is lost in thought, her eyes wistful and far away. Señor José pushes her thighs a little apart and pinches them.

"With Paquito in the day nursery, things would be different."

Paquito is the girl's youngest brother. There are five brothers and sisters, with Purita herself, six. Ramón, the eldest, is twenty-two—he is doing his military service in Morocco; then comes Mariana, who is eighteen and an invalid, poor thing, tied to her bed; then Julio, an apprentice at a printer's, who is going on fourteen; Rosita, who is eleven; and Paquito, who is nine. Purita is the second eldest, she is twenty, although she may look a little more than her age.

The six live on their own. Their father was shot against a wall for one of those things, and the mother died of T.B. and undernourishment in 1941.

Julio gets four pesetas a day at the printer's. The rest of the money Purita has to scratch together by walking the streets all day and coming to port after supper at Doña Jesusa's house.

The children live in a garret on the Calle de la Ternera, Purita in a lodging house, where she is freer and can get telephone messages. About noon every morning Purita goes to see them. Occasionally, when she has no date, she has lunch with them; at the lodging house they keep her lunch for her so that she can have it instead of supper if she likes.

Señor José has had his hand down the girl's low neckline for some time.

"Shall we go now?"

"If you want to."

Señor José helps the girl into her cotton overcoat.

"Only for a little while, eh? The wife's smelling a rat as it is."

"Just as you like."

"Here, that's for you."

Señor José stows a twenty-five-peseta note into Purita's handbag, which has a blue dye that tends to stain the hands.

"May God reward you."

At the door of the room the pair say good-by.

"Tell me, what's your name?"

"José Sanz Madrid. And yours? Is your name really Purita?"

"Yes. Why should I tell you a lie? My name's Pura Bartolomé Alonso."

The two stay there for a brief moment, both staring at the umbrella stand.

"Well, I must go."

" 'Bye, Pepe. Won't you give me a kiss?"

"Yes, dear."

"And listen, do give me a ring as soon as you've news about Paquito."

"Of course, don't fret, I'll ring you up here."

Doña Matilde shouts out to her boarders: "Don Tesi! Don Ventura! Supper's ready!"

The moment she sees Don Tesifonte, she tells him: "I've ordered liver for tomorrow, let's see how you like that."

The captain does not even look at her, his mind is occupied with other things.

"Yes, that young fellow may be right. Hanging about here like a big booby isn't the way to have conquests, and that's a fact."

Doña Montserrat has had her bag stolen during the Adoration of the Blessed Sacrament. It's a disgrace, nowadays there are thieves even in church. There wasn't more in it than three pesetas and a few coppers, but the bag itself was still quite good, quite serviceable.

They had already started on the *Tantum Ergo*—which Doña Montserrat's irreverent nephew José María used to sing to the tune of the German national anthem—and the only people left in the seats were a few women who stayed behind to perform their acts of private devotion.

Doña Montserrat was meditating on the text she had just read: "This Thursday brings to the soul the fragrance of lilies, and with it the sweet taste of the tears of perfect contrition. In innocence an angel, in penitence rivaling the austerities of the Thebaid . . ."

Doña Montserrat turned her head, and her bag had gone. At first she hardly noticed it; her imagination was too full of transmutations, apparitions, and disappearances.

At home, Julita puts her notebook away again and, like Doña Matilde's boarders, goes to supper.

Her mother tenderly pinches her cheek. "Have you been crying? Your eyes look a bit red."

Julita answers, with a pout: "No, Mamma, I've been thinking."

Doña Visi smiles with a roguish air. "Of him?"

"Yes."

The two women link arms.

"Won't you tell me his name?"

"Ventura."

"Oh, you sly puss, that's why you picked the name Ventura for the Chinese baby!"

The girl averts her eyes.

"Yes."

"Then you must have known him quite some time?"

"Oh, yes, we've seen each other off and on for the last six or eight weeks."

Her mother turns almost grave.

"And how is it you never told me about it?"

"I didn't want to say anything to you as long as he hadn't declared himself."

"That's quite true. I am silly. You were absolutely right, darling, it's best not to say anything till the moment things are quite clear and settled. Women have to be so careful."

Julita feels a cramp in her legs and a slight sensation of heat in her chest.

"Yes, Mamma, very careful indeed."

Again, Doña Visi smiles and asks: "Tell me, what does he do?"

"He's preparing for an exam as a notary."

"It would be grand if he got an assignment."

"Well, we shall see if he's lucky, Mamma. I've made a vow

that I'll light two candles if he gets placed in the first category, and one candle if he only gets into the second."

"Quite right of you, darling. Pray to God and wield the sword. I'll make the same vow myself. But now tell me, what's his surname?"

"Aguado."

"That's rather nice: Ventura Aguado."

Doña Visi laughs excitedly. "Oh, my dear, what a prospect! Julita Moisés de Aguado—have you thought of that?"

The girl has a faraway look. "Oh, yes."

Rapidly, afraid that it may all be a dream and shatter any moment into as many pieces as a smashed electric bulb, her mother starts to count her chicks before they are hatched.

"And if your first-born is a boy, Julita, then we'll call him Roque after his grandfather. Roque Aguado Moisés. What a joy that would be! Oh, when your father hears of this, how pleased he'll be!"

Now that Julita has reached the other side, has crossed her river, she speaks of herself as of another person; nothing else matters to her but her mother's simple candor.

"If it's a girl, I'll call her after you, Mamma. Visitación Aguado Moisés doesn't sound so bad either."

"Thank you, darling, oh, thank you. I'm so touched! But let's pray for a boy; there's always a great need for men."

Again the girl feels her legs trembling. "Yes, Mamma, there's a great need."

With her hands clasped over her stomach, her mother says: "Just think—perhaps God will grant him a vocation."

"Who knows?"

Doña Visi lifts her eyes to the heights above. The ceiling, the room's smooth sky, shows several damp patches.

"All my life I have longed to have a son who's a priest."

At this moment, Doña Visi is the happiest woman in Madrid. She takes her daughter by the waist—very much like Ventura does when they are at Doña Celia's—and sways her to and fro like a small child.

"Maybe it will be my grandson, pet. Perhaps it will."

Both women laugh, locked in a tender embrace.

"Oh, I do so want to live to see it!"

Julita means to improve on her handiwork.

"Yes, Mamma, life's full of delightful things."

She drops her voice, giving it a muted, solemn fall.

"I do believe my meeting with Ventura"—there is a faint buzzing in the girl's ears—"has been my good fortune."

Her mother chooses to sound the note of common sense.

"We shall see, darling, we shall see. Pray God you're right. We must have faith in Him. Yes—why shouldn't it be so? A little grandson who shall be a priest and edify us all by his example! A great orator in the pulpit. It sounds like a joke now, but one day we may well read an announcement of spiritual exercises conducted by the Reverend Father Roque Aguado Moisés. I would be an old woman by then, but my heart would be bursting with pride!"

"And mine too, Mamma."

Martin quickly recovers and walks on, proud of himself.

"A good lesson for her. Ha, ha!"

Martin quickens his step. He is almost running, sometimes he gives a little hop.

"I wonder what that wild sow has got to say after this."

The wild sow is Doña Rosa.

On reaching the Glorieta de San Bernardo, Martin remembers the present for Nati.

Perhaps Rómulo is still in his shop. Rómulo is a second-hand bookseller who sometimes has an interesting print in his cubbyhole.

Martin makes for Rómulo's lair, turning down to the right after the university.

On the door hangs a notice that says: "Closed. Messages to be handed in at the back door." The light is on in the shop. Rómulo must be tidying up his papers or sorting out an order.

Martin knocks at the small back door that leads into the courtyard.

"Hello there, Rómulo."

"Oh, hello, Martin. How nice to see you."

Martin produces his cigarettes and the two men smoke, sitting close to the brazier which Rómulo has brought out from under the table.

"I was just writing to my sister, the one in Jaén. Nowadays I'm living in this place and don't go out except for meals. Sometimes I don't feel like eating and then I don't stir from here all day long. They bring me coffee from across the street, and that's all."

Martin looks at some books lying on a rush-bottomed chair with its back all to pieces, which is only good to put things on.

"Not much here."

"No, there isn't. This thing by Romanones, A *Lifetime's Jottings*, is quite interesting. It's very rare."

"Oh, yes."

Martin puts the books on the floor.

"Listen, I'd like an engraving, but a nice one."

"How much d'you want to spend on it?"

"Twenty to twenty-five."

"For twenty-five I can let you have one that's quite charming. It isn't very large, I admit, but it's genuine. What's more, it's framed and all that, just as I bought it. If you want it for a present, it's the very thing."

"Yes, it's meant to be a present for a girl."

"For a girl? Well, if she isn't a cloistered nun it's absolutely right, I'll show it to you. But first let's smoke our cigarettes in peace, there's no hurry about it."

"What's it like?"

"You'll see it in a minute. It's a Venus with several small figures underneath, and some verses in Tuscan or Provençal, I don't know which."

Rómulo leaves his cigarette on the table and switches on the light in the passage. He comes back immediately with a frame which he wipes with the sleeve of his overall.

"Look."

The print is attractive and it is tinted.

"The coloring was done at the same period as the print."

"It looks like it."

"Oh, yes, there's no doubt about that."

The engraving shows a fair-haired Venus, completely naked and with a wreath on her head. She is standing, surrounded by a gilded ornamental border. Her tresses flow down her back to her knees. On her belly there is a drawing of the four points of the compass; it is all highly symbolic. Her right hand holds a flower, her left hand a book. Her body is outlined against a blue, starry sky. Still within the ornamental border, but lower down, are two small circles, the one underneath the book containing the sign of Taurus, the one underneath the flower, the sign of Libra. The bottom part of the engraving shows a meadow surrounded by trees; two musicians are playing, one the lute and the other the harp, while three couples, two seated and the third sauntering, are deep in conversation. In the upper corners two angels are blowing with puffed cheeks. Right at the bottom are four lines of unintelligible verse.

"What does it say here?"

"It's written on the back. I got Rodríguez Entrena to translate it for me, you know, the professor at the Cardinal Cisneros Institute."

The penciled note on the back reads:

"Venus, passion's grenade, sets afire
Gentle hearts that music doth inspire,
Through the joys of dance and lazy play
Leading them to love the sweetest way."

"Do you like it?"

"I love that sort of thing. The great charm of all such verse is its vagueness, don't you think?"

"I entirely agree."

Martin takes out his packet of cigarettes again.

"You're well off for tobacco."

"Today, yes. Some days I haven't got a shred and have to pick up the stubs my brother-in-law leaves about, as you well know."

Rómulo gives no answer, it seems the wiser course to him. He knows that Marco loses his head when he touches the subject of his brother-in-law.

"For how much will you let me have it?"

"Well, let's say twenty. I told you it was twenty-five, but if you give me twenty, it's yours. I paid fifteen for it and it's been sitting on the shelf there nearly a year. Is twenty all right for you?"

"Good, give me five pesetas change."

Martin puts his hand in his pocket. For an instant he stays still, frowning as though in thought. He pulls out his handkerchief and spreads it on his knees.

"I'd swear I had it in here."

He gets up.

"I can't understand . . ."

He searches in his trouser pockets and turns out their linings.

"Well, that does it. It's the last straw."

"What's the matter with you?"

"Nothing. I'd rather not think about it."

Martin looks through the pockets of his jacket, takes out his old, dilapidated wallet stuffed with his friends' visiting cards and newspaper cuttings.

"That's finished me."

"Have you lost something?"

"The twenty-five pesetas . . ."

Julita has a queer sensation. At times she feels something like a depression, and at times she has to make an effort not to smile.

"The human brain," she thinks, "is by no means a perfect instrument. If one could read the thoughts in people's minds like a book . . . No, it's better as it is, it's better we can't read anything and don't understand one another except for the things we choose to say, even if they're all damn lies!"

Occasionally Julita likes to use strong words when she is alone.

They walk along the street hand in hand, looking like an uncle with his niece whom he takes out for a walk.

As she goes past the porter's lodge, the girl turns her head away. She is so absorbed in her thoughts that she fails to see the first step of the staircase.

"Take care, don't hurt yourself."

"No."

Doña Celia comes to open the door.

"Good evening, Don Francisco."

"Hello, my dear. Let the girl go in, I want a word with you first."

"Certainly. Go in there, my child, and sit down where you like."

The girl sits down on the edge of an easy chair with green upholstery. She is thirteen years old and her breasts are small and pointed, like tiny roses about to burst the bud. Her name is Merceditas Olivar Vallejo; her girl friends call her Merche. She lost her whole family in the war. Some are dead, others in exile. Merche lives with her grandmother's sister-in-law, an old lady swathed in lace and painted like a monkey; she wears a wig and her name is Doña Carmen. Among her neighbors Doña Carmen is known by the unpleasant nickname of "Old Corpse hair." The children in her street prefer to call her the "Grasshopper."

Doña Carmen has sold Merceditas for five hundred pesetas, and Don Francisco, the one with the popular clinic, has bought her. She told the man: "First fruits, Don Francisco, first fruits. A carnation in bud."

And to the girl she said: "Look, child, all that Don Francisco wants is just to play. Anyway, it's got to happen one day, don't you see?"

The Moisés family has a gay time at supper tonight. Doña Visi is radiant, Julita all smiles, almost blushing. Inside her head, her thoughts go marching on.

Don Roque and his other two daughters have caught the infection of gaiety, without knowing the cause. Only at certain moments does Don Roque recall the words Julita said to him on the stairs: "From . . . from the photographer's." And then the fork trembles between his fingers; until this is over, he dare not look at his daughter.

After she has gone to bed, Doña Visi takes a long time to go to sleep. Her head seems to be spinning round the one subject.

"Do you know our girl has got herself a young man?"

"Julita, you mean?"

"Yes, and he's going to be a notary."

Don Roque turns over between the sheets.

"Now, don't you set the bells ringing yet. I know you're fond of giving out every piece of news straight away through the town crier. Let's first wait and see what comes of it."

"Oh, but you always pour cold water on everything!"

Doña Visi's sleep is full of sweet dreams. After several hours she is wakened by the sound of a small bell that calls a convent of poor nuns to the first prayer at daybreak.

Doña Visi is in a mood to see in everything good omens, happy auguries, and reliable signs of joy and future blessings.

Chapter Six

MORNING.
Half asleep, Martin hears the stir of the waking city. It is pleasant to listen, lying between the sheets next to a live woman, a live and naked woman, and to hear the sounds of the city, its rioting heartbeat. The carts of the garbagemen coming down from Fuencarral and Chamartín, coming up from Las Ventas and Las Injurias, emerging from the sad, desolate landscape of the cemetery, and passing—after hours on the roads, in the cold—at the slow, dejected trot of a gaunt horse or a gray, worried-looking donkey. And the voices of women hawkers who got up early and are on their way to set up little fruit stalls in the Calle del General Porlier. And the first, distant, indistinct motor horns. And the shouts of children going to school, satchels on their backs and morning snacks, fresh and sweet smelling, in their pockets.

In Martin's head the bustle in the house, closer at hand, wakes a kindly echo. Doña Jesusa, who is an early riser and takes a nap after lunch to make up for it, organizes the work of her charwomen, some of them old whores in their decline, but the rest affectionate, meek, domesticated mothers of families. In the mornings, Doña Jesusa has in seven women to help. Her two servant maids sleep till lunch time, till two in the afternoon, in whatever bed it happens to be: a mysterious bed recently left vacant, as a grave may be left, with an entire deep sea of grief caught prisoner between its iron headrails, and with the horsehair of its mattress still retaining the groan of the young husband who, almost unthinkingly, deceived his wife for the first time—and she an enchanting creature—with a common tart covered with boils and sores like a mule. Deceived his wife who was waiting up for him like every other night, knitting by the dying afterglow of the brazier, rocking the baby's cradle with her foot, reading an endlessly long novel about love, and pondering difficult, complicated economic stratagems that would allow her, with a little luck, to buy a pair of stockings.

Doña Jesusa, who is orderliness personified, shares out work among her daily help. In her house the bed linen is washed every day; each bed has two complete sets which are most carefully darned on the occasions when a client tears them— perhaps even on purpose, for it takes all kinds to make a world. In these days it is impossible to get bed linen. You may find sheets or material for pillow cases on the junk market, but at prohibitive prices.

Doña Jesusa employs five washerwomen and two who do the ironing, and keeps them busy from eight in the morning till one in the afternoon. They earn three pesetas each, but the work does not kill them. The two ironers have the daintier hands, and put brilliantine on their hair; they have not resigned themselves to being finished. They have poor health and are prematurely aged. Both started their career on the streets when little more than children, and neither of them ever managed to put money by. And now they have to pay for it. While they work, they sing like crickets and drink whole buckets of wine like cavalry sergeants.

One is called Margarita. Her father, now dead, used to work as a porter at the Delicias Station. When she was fifteen she had a boy friend named José; his Christian name is all she knows of him. He was a young man who frequented the open-air dances at La Bombilla to pick up girls; one Sunday he took Margarita into the underbrush in El Pardo, and after that he chucked her. She began to go off the rails altogether and ended by trailing her handbag round the bars in the Plaza de Antón Martín. What came afterwards is a very vulgar story, very vulgar indeed.

The other's name is Dorita. She was seduced by a seminarist spending his vacation in their home village. The seminarist, who is no longer alive, had the name of Cojoncio Alba. His Christian name had been a stupid joke of his father's, who was a great brute. He bet his friends a supper that he would christen his son Cojoncio, and he won the bet. On the day of the boy's christening, Don Estanislao Alba, the father, and his cronies got roaringly drunk. They shouted, "Death to the King," and cheered the Federal Republic. The poor mother, Doña Conchita Ibáñez, who was a saint, wept and could say nothing except: "Oh, what a disgrace, what a disgrace! My husband intoxicated on a blessed day like this!"

Even many years later she would lament, on every anniversary of the christening: "Oh, what a disgrace, what a disgrace! My husband intoxicated on a day like this!"

The seminarist, who later was to become a canon at León Cathedral, showed Dorita a few gaudily colored stamps depicting the life of St. Joseph of Calasanz, and so enticed her to the banks of the river Curueño, to one of the meadows, where things happened as they were bound to happen. Dorita and the seminarist both came from Valdetejo in the province of León. When the girl went with him she had a presentiment that it would lead to no good, but she let herself be taken along; she walked in a kind of foolish daze.

Dorita had a son, and on his next vacation the seminarist refused even to see her when he came to their village.

"She's a wicked woman," he said, "the spawn of the Evil One, and capable of dragging the most temperate man to perdition with her artful wiles. Let us avert our eyes from her."

Her parents showed Dorita the door and for a while she tramped round the countryside with the baby at her breast. The little thing went and died one night, in one of those caves above the river Burejo in the province of Palencia. The mother told no one anything. She tied stones round the dead baby's neck and threw it into the river as food for the trout. Afterwards, when there was no longer anything to be done, she began to weep and stayed in the cave five days, seeing nobody and eating nothing.

Dorita was then sixteen. She had the wistful, dreamy expression of a masterless dog, a stray animal.

For some time she dragged herself round the brothels of Valladolid and Salamanca, like a battered piece of furniture, until she had collected enough money for the fare and could go to Madrid. Here she worked in a house on the Calle de la Madera, on the left-hand side going down, which was known as the League of Nations because so many of the girls were foreigners: Frenchwomen, Poles, Italians, one Russian, one or the other dark, mustachioed Portuguese, but chiefly Frenchwomen—strong Alsatians looking like cowgirls, decent lasses from Normandy who had turned prostitutes to earn money for a wedding dress, sickly Parisiennes, some with a glittering past, who felt deep scorn for the chauffeur or shopkeeper when he fetched his good seven pesetas out of his pocket. She left this house because Don Nicolás de Pablos, a rich villager from Valdepeñas, took her away to marry her at the registrar's.

"What I want," said Don Nicolás to his nephew Pedrito, who wrote exquisite verse and studied philosophy and literature, "is a really hot piece who knows how to give me a good time, if you get my meaning, a wench with firm flesh one can hold on to, and nothing flabby about her. All the rest is flim-flam and only good for literary games."

Dorita gave her husband three children, but all three were born dead. The poor girl gave birth the wrong way round, so that the babies came out feet first and were, of course, smothered on their way.

Don Nicolás left Spain in '39 because he was suspected of being a Mason, and nothing was ever heard of him after. When the little money he had left behind was eaten up, Dorita, not daring to approach her husband's family, had once more to go out on the streets. Yet although she was very willing and tried hard to please, she could not get a regular clientèle. This was at the beginning of 1940, and she was no longer exactly young. Moreover, there was plenty of competition from very attractive young girls. And from many young ladies, who did it for nothing, simply for their own amusement, and so took the bread out of the mouths of others.

Dorita tramped round Madrid till she met Doña Jesusa.

"I'm looking for another reliable woman to do my ironing for me. You can take it on. All you have to do is dry the sheets with the iron and press them a bit. I'll give you three pesetas, but there's work every day, and you'll have the afternoons free. And the nights."

In the afternoons, Dorita now accompanies a crippled lady on her walks in the Paseo de Recoletos or to the Café María Cristina to hear a little music. For this she is paid two pesetas and the price of a light coffee by the lady, who herself drinks hot chocolate. The lady's name is Doña Salvadora; she used to be a midwife. She has a foul temper and does nothing but complain and grumble. She constantly uses bad language and says that the world is only fit to be burned because there is no good in it. Dorita bears with her and agrees to everything she says; after all, she has to safeguard her two pesetas and her nice cup of coffee in the afternoons.

The two ironers, each at her own table, sing as they work and bang their flatirons on the patched-up sheets. Sometimes they talk.

"I sold all my rations yesterday. I don't want them. I got four-fifty for my half pound of sugar. And three for my half-pint of olive oil. The seven ounces of dry beans I got rid of for two; they were maggoty. But I'm keeping the coffee."

"I've given my rations to my daughter, I always give her the whole lot. She takes me out for a meal once every week."

From the attic room, Martin hears them. He cannot make out what they say. He hears their off-key singing and their thumps on the tables. He has been awake for a long time, but without opening his eyes. He prefers to feel the movements of Pura, who gives him an occasional kiss, taking care not to wake him, and pretends to be asleep so that he should not have to move. He is aware of the girl's hair on his face, of her naked body under the sheet, of her breath that is at times a faint, almost imperceptible snore.

In such a manner he lets more time go by; this is his first and only contented night in many months. Now he feels a new man, as if he were ten years younger, a mere boy. He smiles and opens one eye, slowly and gradually.

Pura, with her elbows propped on the pillow, is contemplating him. As she sees that he is awake, she too smiles.

"How did you sleep?"

"Very well, Purita. And you?"

"I did, too. It's nice with a man like you. You don't bother a girl."

"Never mind. Tell me something else."

"Just as you like."

They say nothing for a short while. Pura gives him another kiss. "You're a romantic."

Martin smiles, with something near sadness. "No, simply a sentimentalist."

Martin strokes her face. "You're pale, you look like a bride."

"Don't be silly."

"Yes, just like a new bride."

Pura turns grave. "Well, I'm not."

Martin kisses her eyes gently, like a poet of sixteen.

"For me you are, Pura. Of course you are."

The girl, profoundly grateful to him, gives him a smile of wistful resignation. "If you say so. It wouldn't be so bad either."

Martin sits up in bed. "Do you know a poem by Juan Ramón that begins, 'Lofty and tender image of consolation'?"

"No, Who's Juan Ramón?"

"A poet."

"He writes verse, you mean?"

"Of course."

Martin glances at Pura almost in fury, but only for an instant. "Listen:

'Lofty and tender image of consolation,
    Dawn breaking over all my sorrows' sea,

Lily of peace, whose scent is purity,
Divine reward for my long tribulation!' "

"How sad that is, and how beautiful."
"You like it?"
"And how!"
"Another time I'll tell you the rest."

With his body stripped, Señor Ramón is washing in a deep
cauldron full of cold water, splashing it over himself.

Señor Ramón is a strong man with a hard body, a vigorous
eater who never catches colds, a man who drinks his wine,
plays dominoes, pinches the servant girls' bottoms, gets up at
dawn, and has worked all his life.

Señor Ramón is no boy any more. Now that he is a rich
man, he no longer watches the sweet-smelling, unsanitary
oven where the bread is baked; since the end of the war he
stays in the shop all the time. He looks after it with loving
care, tries to satisfy all his customers, and has worked out a
fanciful but meticulous order of service according to age, standing, circumstances, and even looks.

"Get up, girl. What d'you mean by staying in bed at this
time of day, like a young lady?"

The girl gets up without a word and has a quick wash in
the kitchen.

In the mornings the girl has a faint little cough, almost
unnoticeable. Occasionally she catches a slight chill, and then
her cough sounds more hoarse, as though dryer.

"When will you give up that wretched consumptive?" her
mother asks her on some mornings.

And then the girl, who is gentle as a flower and, like a
flower, capable of letting herself be torn open without a sound,
is overcome by a desire to kill her mother.

"I wish you would die, you poisonous old snake," she says
under her breath.

In her thin cotton overcoat, Victorita runs along to the El Porvenir printing house on the Calle de la Madera, where she works as a packer and has to be on her feet all the blessed day long.

There are times when Victorita is colder than usual and feels a need to cry, an immense need to cry.

Doña Rosa is a fairly early riser; she goes to seven o'clock Mass every morning.

At this time of the year, Doña Rosa sleeps in a warm nightdress, a flannel nightgown of her own invention.

On her way back from church Doña Rosa buys herself breakfast fritters, enters her café through the side entrance— her café that looks like a deserted cemetery, with the chairs upside down on the tables, and the coffee urn and the piano sheathed in covers—pours herself a large glass of *anís*, and has her breakfast.

While she has it, Doña Rosa thinks how uncertain these times are; she thinks about the war, which the Germans seem to be losing, God forbid; she thinks that the waiters, the manager, the server, the musicians, and even the messenger boy all come with more demands, claims, pretensions, and hoity-toity ideas every day there is.

"But it's me who's the boss here, whether you like it or not. If I want, I can pour myself another glass, and that's nobody's business but mine. And if I want to I can throw this bottle at the mirror. If I don't do it, it's because I don't want to. And if I like, I can shut up the place for good, and then not another coffee gets served here, not if it were to God Almighty Himself. It's all mine, and good hard work it cost me to get it going."

In the early morning Doña Rosa feels the café more hers than at any other time.

"The café is like the cat, only bigger. It's mine, as much as the cat is. I can give it black pudding or beat it to death, just as I feel like."

*　　*　　*　　*

Don Roberto González has to reckon that it takes him half an hour's walk from his house to the Council offices. Unless he is very tired, Don Roberto González goes everywhere on foot. By taking a little walk you stretch your legs and you save one-twenty a day, thirty-six pesetas a month, very nearly four hundred in the course of a year.

Don Roberto breakfasts on a cup of malt coffee with very hot milk and half a small French loaf. The other half he takes along with a little sheep cheese from La Mancha, to have a snack in the middle of the morning.

Don Roberto does not complain; others are worse off. After all, he has his health, which is the main thing.

The boy who sings flamenco songs sleeps under a bridge on the road to the cemetery. The boy who sings flamenco belongs to a sort of family of gypsies, the sort of clan in which every member fends for himself as best he can, with complete freedom and autonomy.

The boy who sings flamenco gets wet when it rains, frozen when it is cold, grilled in August when the meager shade under the bridge gives him scant shelter: this is the old Law of the God of Sinai.

The boy who sings flamenco has one foot that is slightly twisted. He stumbled over a pile of brushwood, felt a sharp pain, and went limping for some time. . . .

Purita strokes Martin's forehead.

"I've got five pesetas or so in my bag. Would you like me to send for something for breakfast?"

In his contentment Martin has lost his shame. It happens to everybody.

"Please, do."

"What would you like? Coffee and fritters?"

Martin gives a little laugh. He is very nervous.

"No, coffee and two buns, don't you think?"

"Whatever you like is all right for me."

Purita kisses Martin. Martin jumps out of bed, takes a turn round the room, and goes back into bed.

"Give me another kiss."

"As many as you like, silly."

Completely unembarrassed, Martin pulls out the envelope he has crammed with butts, and rolls himself a cigarette. Purita does not dare to make any comment. Martin's eyes have a glitter, as of triumph.

In the mortuary, Doña Margot, her eyes open, sleeps the sleep of the just on the cold marble of one of the slabs. The bodies in the mortuary look, not like dead people, they look like murdered dummies, like dolls with their clockwork run down.

A beheaded puppet is a sadder sight than a dead human being.

Señorita Elvira wakes early, but does not get up. Señorita Elvira likes to stay in bed, well wrapped up, thinking of her problems or reading *The Mysteries of Paris*, with one hand just a little outside the blanket to hold the fat, grease-stained, battered tome.

The morning unfolds slowly; it creeps like a caterpillar over the hearts of the men and women in the city; it beats, almost caressingly, against the newly wakened eyes, eyes which never once discover new horizons, new landscapes, new settings.

And yet, this morning, this eternally repeated morning, has its little game changing the face of the city, of that tomb, that greased pole, that hive. . . .

May God have mercy on us all!

Finale

IT IS three or four days later. A certain Christmas coloring has begun to tinge the air. Over Madrid, which is like an old plant with soft, green young shoots, there ring at times, through all the bustling noise of the streets, the sweet and kindly peals of a chapel bell. People pass each other in a hurry. Not one thinks of the man next to him who, maybe, walks with his eyes fixed on the ground: with his stomach ruined, or a cyst in his lungs, or a screw loose in his head.

Don Roberto reads the newspaper while he has breakfast. Then he goes in to say good-by to Filo, his wife, who is staying in bed because she is half sick.

"I've read it now, the thing's quite clear. We'll have to do something for the lad, you try to think about it. He doesn't deserve it, but all the same . . ."

Filo weeps while two of her children stand at the side of the bed and stare, uncomprehendingly; her eyes are full of tears, her look vaguely sad and forlorn, like a heifer's that still breathes when her blood is already steaming up from the flagstones and passes her tongue in a last, halting movement over the dirt crust on the overall of the slaughterer who has hurt her with the indifference of a judge—a cigarette stuck between his lips, his mind on one of the servant girls, his muddy voice humming a romantic song from a musical comedy.

Nobody remembers the dead who have been under the ground for a year.

You may hear in the family circle: "Don't forget, tomorrow is poor Mamma's anniversary."

It is always a sister, the saddest among the lot, who keeps count. . . .

Every day Doña Rosa goes to the Calle de la Corredera for her shopping, with her maid in her wake. Doña Rosa goes to the market after having done her chores at the café; she prefers to descend on the stalls when the crowd is thinning out and the morning well advanced.

Sometimes she meets her sister in the market. Doña Rosa makes a point of asking after her nieces. One day she said to Doña Visi: "And what about Julita?"

"Nothing special."

"That girl needs a young man."

Another time—it was two days ago—Doña Visi pounced on Doña Rosa as soon as she saw her, beaming with joy. "D'you know, the girl has found a young man!"

"Has she?"

"Yes."

"What's he like?"

"A splendid fellow, my dear! I'm absolutely delighted."

"That's fine. I hope you're right and things won't take a bad turn."

"But why should they take a bad turn?"

"I couldn't tell. It's just the way people are nowadays."

"Oh, Rosa, you always have to paint things so black!"

"No, it's simply that I like to wait till things have actually happened. You see, if they turn out well, so much the better."

"Yes, I see."

"And if they don't . . ."

"If they don't this time, there'll be someone else, I daresay."

"Yes. Provided this one doesn't get her into trouble."

There are still trolley cars left in which people face each other seated in two long rows, looking at one another with thoroughness and even curiosity.

"The man over there has got the face of a cuckold, his wife must have run off with somebody. Perhaps with a racing cyclist. Or with a clerk at the Food Office."

If the journey is long, people grow quite fond of one another. It is odd that it should make any difference, but we always feel a bit sorry when the woman who looked so unhappy gets out at one of the stops, and we realize that we have seen the last of her, possibly for our whole life.

"She must be badly off. Perhaps her husband's out of work. No doubt they've more children than they can cope with."

Each time there is a youngish woman in the trolley who is fat, much made up, and overdressed. She would carry a big handbag of green leather, wear lizard-skin shoes, and have a beauty spot on her cheek.

"She looks like the wife of a rich pawnbroker. Or perhaps she looks like the mistress of a doctor; doctors always go in for very showy mistresses, just as if they wanted to tell the world: 'Here's an eyeful for you, eh? Have you had a good look? First-class stock!' "

Martin has taken the trolley at Atocha. When he comes to Las Ventas he gets out and begins to walk along the Great East Road. He is on his way to the cemetery to visit his mother's grave. Doña Filomena López de Marco died some time ago, a few days before Christmas Eve.

Pablo Alonso folds the paper and rings the bell. Laurita slips under the blankets. It still makes her feel somewhat ashamed to let the maid see her in bed. After all, it must be remembered that she has not been more than two days in this house; the boarding house on the Calle de Preciados, where she went after leaving her porter's lodge in the Calle de Lagasca, had turned out to be too uncomfortable.

"May I?"

"Come in. Is Señor Marco here?"

"No, sir, he went out a little while ago. He asked me to give him one of your old ties, sir, a black one."

"Did you give it to him?"

"Yes, sir."

"Right. Now pour me a bath."

The maid leaves the room.

"I must go out, Laurita. Poor chap! That's the last straw."

"Poor boy! D'you think you'll find him?"

"I don't know, I'll look in at the Central Post Office and the Bank of Spain, that's where he usually spends his mornings."

Near the Great East Road stand some wretched hovels made of old tin cans and bits of planks. A few children play about, throwing stones into the puddles left by the rain. In summer, before the Abroñigal dries out completely, they fish for frogs with sticks and paddle in the dirty, evil-smelling trickle of water. Women are raking through piles of refuse. Here and there an aging man, perhaps an invalid, sits on an upturned bucket at the door of a shanty and spreads a heap of cigarette butts out on a newspaper to dry in the lukewarm morning sun.

"They're unconscious of it, they're unconscious . . ."

Martin, who had been searching for a rhyme on *laurel* for a sonnet to his mother he had just begun, thinks of the hackneyed statement that the problem is one of distribution, not of production.

"Really, these people are worse off than I am. It's appalling that such things can exist!"

Paco arrives at the bar on the Calle de Narváez out of breath, with his tongue hanging out of his mouth. The barkeeper,

Celestino Ortiz, is just serving the policeman García with a glass of Cazalla brandy.

"Too much alcohol is bad for the molecules of the human body, of which there are three kinds, as I told you before: molecules of the blood, molecules of muscle tissue, and molecules of nerve tissue; it burns them up and ruins them. But a little drop of spirits now and then is good for warming the stomach . . ."

"That's what I say."

". . . and for lightening up the mysterious zones of the human brain."

The policeman Julio García is entranced.

"We are told that when the ancient philosophers of Greece and Rome and Carthage wanted to attain supernatural powers . . ."

The door swings violently open and a great gust of cold air blows across the counter.

"That door!"

"Hello, Señor Celestino!"

The barkeeper cuts him short. Ortiz is very particular about modes of address. Potentially he is something like a *chef de protocole*.

"Friend Celestino, please."

"All right, leave it. Has Martin been here?"

"No, he hasn't been since the other day, I suppose he got too angry then. I'm not happy about it, believe me."

Paco turns his back to the policeman.

"Look, read this."

Paco gives him a folded newspaper.

"Down there."

Celestino reads slowly, with knitted brows.

"That's bad."

"I should say so."

"What do you mean to do?"

"I don't know. Have you an idea? I believe the best thing is to have a talk with his sister, don't you? If we could only pack him off to Barcelona tomorrow!"

In the Calle de Torrijos, a dog is slowly dying in the irrigation gutter at the foot of a tree. A taxi ran right over his belly. His eyes are pleading, his tongue lolling out. Several small boys are prodding it with their feet; two or three dozen people watch the scene.

Doña Jesusa runs across Purita Bartolomé.

"What's going on here?"

"Nothing, a mongrel with a broken back."

"Poor thing!"

Doña Jesusa takes Purita by her arm.

"Have you heard about Martin?"

"No, what's the matter with him?"

"Listen."

Doña Jesusa reads out a few lines from a newspaper to Purita.

"And what will happen now?"

"I don't know, dearie. I'm afraid it won't be anything good. Have you seen him?"

"Not since the other day."

A couple of garbagemen come up to the group clustered round the dying dog, pick it up by its hind legs and throw it into their cart. In sailing through the air the poor beast gives a howl of deep, hopeless pain. The group of people stare at the garbagemen and then disperse. Each one goes his separate way. Amid the crowd there may have been a pale-faced boy who enjoyed—with an impalpable, sinister smile—the spectacle of the dog's slow, endless dying.

Ventura Aguado talks to his girl friend Julita over the telephone.

"Do you mean now, at once?"

"Yes, my girl, this very moment. In just under half an hour I'll be at Bilbao underground station. Don't be late."

"No, no, don't worry. 'Bye."

"Good-by—blow me a kiss."

"Here you are, you spoiled boy."

Half an hour later Ventura comes to the entrance of Bilbao station and finds Julita waiting for him. The girl has been dying with curiosity, and was a little worried as well. What could be the matter?

"Have you been here long?"

"Not more than five minutes. What's happened?"

"I'll tell you in a second. Let's go in here."

The couple go into a beerhouse and sit down at the back, at a table almost in darkness.

"Read this."

Ventura lights a match so that the girl may read.

"Well, your friend's in for it."

"That's the whole news. That's what I called you up for."

Julita thinks it over. "What will he do now?"

"I don't know, I haven't even seen him."

The girl clutches her lover's hand and takes a puff at her cigarette.

"What rotten luck!"

"Yes, it never rains but it pours. . . . I thought you might call on his sister. She lives on the Calle de Ibiza."

"But I don't know her."

"Never mind, tell her you come from me. It would be best if you went there now. Have you got any money?"

"No."

"Here's ten pesetas. Go both ways by taxi, the quicker we are, the better. We'll have to hide him, there's no other way."

"Yes, but . . . won't we get into trouble?"

"I don't know, but it's the only thing to do. If Martin's left alone, he's capable of doing something foolish."

"All right, all right. Have it your way."

"Come on, get going."

"What's the number of the house?"

"I don't know. It's the corner of the second turning on the left as you go up from the Calle de Narváez, I don't know its name. It's on the other side of the street, the one with the even numbers, just after the crossing. Her husband's name is González, Roberto González."

"Are you going to wait for me here?"

"Yes. I'll first go and see a friend of mine who's got his fingers in many pies, and I'll be back here within half an hour."

Señor Ramón is talking with Don Roberto, who has not been to his office, after asking his chief by telephone to give him the day off.

"It's something extremely urgent, Don José, I assure you; extremely urgent and extremely unpleasant. You know yourself that I would never neglect my work for a trifling reason. It's a family matter."

"It's perfectly all right. You stay away. I'll tell Díaz to keep an eye on your section."

"Many thanks, Don José, and God reward you. I won't fail to repay you for your kindness."

"Not at all, man, not at all. We're here to help one another as friends. The important thing is that you settle your problem."

"Many thanks, Don José, I'll do my best. . . ."

Señor Ramón looks worried. "See here, González, if you ask me to do it I'll hide him here for a day or two, but after that he'll have to find another place. It's no great matter because I'm the boss here. But if Paulina finds out, she'll be as mad as hell."

Martin walks down the long lanes of the cemetery. Sitting at the door of the chapel, the priest is immersed in a Wild West story. The sparrows are chirping in the mild December sun, they hop from one cross to the next and swing on the bare branches of the trees. A very young girl rides a bicycle down a path; in her immature voice she sings a gay hit song. Everything else is gentle silence, welcome silence. Martin has an ineffable sense of well-being.

Petrita talks to her mistress, to Filo: "What's the matter with you, Señorita?"

"Nothing. The baby isn't well, that's all."

Petrita smiles an affectionate smile. "There's nothing wrong with the baby, but with you there's something wrong, Señorita."

Filo touches her eyes with her handkerchief. "This life is one long trouble, my dear. But you're too much of a child to understand that."

Rómulo reads the newspaper in his secondhand bookshop.

" '*London*: Moscow Radio reports a conference between Churchill, Roosevelt, and Stalin some days ago.'

"That fellow Churchill is the very devil. Here and there and everywhere, as if he were a mere chicken, and all that at his age!

" '*The Führer's Headquarters*: In the region of Gomel, in the central sector of the Eastern front, our forces have evacuated the towns of . . .'

"Oooh, oooh, I'm smelling a rat.

" '*London*: President Roosevelt has arrived at Malta in his giant Douglas plane.'

"What a man! I bet my dear life that plane's got everything, including a lavatory."

Rómulo turns over the page and runs his eye rather wearily down the columns.

He stops at a few short, crowded lines. There is a dry lump in his throat and a droning in his ears.

"That's the last straw. Some guys are jinxed."

Martin has reached his mother's grave. The inscription seems to weather well: "R.I.P. Doña Filomena López Moreno, widow of Don Sebastián Marco Fernández. Died Madrid, 20 December 1934."

Martin does not go every year to pay a visit to his mother's remains on the anniversary of her death. He goes when he remembers.

Martin takes off his hat. A slight sensation of repose fills his body with placid calm. Far away, beyond the cemetery walls, stretches the gray-brown plain on which the sun lies broadly, as if it had gone to bed. The air is cold, but not icy. As he stands there, his hat in his hand, Martin senses on his forehead a light caress, almost forgotten, an old caress of his childhood days.

"It's very good to be here," he thinks. "I shall come more often."

He is about to start whistling, but stops himself in time.

Martin looks to both sides of the grave.

"Josefina de la Peña Ruiz went to heaven on May 3, 1943, in the twelfth year of her childhood."

"Like the little girl on the bicycle. Perhaps they were chums, perhaps this one told the other, a few days before she died, one of those things little girls of eleven are keen about: 'When I'm grown up and married . . .' "

"The Illustrious Señor Don Raúl Soria Bueno. Expired in Madrid . . ."

"An illustrious man rotting away in a box."

Martin realizes that he does not make sense.

"Stop it, Martin, keep quiet."

He raises his eyes once more and concentrates on the memory of his mother. He does not think of her in her last years, but rather sees her as she was at the age of thirty-five. . . .

"Our Father which art in Heaven, hallowed be Thy name, Thy Kingdom come, as we forgive them that trespass against us . . . no, I don't think that can be right."

Martin starts again and again gets it wrong; at this moment he would give ten years of his life to remember the paternoster.

He shuts his eyes and presses his eyelids tightly together. Suddenly he breaks into speech, in a subdued voice.

"My mother which art in the grave, I carry you in my heart and pray God to receive you into Eternal Glory as you deserve. Amen."

Martin smiles. He is delighted with the prayer he has just made up.

" 'My mother which art in the grave, I pray God . . .' No, it wasn't like that."

Martin frowns. "How did it go?"

Filo is still in tears.

"I don't know what to do. My husband's gone out to see a friend. My brother hasn't done anything, believe me. It must be a mistake, nobody's infallible. His affairs are in order. . . ."

Julita does not know what to say.

"I quite agree, they simply must have made a mistake. All the same, I do think one ought to do something, or see somebody. . . . That's only my opinion, of course."

"Yes, we'll see what Roberto says when he comes back."

Suddenly Filo's tears begin to flow faster. The baby in her arms cries, too.

"All I can think of is to pray to Our Lady of Perpetual Help; she's always helped me out of my troubles."

Roberto and Señor Ramón have jointly made up their minds. Since Martin's case could not possibly be anything grave, it will be best for him to report to the police at once, without further ado. Why should he try to run away when there's nothing serious to conceal? They might wait a couple of days—which Martin could perfectly well spend at Señor Ramón's place—and after that (why not?) he would report to the police accompanied by Captain Ovejero, that is, Don Tesifonte, who is the last man to say No and who is, after all, a guarantee.

"It seems very reasonable to me, Señor Ramón. Thank you very much. You're a sound man."

"No, no, it's simply that this seems the best way to me."

"And to me. Believe me, you've taken a great weight off my mind. . . ."

Celestino has written three letters and intends to write three more. The case of Martin occupies his mind.

"If he doesn't pay me, that's that, but I can't leave him in the lurch."

Martin strolls down the gentle slopes of the cemetery with his hands in his pockets.

"I'm going to pull myself together. The best way is to do a spot of work each day. If they'd take me in at some office I really would accept the job. Not at first, of course, but later on I could even do some writing there at odd times, especially if the heating is good. I'll talk to Pablo about it, he's sure to know of something. It ought to be a pretty good thing to work for one of the Syndicates, they pay all the extra benefits according to law."

Martin's mother has been erased from his mind.

"Another good job would be with the National Pensions Institute, but it must be harder to get in there. All these places are better to work in than a bank. Banks exploit their staff; if one's late for work one day they take it off one's pay next time. Then there are bound to be some private firms where it's not too difficult to make good. What would suit me is a publicity job, running a press campaign. 'Are you suffering from insomnia? If you do, it is because you choose to. So-and-so tablets—Marco tablets, for instance—will make you content without doing the slightest harm to your heart.' "

Martin waxes enthusiastic about the idea. At the cemetery gate he turns to an attendant.

"Do you happen to have a newspaper on you? If you're finished with it, I'd like to buy it from you. There's something I want to see."

"Yes, I've read it. Here you are."

"Thank you so much."

Martin rushes out. In the small park outside the cemetery gate he sits down on a garden bench and unfolds his paper.

"The press sometimes has very good hints for people like me who're looking for a job."

Martin is aware that he is going too fast, and tries to put on the brakes.

"Now I'm going to read through the news. What's meant to happen will happen. Anyway, getting up early doesn't make the sun rise earlier."

Martin is enchanted with himself.

"Today I'm really in good form and put things well. It must be the country air."

Martin rolls himself a cigarette and begins to read the paper.

"Wars are sheer barbarism. Every one loses, and no one advances civilization an inch."

He smiles within himself. He is going from strength to strength. Every now and then he reflects on something he has read, with his eyes fixed on the horizon.

"Oh, well, let's go on."

Martin reads every line, everything interests him: foreign reports, the editorials, extracts from public speeches, news of theater and film premieres, football. . . . Martin notes that, on going to the outskirts of the town and breathing a purer air, life assumes softer, more delicate shades than while one lives walled up in the city.

Martin folds up the paper, puts it into his coat pocket, and walks away. Today he is more knowledgeable than ever before, he would be capable of holding his own in any conversation about current affairs. He has read the newspaper from top to bottom. He leaves only the advertisement section for later, to be read in peace somewhere in a café where he would be able to note down an address or make a telephone call if necessary. The section containing the advertisements, the public notices and decrees, and the list of rations to be issued in the villages of the "Outer Belt" is the only part of the paper Martin has not read.

In the Plaza de Toros he sees a group of young girls who stare at him.

"Hello, lovelies!"

"Hello, Mr. Tourist!"

Martin's heart leaps in him. He is happy. He walks up the Calle de Alcalá at a lively pace, whistling the *Madelón*.

"Today my people will see I'm a different man."

His people have been thinking somewhat along the same lines.

Martin has walked a long way. He stops in front of a jeweler's show window.

"When I've got a job and earn good money, I'll buy a pair of earrings for Filo; and another pair for Purita."

He taps his newspaper and smiles. "There may be just the thing in here!"

A vague presentiment makes Martin unwilling to hurry. . . . In his pocket he still has the newspaper of which he has not yet read the section containing the advertisements and the public notices. And the ration orders for the villages of the Outer Belt.

"Ha, ha! The villages of the Outer Belt. What a funny expression! The villages of the Outer Belt!"

Madrid, 1945–1950